STOLEN TIME

THE WITCHES OF MINGUS MOUNTAIN - BOOK 1

CHRISTINE POPE

STOLEN TIME

Copyright © 2024 by Christine Pope

ISBN: 978-1-946435-79-8

Published by Dark Valentine Press

Cover design by Indie Author Services

Book formatting by Indie Author Services

1

INTO THE DARK

"I DARE YOU TO GO IN," MY FRIEND BELLAMY said, and I shot her a side-eyed glance.

"What is this, fifth grade?"

She only grinned, unfazed by the dig. We were standing at a boarded-up shaft to the abandoned United Verde Mine above Jerome, Arizona, a site that was off-limits to pretty much everyone…not that the "keep out" signs and the barbed wire stopped members of the McAllister witch clan from coming up here and poking around from time to time, or merely checking on the isolated spot to make sure no wayward tourists had gone out of bounds and started wandering around where it wasn't safe.

Bellamy had lived her whole life in the former mining town—her two dads owned the sweet shop down on Main Street, and I had to believe the United Verde was old hat to her by now. But since I'd only arrived in Jerome a month ago, much of it was still new to me, even though, like most other members of the Wilcox witch clan, I'd come here to visit and explore at least once a year throughout most of my childhood, depending on what my family's vacation schedule looked like.

After I graduated from Northern Pines University at the end of May, I really hadn't known what I wanted to do with myself. When I heard that Rachel McAllister, who'd run McAllister Mercantile in the heart of Jerome for longer than a lot of us had been alive, was looking for some additional help at her store, I decided to go for it. Why she'd chosen me when I had to believe there were plenty of other McAllisters who might have wanted the job, I still wasn't sure.

I hadn't asked too many questions, though. It was enough for me to be living in Jerome—I'd lucked out and was able to rent the same darling little bungalow my cousin Lucas's wife Margot still owned, just a block south of Main Street—and to allow myself to be on autopilot for a while. My parents weren't entirely thrilled that I'd decided to bail on Flagstaff, but it wasn't as if I'd moved to Africa or something.

Not that I could have done anything so extreme even if I'd wanted to. Witches stuck to their clans' territories, and the only reason why things were a little different here in Arizona was that the *prima*—head witch of the McAllisters—just happened to be married to the *primus*—head warlock—of the Wilcox family. We were also on friendly terms with the de la Pazes, who lived in the Phoenix area and points south of that, so at least we could wander around the state pretty much as we liked, and even into New Mexico as well, since they'd come to our aid back before I was even born, when all the Arizona clans had been fighting the dark warlock Joaquin Escobar and had been on the brink of losing...until the Castillos stepped in to lend their assistance.

Bellamy was Rachel's other shop assistant, and the two of us hit it off right away. It probably helped that she was only a year younger than I, although she had decided against going to a four-year university and was instead getting her certification in enology at the local community college.

"More future in that kind of thing around here anyway," she'd told me not too long after I came to work at the store, which was true enough. The wine industry was positively hopping in the Verde Valley, and since the area had gained AVA—"American Viticultural Area"—status, it was becoming almost as popular as Napa or Sonoma.

She also worked two nights a week at the tasting room down the block from Rachel's store, so it had become a hangout of mine as well, a place where we could continue our chats, except she got paid for doing so.

This particular Thursday night, however, she didn't have a shift at the tasting room, which was why she'd suggested we go take a look at the abandoned United Verde mine. At first, I'd demurred —when I was a kid, maybe around eight or nine, my parents had taken the family to the Gold King Mine just outside Jerome, which had once been a separate settlement, and I didn't see the point in visiting something that seemed way too similar— but Bellamy had told me that wasn't the reality of the situation at all.

"The Gold King is just a tourist attraction," she said. "I mean, it was a mining settlement once, but it's been defunct a lot longer than the United Verde, which was a working mine until the 1950s. When it was closed…it was just closed, and that's it. Most of it was open pit mines, and there isn't much to see. But there are also some exploratory shafts they dug and then boarded up, and those are kind of creepy."

I had to admit I wasn't sure whether I was in the mood for "creepy." People had always told me Jerome was super-haunted—and Angela, the McAllister *prima,* had a special talent for talking to ghosts, which probably had been handy while she was growing up there—but even though I'd been living in the former mining town for almost a month now, I hadn't seen even a single sign of a ghost. True, Margot had told me no one had ever died in her bungalow, at least as far as she knew, and I had to admit Rachel had so imprinted her presence on the big brick building her store occupied that I doubted any ghost would have the guts to try haunting the place.

But it had been awfully hot this past week… June in the Verde Valley was often like that…and I thought going up to the mine and checking out one of those abandoned shafts might be a little cooler than trying to sit on a patio somewhere and have drinks.

Which was why Bellamy and I now stood outside the shaft she'd said was the easiest to access. I had to admit it didn't look very inviting; my brain had manufactured images of a gaping hole in the steep hillside, but of course, that wasn't how it was set up at all. No, the entrance had been covered with some weathered boards, and barbed-wire fencing provided an additional perimeter about a dozen feet back from the actual opening.

That barbed wire hadn't offered too much of a deterrent, since Bellamy had gone unerringly to a section off to one side and stepped down on the bottom strand of wire and deftly pulled up the one above it, showing that she—and probably generations of other McAllisters—had been doing that very same thing for a long time.

While the fence hadn't proved to be much of a barrier, I couldn't say the same for the boards that concealed the opening to the mine.

"Even if I wanted to, how am I supposed to get in there?" I asked, and she just grinned. She had long hair in the bright copper shade that showed up in the McAllister clan from time to time, although I supposed it might also have come from the egg donor who had been her mother. Obviously, Kirby and Matthew couldn't have children on their own, and they'd known Kirby would need to be their child's biological father, or there wouldn't have been any chance of the baby inheriting the McAllister clan's magic.

Bellamy had been perfectly frank about her situation, as if it wasn't any big deal, and I supposed it wasn't. After all, she might not have known who her mother was, but I had my own craziness in my family tree, considering how my father, Robert Rowe, had been born in the eighteen hundreds but had come to live in the twenty-first century after my mother rescued me when she time-traveled to 1884 and brought him back to modern-day Flagstaff with her.

"Like this," Bellamy said, and stepped forward so she could grasp one of the plywood boards and pull it away from the opening.

Clearly, the majority of the nails that had been holding it in place were just for show. With the sheet of plywood set off to one side, I now could see the dark opening that yawned in the hillside, and a shiver went down my back despite the lingering heat of the day. With Mingus Mountain towering above us, Jerome and part of Clarkdale and Cottonwood below were already in shadow, although the sun wouldn't actually set for at least another forty-five minutes or so.

"You've really gone in there?" I asked, knowing how dubious I sounded.

"Lots of times," she said blithely. "My cousins and I would come here and play Truth or Dare, or just sort of hang out when we needed a place to be away from everyone else. And it's kind of a thing to go in the mine and stay there alone for at least an hour, just to prove you can do it."

That sounded like a kind of whack rite of passage to me, but I supposed every clan had its quirks. Also, while I thought Jerome was absolutely darling, with its various hundred-plus-year-old houses and buildings and sloped sidewalks and absolute lack of anything resembling a true right angle, I had to admit that it probably didn't offer much to do except go exploring. Growing up there would have been very different from my own childhood; the big house in Flagstaff where I'd been raised was less than a mile away from shopping and a movie theater and a variety of diversions.

"So if I do this," I asked, "does that make me an honorary McAllister or something?"

Bellamy's grin only broadened. "I'd say you already are, kind of, since you're working at Rachel's store."

The question had been dancing around in my mind anyway, so I figured I might as well go ahead and ask it. If nothing else, prolonging our conversation would postpone the moment when I had to go into that dark, gaping hole in the side of Cleopatra Hill.

"Why did Rachel hire me, anyway?" I said. "I mean, there must have been plenty of McAllisters who wanted the job."

Bellamy shrugged. With the light fading fast, her coppery hair wasn't nearly as bright as it had looked even a couple of minutes earlier.

"You'd be surprised," she responded. "I mean, a lot of my cousins have worked there part-time to help out, or to earn some extra money over the holidays or whatever. But most of them really aren't interested in doing the retail thing unless it involves owning their own business."

Like her parents, who had been running the treat shop on Main Street since before she was born.

"Why did *you* take the job, really?" Bellamy asked next. "I can't believe there wasn't plenty for you to do in Flagstaff."

There was, of course. True, a lot of people would probably argue that a history major didn't make me a shoo-in to work in a law office or even at my cousin Jake's witch-finding operation across the street from Wheeler Park in Flagstaff's historic district, but I knew someone in the Wilcox clan would have found me a job if I'd asked. That was just how we rolled—how most witch clans rolled, from what I'd been able to tell. We always looked out for one another.

After graduation, though, I'd found myself longing for a change of scenery, and when the job at McAllister Mercantile came up, I thought it must be fate.

Or maybe just really good timing.

Also, it was plain, honest work, the kind of thing that allowed me not to think about very much. And most of the time, not thinking was the best way to ensure there weren't any more incidents.

All witches had certain magical talents they shared, like unlocking doors or lighting a candle with just a thought. Once you got past the basics, though, things became more specialized, with every witch and warlock having their own particular gift...and, every once in a great while, being lucky enough to have two, the way I did. The one I'd inherited from my father involved being able to hide my witch powers from other witches and warlocks, something I'd never really needed, although I assumed it might come in useful at some point.

My mother's power was also an unusual one—she had the ability to give herself an extra five minutes whenever she liked, while time froze for everyone around her—and I'd inherited something like it...except my supposed "talent" wasn't useful in any way I'd been able to determine.

Yes, I could manipulate time, but rather than having it stand still for everyone around me, I instead sometimes went into the future and sometimes into the past, not with any real rhyme or reason. True, sooner or later, I either snapped back to where I was supposed to be or the rest of the world caught up with me, but because I couldn't control those jaunts in time, I'd caused quite a lot of havoc in my family. The worst incident had occurred when I was twelve and went a week into the future and thought I'd only been there for a couple of hours...only to discover upon my return that I'd been gone for nearly seven whole days.

My parents, understandably, had freaked out, and after that, I basically did whatever I could to prevent my weird, annoying magical talent from asserting itself. On a couple of occasions, I still screwed up and lost control, but because the time involved had only been a few minutes or at most an hour, it wasn't too big of a deal.

Which was why I thought having a nice, low-stress job far away from any surroundings that might trigger me was probably the best thing to help me cope with the situation. Over the years, I'd gotten my supposed "gift" under control, and yet I still couldn't quite trust it not to pop up at inopportune moments even though I hadn't had a slip since I was around fourteen, almost eight years ago now.

"Haven't you ever wanted a change of scenery?" I asked, and now Bellamy smiled again.

"All the time," she said, her tone cheerful. "I suppose that's partly why I wanted to go into the wine industry. Sure, I'll stay in the Verde Valley once I find something permanent—although I guess I could also go down to wine country in the south, maybe Sonoita, since the de la Pazes are pretty cool with us being in their territory—but wherever I end up, I don't think it'll be Jerome. Page Springs would be nice."

I couldn't disagree with that comment. No, I hadn't spent a lot of time in the small community about fifteen minutes outside Sedona, but it was a pretty place, with the Verde River flowing through a narrow valley and vineyards and wineries scattered on either side of the winding country road that bisected the area.

"Well, that's how I feel about Jerome, I guess," I said. "I always liked it when I visited, and being here gives me a chance to try something new."

"Speaking of which," Bellamy replied, still smiling, "that's why you should check out the mine."

A flicker of worry went through my body. "Aren't you coming in with me?"

"Not at first," she said. "You should really go in and experience it for yourself the first couple of minutes. But don't worry—I'll follow along soon enough."

Her words reassured me a little…a very little. However, even though this wasn't fifth grade and I was a grown woman of twenty-two, I also didn't want to look like an utter chickenshit in front of Bellamy McAllister, not when she made all this sound like child's play.

And it wasn't as if I was afraid of the dark. No, I didn't have some kind of witchy night vision—although that would have been a cool talent to have—but I knew there wasn't anything in the mine shaft that would hurt me.

Except snakes. And rats. And probably bats, too, although I wasn't afraid of bats. Honestly, I wasn't all that afraid of snakes or rats, either, even if I didn't want them running over my foot.

Or biting me, although the sturdy hiking boots I wore probably would have foiled a strike by a rattler as long as it didn't aim too high.

I tried to reassure myself that a rattlesnake would have settled down for the night by now, although I couldn't be sure. Maybe it was still warm enough that any snakes in the immediate vicinity might still be up and about, looking for a nice, juicy rodent before they slithered off to their burrows to await the arrival of another day.

As best I could, I shut down that line of thought. Psyching myself out before I even took a single step inside the mine probably wasn't a very good idea.

"Here," Bellamy said as she handed over a small flashlight, the kind of thing you could easily stash inside your purse without it taking up too much room. "This'll make it easier."

That was for sure. Suddenly, the prospect of stepping inside the mine opening didn't seem quite as scary. I'd already planned to use the light on my phone to illuminate my surroundings, but I knew it wouldn't have been anywhere as bright as the flashlight my friend had just given me.

"Thanks."

Now that I was more or less properly outfitted to go in, I knew any other delays would be way too obvious. Besides, tons of McAllister kids had gone in the mine before me. Did I really want to be scared off by something that didn't even frighten a twelve-year-old?

It seemed I'd answered my own question.

"'Once more into the breach,'" I quipped, and Bellamy raised an eyebrow.

"Huh?"

"Shakespeare," I said briefly. Well, not everyone had a displaced warlock from the nineteenth century for a father, someone who'd made sure that I and my older sister Jessica and my little brother Patrick were well-versed in the classics.

Flashlight in hand, I moved closer to the opening and shone it inside. To be honest, the shaft didn't appear all that impressive—just a space about fifteen feet wide or so, with some sketchy-looking timbers holding up the rock sides, and more rocks strewn on the ground below. I recalled Bellamy's comment about how shafts like these had been dug to look for additional deposits of the copper and silver and gold hidden in the hill.

They probably hadn't found much, or this part of the hillside would have been blasted open as well.

"It's not going to bite," came her voice from behind me, and I shook my head.

"That you know of."

But since there wasn't any point in drawing this out, I went ahead and squeezed through the opening she'd made by pulling back that one piece of plywood. Almost at once, the temperature seemed to drop a good ten degrees...or maybe that was just my inner heebie-jeebies taking over.

Because I couldn't lie—the place was creepy. Maybe it was the utter darkness, broken only by the narrow beam of the flashlight Bellamy had given me, or maybe the oddly musty scent of cold stone and confined spaces.

Or maybe it was only that I couldn't tell how deep the shaft went.

It can't be that deep, I told myself as I took a gingerly step forward, then another. *This was an exploratory shaft, so it's not like they would have been drilling hundreds of feet inside the mountain.*

At least, that was what I wanted to believe. Since what I knew about mining probably would have fit in the palm of my hand, I couldn't know for sure.

Another cautious step. I paused and shone the flashlight all around me, but everything still looked pretty much the same—evenly spaced timbers along the wall that were beginning to show signs of rot, loose stones and gravel spread over the ground beneath my feet.

On one wall, though, I noticed something that seemed to be chalk markings on the dark surface. I headed over there, figuring I might as well take a look, even though I guessed the scrawls were probably graffiti left behind by some long-ago McAllister coming in here to get their wiggles out.

It didn't look like graffiti, though. No, it looked like purposeful markings of some kind, numbers and letters that didn't appear to be real words but possibly abbreviations. At the end were the letters SLM and the number 26.

Initials and a date?

Possibly. It didn't seem too out of bounds to guess that it might have been an inscription left behind by a long-ago surveyor or someone else who worked for the mine.

For some reason, seeing that physical evidence left behind by someone who'd been working here made me feel a little better. True, the shaft was still creepy and not the sort of place I'd want to hang out, but really, it was just a place that people had surveyed and moved on. Nothing to see here.

A little lighter of spirit, I shone the flashlight around again. It looked as though there was another set of markings on the opposite wall, and I hurried over to take a look.

Except with my flashlight fixed on the wall and not on the uneven ground at my feet, I didn't notice the gaping crack in the stone surface until it was too late. The toe of my hiking boot caught in the fissure, and I went down hard, my head smacking against the rocks.

The last thing I remembered was the metallic clank of the flashlight as it fell from my limp fingers.

2

A TIME TO HEAL

Seth Lewis McAllister paused at the entrance to the new shaft they'd sunk only the week before. He already knew they weren't going to continue exploring in this area, not when the amounts of copper the surveyors had found had proved it wasn't worth wasting money on this branch of the mine, but he wanted to go inside one more time to take a few additional samples, just in case. Technically, he wasn't a surveyor or a geologist, just a recently promoted foreman at the United Verde, and yet he thought if he was able to prove that the operation could be expanded here after all, it might mean a decent bonus, or maybe even another promotion.

Jerome was booming, and he wanted to boom right along with it. Maybe then he'd feel as if it was safe to start thinking about settling down.

The day shift had already gone home, which was why he'd taken the detour over here. He'd said goodbye to his men and watched them troop down the hill to their various rented homes and boarding houses, and once he knew he was safely out of eyeshot, had walked back up to the place, hidden by a curve of the hill, where the mine shaft was located.

It stood exposed to the sun and the wind, mostly because everyone working at the United Verde knew it was going to either get boarded up or filled in within the next couple of weeks, whenever they got around to it.

Not if he could prove them wrong, though.

He paused to fish a box of matches out of his pants pocket and lit one of the lanterns sitting on the ground closest to the entrance. The surveyors had already noted that the excavation was free of any flammable gases, so using the lantern wouldn't be a problem.

As he turned away from the lantern and raised his arm to shine the light around the interior of the shaft, however, he realized he wasn't alone.

Lying on the floor of the tunnel was the limp form of a woman. She faced away from the entrance, so all he could see was a spill of long brown hair against the dirt and one outflung arm. Even from this distance, he immediately noticed she was dressed oddly, in blue denim pants not too dissimilar from the dungarees many of his fellow miners wore and a light-colored blouse that did nothing to cover her arms.

For all that Jerome was a rough and ready town, with more than its fair share of women who were, as his father liked to obliquely say, "no better than they should be," Seth couldn't recall ever seeing a woman who wore those sorts of pants. At fairly regular intervals, tourists came through Jerome from the East Coast or even from Los Angeles to the west, and the women were often decked out in what had been to his eyes some fairly outlandish getups, but even they hadn't been sporting a tightly fitting pair of trousers like these.

Frowning, he moved toward the strange woman, even as he called out, "Hello?"

No response, not even a twitch.

Worried now, he hurried over to her and knelt on the far side of the spot where she lay so he could get a better look at her and assess whether she'd been hurt in some way. As he set the lantern down on the floor of the mineshaft, its warm glow caught her face.

She was beautiful. Eyes shut, which meant he couldn't see what color they were, but even when slack, her mouth was full and rosy, her nose straight and delicately molded, her face almost heart-shaped because of its wide cheekbones, but softened by a more rounded chin.

And no real sign that she'd been injured—no bruises, no blood. Nothing to explain why she appeared to be in a deep faint, or how in the world she could have ended up here.

"Hello?" he ventured again.

Not even a flutter of the long lashes against her cheeks. For one awful moment, he wondered if she was dead, but then he saw the rise and fall of her chest under the sleeveless buttoned shirt she wore, and he knew she still walked among the living.

For now, anyway.

Could he risk moving her? Even though she didn't appear to be hurt, he knew that carrying her could be a problem if she'd suffered some kind of back or neck injury. On the other hand, leaving her here in the tunnel while he went to fetch help didn't seem like a very good idea, either, not with everyone gone for the day.

And unfortunately, his gift for moving from place to place, one that had emerged on his twelfth birthday, wouldn't help him now. Over the years, he'd done a lot of work to test its limits, and about the most he could carry with him was forty pounds. That was a decent amount, but definitely not enough for him to take the woman down the hill to safety.

He reached out to lay his fingers against the strange woman's throat. Her pulse was strong and steady, so whatever had happened to her, it didn't seem as if it had put her in any immediate danger.

She should be able to hang on until he came back in his car.

With that plan settled, he blinked himself into his bungalow's kitchen, then went down the back steps to the detached garage he'd had built a little over a year ago, right after he purchased the convertible Dodge that was his pride and joy. He didn't much like the delay involved in having to open the garage door and back out the car, then hurry over so he could close the door again, but he tried to reassure himself that the woman he'd found had seemed stable enough, and really this whole expedition would only take about ten minutes or so.

The streets were pretty much deserted by that point, with his fellow miners done with their shifts for the day and most of Jerome's denizens safely tucked inside having their dinners. Seth was glad about that, just because he really didn't feel like explaining why he was taking his car up to the mine.

When he returned, it didn't look as though she'd moved at all.

Was that a good sign?

Since there wasn't anything else he could do, he knelt and slid his arms under the woman, then lifted her from the ground as carefully as he could. During this procedure, she didn't stir, not even the slightest bit, and his worry deepened.

What had happened to her?

He wasn't a doctor or a healer, only a man who'd decided to buck tradition and work at the United Verde rather than the store that had been in his family for going on three generations now. But the McAllister healer, his cousin Helen O'Dowd, should be able to determine what had caused the strange woman's ongoing faint.

She was very light in his arms, not much of a burden for someone who'd done hard physical work from the time he was seventeen. Stepping as gently as he could, he headed back to his car and then laid her down in the back seat. During all this, she'd been as limp and unmoving as a rag doll, and he murmured a prayer to the goddess Brigid under his breath that the woman he found wouldn't be harmed by the trip down the hill to his bungalow.

A lone car passed him as he drove down into town, but he didn't recognize it, and guessed the vehicle probably belonged to either a tourist or someone from Prescott who'd been doing business in the Verde Valley but now wanted to get over the mountain before true night fell. His street was similarly deserted, with no one to take any note of him carrying the woman into the house.

The familiar space surrounded him, with its windows open to the evening breeze and the few pieces of furniture he'd been able to acquire carefully set in the space. Chief among them was the sofa, purchased only a few months earlier at a store down in Cottonwood. It was still quite a novelty to have a shop like that nearby at all, rather than having to make the perilous drive up and over Mingus Mountain to Prescott to purchase those items you didn't want to build for yourself. Several members of his clan were expert woodworkers, and they were the ones who had provided the table and chairs in the dining room and the cabinet which held a few pieces of mismatched china his mother had provided for him, but the couch—that was the item he was most proud of, since he'd paid for it with the money he'd earned in his new position as one of the foremen at the mine.

He laid the woman down on the sofa and then, as carefully as he could, unlaced the sturdy boots she was wearing. The laces felt odd under his fingers, too silky to be cotton, definitely not leather. And the soles were also strange—while he could tell they were some kind of rubber, they felt far springier than any rubber-soled shoes or boots he'd ever seen.

Who was she?

First things first. Although some of the houses in Jerome now had telephones, his wasn't among them. Seth had decided it was a luxury he couldn't afford, and besides, the town was small enough that you could get pretty much anywhere you needed to be in ten minutes or less.

And Helen's home was much closer than that —just a few houses down the street, in fact.

By that time, night was truly beginning to fall, and he had the uneasy feeling he might be interrupting Helen's supper with her young family. It couldn't be helped, though—part of being a clan healer was knowing that you might be intruded upon at any time to treat an ailing family member. They did their best to make her cures for their various coughs and colds and bumps and bruises seem as if it was all perfectly natural, nothing more than folk medicine that had been in the family for generations, for while the McAllisters were the dominant group in the town, there were still plenty of strangers living in Jerome as well, people who could never be allowed to learn that there was a little something more to the McAllister clan than met the eye.

Helen's home was much larger than the

bungalow Seth had purchased a few months back, a handsome white four-square house with green shutters and a flourishing oak tree in the front yard. Her husband Calum had come to America only a decade earlier and arrived in Jerome the way so many others had, seeking to make his fortune in the copper mines. He'd done very well for himself, and although Seth had heard that anti-Irish sentiment ran high in other parts of the country, the McAllisters were always happy to welcome nonmagical spouses here and there, as it kept their clan from getting inbred.

Calum was the one who answered the door in response to Seth's knock, and a certain resignation entered his bright blue eyes as he saw who stood on his front porch.

"An accident at the mine?" he asked. His brogue had softened during his years here in Arizona, but it was still clear to anyone who heard him that he'd been born a long way away from Jerome or the Verde Valley.

"No, nothing like that," Seth replied. "It's very strange—I went into the exploratory shaft we opened up last week, and I found a woman lying on the ground inside. She appears to have fainted. I have her resting on the couch at my house, but I need Helen to take a look at her and see if she can find out what's wrong."

"Just a moment, then," Calum said. "Come wait inside—I'll fetch her."

Seth did as requested and entered the foyer, which was decorated with a matching pair of small tables with marble tops, tables he knew his cousin Helen had had shipped here all the way from San Francisco. On top of each table was a lush Boston fern. The clan healer took great pride in her houseplants, and tended them nearly as fiercely as she did her three children.

As if his thoughts had summoned her, Helen appeared a minute later. Like many of his fellow McAllisters, she had sandy blonde hair and blue eyes, and had often been referred to as the beauty of the family, with her porcelain-doll features. However, Seth knew those delicate looks hid a woman of great intensity and drive.

"You found someone in the mines?" she asked as she reached for a cardigan that hung from the coat rack in the corner of the foyer. Seth didn't think the warm June evening merited such a covering, but perhaps she didn't want to go outside in just her housedress.

"Yes, a woman," he said. "I've never seen her before, so I have no idea who she is."

Because he knew if he'd seen the woman's face in the past, he would never have forgotten it.

Helen only said, "Hmm," and waited for him to open the door so they could head outside.

Their street was located a block below the main thoroughfare, but even that distance—and the numerous trees that had been planted to both stabilize the ground and muffle sound—couldn't quite hide the noise emanating from all the bars on Main Street.

His cousin looked disapproving, but she didn't say anything as she followed Seth up the steep incline to his bungalow. He hadn't thought to turn on a light—their little side street had been electrified only the year before—so the house was quite dark as they approached.

What if the strange woman had awoken while he was gone, panicked to find herself in an unfamiliar place, and had fled?

She can't have gotten very far, he reassured himself. *If she's not there, we'll have all the McAllisters out looking for her.*

But when he and Helen entered the living room and he hurriedly crossed the space to turn on the single electric light on its side table, he saw at once that the strange woman still lay on the sofa. From what he could tell, it didn't look as though she'd moved at all.

Helen's finely arched brows drew together, and she went over to the woman and laid a gentle hand on her forehead. Because Seth had seen his cousin do the same thing with many other patients before this, he knew this was her way of reaching out with her gift into a person's body to sense what was wrong with them and how she might heal whatever ailment they might be suffering.

Now, though, her frown only deepened, as if she wasn't quite sure of what she had found. A moment passed, one that seemed interminably long, although that might have only been because of the heavy ticking of the clock on the mantel.

At last she said, "It is very strange. I can't detect anything truly wrong with her, and yet it's clear she's in a deep faint of some kind. I think all we can do is wait for her to wake up."

That was not what Seth had wanted to hear... especially since he couldn't recall a time when Helen hadn't been able to immediately pinpoint what was wrong with a person and take steps to correct it.

"There's nothing you can do?"

His cousin lifted her hand from the strange woman's forehead and gave him a very direct look. "I could try to force her awake, but I fear that might do more harm than good. It seems better to me that you allow her to regain consciousness naturally. This faint doesn't seem to have any physical cause—there is no bruising, no swelling, nothing to tell me she suffered a blow to the head or anything like that—so there isn't anything for me to heal." Helen paused there, forehead puckering again. "It seems to me that she's suffered some sort of terrible shock, although I can't begin to explain what it might have been. Patience is the best remedy here."

As his father had lectured him on more than one occasion, patience was a virtue Seth often struggled with. "So…we're just supposed to leave her lying on my sofa?"

Now Helen smiled, although he hoped it wasn't because she was amused by his predicament. "For now. When she wakes, we can decide what to do next. I'm sure she must have people who are concerned about her. She can tell us where she comes from, and we can figure out from there how to get her home." A shake of the head, followed by, "Jerome is not the sort of place where a pretty young woman should be wandering around by herself."

No, it wasn't. Or rather, while most everyone associated with the various mining camps knew to leave the McAllister women alone—and if they were a newcomer unfamiliar with the town's unspoken rules, they found out soon enough—those same protections wouldn't be afforded to a civilian woman, someone unconnected to the clan.

For he knew the stranger he'd found wasn't a witch. She definitely wasn't a McAllister, and although he'd had little reason to connect with a witch or warlock outside their clan, isolated as they were here, he still knew that he and everyone else who'd come from a witch family would experience some sort of telltale when they encountered a magical stranger, whether it was a tingle at the back of their neck or a ringing in their ears or even a small flash of light.

He hadn't felt anything like that when he found the stranger or when he picked her up, which meant she must be a civilian.

"In the meantime," Helen went on briskly, "you should go see your parents and see if they can get you some clothes from the mercantile so she can put on proper garments when she wakes up. I have no idea who she is or where she came from, but it's very odd that she allowed herself to be seen in public like that."

A point Seth had to agree with. Yes, there was some part of him—one he didn't quite wish to acknowledge—that enjoyed seeing her long, slim legs in the close-fitting trousers and the smooth curve of her bare arms in that lightweight blouse, but he knew it was not the sort of outfit that should be seen in public, especially in a town full of unmarried men who still had physical needs that required attention.

"I'm not sure I should leave her alone again," he said, knowing how dubious he sounded. "What if she wakes up while I'm away?"

Helen made a waving motion with one hand, dismissing his worries. "I'll stay here with her," she replied. "It's not as if my dinner hasn't already been interrupted, so a few more minutes won't be any problem."

Faced with that declaration, Seth knew there was no point in arguing further. Besides, while he'd walked down to his cousin's house the ordinary way because the clan had long ago agreed that he couldn't just blink himself into other people's homes without so much as a by-your-leave, he knew such strictures didn't bind him when it came to appearing in the apartment over the mercantile that had been his childhood home. He could be there and back very quickly, even accounting for the time it would take his mother to locate some proper garments for the strange woman.

"Very well," he said. "I'll be as fast as I can."

With that, he imagined the sitting room of the apartment, the comfortably worn furniture that contrasted with the big, shiny radio in its cabinet that had been given a place of honor on the wall opposite the fireplace. At this hour, he guessed his mother and father and his older brother Charles would all be sitting down to dinner, so appearing in the sitting room wouldn't be quite as much of a disruption.

Immediately, he stood in those familiar

surroundings, and took a moment to get his bearings. As he'd thought, the clinks of silverware and murmur of voices came clearly to his ears, even over the static-y sound of a jazz orchestra coming through the radio's speaker.

Steeling himself, Seth made his way to the dining room. As always, his father sat at the head of the table, with his mother to his right and Charles immediately across from her. As soon as he paused at the entrance, his mother caught sight of him and set down her fork.

"Seth!" she exclaimed, and began to rise from her seat. "I didn't know you were coming to dinner tonight."

"I wasn't," he told her. It was on his lips to add that there was no reason for her to get up from her chair, but then he realized she would have had to leave the table at some point to fetch the necessary clothing from the store downstairs. "I'm sorry for the intrusion, but I need your help."

"What's wrong?" his father asked. Like both his sons, he was tall and blue-eyed, although his brown hair had already begun to gray at the temples, and he wasn't quite as slim as he'd been when he inherited the mercantile from Seth's grandfather some eight years earlier.

As quickly as he could, Seth explained the situation. Through it all, his father wore an increasing frown, while his mother only appeared concerned.

Before either of them could respond, however, Charles spoke up. Although barely a year separated the two men, he had always taken his responsibilities as the oldest son seriously, and was very concerned with propriety.

"I'm not sure it's a good idea to have this woman staying at your house," he said. "It would appear very improper to anyone looking in from the outside."

Irritation flared, but Seth did his best to push it aside. Getting into an argument now didn't seem like a very good idea.

"I'm not having her move in with me permanently," he responded, knowing there was a snap to his words that he hadn't been able to fully contain. "Once she's awake and we can determine who she is and where she came from, then we can all work to get her back to her people. In the meantime, though, Helen thought—and I agree —that the stranger should at least have a change of clothes."

"She certainly should," his mother agreed. Like Helen, who was Molly McAllister's actual first cousin and not the much looser interpretation of the word that witch clans used to refer to anyone in their families, she was blonde and blue-eyed, and slight enough of stature that people often wondered how she'd been able to produce two sons who were both north of six feet tall. "And I will help you find something for her." She looked over at her husband and other son, adding, "Go ahead and finish your dinner. This shouldn't take very long."

Although from the outside it might have seemed as though Henry McAllister ruled the roost, Seth knew his mother was the real person in charge of their household. While both his father and brother appeared a little put out, neither of them said anything as she looped her arm in his and went downstairs with him to the ground floor of the three-story building.

"Is Helen with her now?" she asked, and Seth nodded.

"Yes. We didn't want to leave the girl alone for too long."

"It all sounds rather sad to me. There was no way to tell who she is?"

He shook his head as they entered the stockroom at the back of the store. "She wasn't carrying a bag and didn't seem to have a wallet of any kind."

Not that having one in her possession would have made much of a difference. While he'd heard some other states required driver's licenses and that people used them as a form of identification, things weren't nearly so formal here in Arizona.

And even if the woman he'd found wasn't from his state, there was a very good chance she didn't even drive. While women were making greater strides in that area, especially after the Great War when so many men had gone overseas to fight, there were still quite a few among the male half of the population who didn't think women had any business being behind the wheel of a car.

His mother made a tutting kind of sound. "How very unfortunate," she said. "But I suppose it's lucky that we just got a new batch of clothing in from New York. There should be several things that will fit her." She stopped there, blue eyes keen on his face. "I don't suppose you have any idea of her size."

The glaring lightbulb his mother had switched on as they entered the stockroom probably did a very good job of illuminating the embarrassed flush that rose to his cheeks. "I, um...." He stopped for a moment to gather himself, doing his best to remember that he was now a grown man of twenty-four and didn't need to act like a foolish schoolboy. "I suppose she's around cousin Daphne's size," he said quickly, naming a relative who was slim and rather tall, and his best guess for an approximation of the strange woman's height and build.

This seemed to be enough information for his mother, who gave a quick nod and then started inspecting the stack of clothing on the big table in the middle of the room, which was the usual dumping ground for new clothing stock that had arrived at the store but hadn't yet been put on display in the mercantile. She pulled out several dresses and a shirtwaist and skirt, and added to those items a selection of undergarments whose presence again made him want to blink and look away.

To his eyes, it seemed like rather a lot for someone who no doubt would be returned to her family as soon as she regained consciousness, but he didn't protest. Molly McAllister knew what she wanted and how to make it happen, and Seth had long ago realized it was best to stay silent and simply let her go about her business.

At last, though, it seemed as if the pile of clothing she'd assembled was enough to satisfy her, because she glanced up at her son and said, "And shoes?"

Thank God he'd taken off the stranger's boots, so at least he had a rough idea of her shoe size. "About like this," he said, holding up two hands to indicate the length of her feet.

His mother looked almost disapproving. "Big feet, then."

Were they? Seth had to admit that he didn't spend a lot of time looking at women's feet, so he didn't have much of a point of reference. "Possibly," he allowed.

Undeterred, Molly went to the shelf where they stored the boxes of shoes that hadn't yet been put on display and rummaged through them for a moment. "These should do," she said, coming back to him with a shoebox tucked under one arm. "Honestly, I'm glad to get this pair off my hands, because no one around here seems to wear this size. But if it works for this woman you found, then all the better."

He took the shoebox, then stood there as his mother piled the rest of the garments she'd collected on top of it. Again, he thought it seemed like an awful lot…and he also couldn't help being a bit worried as to how he was going to get all this back to his house without spilling something.

What would happen if he dropped an unmentionable during one of his eye-blink journeys? Would it disappear forever, or would it simply flutter down from on high, making whoever found it wonder how it could have possibly gotten there?

Probably best not to speculate.

"Thank you, Mother," he said, and she went on her tiptoes to press a kiss against his cheek.

"It's good to help those in need," she replied. "Now, you get back there—and let us all know when she awakes. This is a mystery we need to get solved."

"I will," he promised. Then, because he didn't trust himself to hold onto that pile of clothing for too much longer without dropping something, he took himself away to his house, purposely making sure he'd appear close to the dining table so he could leave the bounty of clothing there once he appeared.

Once he was done, though, he hurried out to the living room, where his cousin Helen still stood close to the woman on the couch.

"She hasn't stirred at all," she said. "But her breathing is fine, and her color is good. As I said before, all we can do is let things run their course."

"Thank you for watching her," Seth replied.

"It's what I do," Helen said simply. "Time for me to get home, though. You just let me know tomorrow if she still hasn't woken up."

He nodded, and his cousin slipped out the front door, presumably heading straight for home so she could finish her now-cold dinner.

Or maybe Calum had put it back on the stovetop to keep warm.

Seth realized he hadn't eaten anything yet. Luckily, though, he had some leftover stew that his mother had sent home with him the day before waiting in the icebox. He'd just have to do his best to heat it up while trying to keep an eye on the woman lying on his couch.

No real need to worry about that, not when she didn't seem to have moved even a fraction of an inch in the time he'd been gone. He pulled up a chair and sat next to her, wondering if the scent of the heated food would wake her up.

It didn't, though, and he finished the entire bowl and set it aside.

Now, as Helen had said, he could only wait.

3

DÉJA VIEWED

I OPENED MY EYES AND BLINKED. THE CEILING above me didn't look familiar at first, and then I remembered how those broad beams in their criss-cross pattern decorated the ceiling in the living room of my rented bungalow in Jerome.

That had been a hell of a dream...or maybe a nightmare. Memories came flooding back to me —the mine shaft high above the former mining town and current tourist destination, the way I'd tripped and fallen...and had felt as though I continued to fall for centuries in the spiraling dark, slipping down a rabbit hole deeper than anything Alice in Wonderland had ever encountered.

But....

The curtains at the windows in the house I'd been renting were filmy and pale, hung there more as accents and to add a little privacy than to keep out any light. In contrast, these were blue-checked gingham, hanging from a simple wooden pole rather than the dark bronze versions that had decorated the bungalow's living room.

I sat up. For a second or two, the not-quite-familiar room spun around me, and I set a hand down on the sofa where I lay to steady myself.

No, that wasn't right, either. I knew the couch at the house I'd been renting had been a warm cognac leather, while this was some kind of silky jacquard fabric, a deep blue to coordinate with the gingham curtains at the windows.

Except…that fireplace was the same, wasn't it? The bungalow had been built in the typical Craftsman style and dated to the late teens of the previous century, and so the fireplace was wide, with built-in bookcases to either side and pretty smoke-blue tile surrounding the firebox. This one looked identical, as far as I was able to tell.

So, maybe there are two houses in Jerome with the same fireplace, I told myself. *Didn't they use to mail-order house kits out of the Sears catalog back then or something like that?*

I supposed that was remotely possible. However, it didn't explain where I was, or how I'd gotten here.

You tripped and fell, I thought then. *And Bellamy went to get help and they took you here.*

Again, mostly plausible. All the same, even if I'd been hurt and my friend had brought the cavalry to pull me out of that mine shaft, it didn't explain why I'd ended up here rather than my house. It wasn't as if I didn't have my keys with me.

Except, I realized in a moment of panic, I didn't. The little bag that had held my cell phone and house keys and I.D. must have slipped off my shoulder when I fell, because it sure as hell wasn't anywhere near where I was sitting.

In consternation, I swung my legs off the side of the couch, determined to stand up despite how swimmy I was feeling. Before I could get any further than that, though, a man came out of the hallway that led to the bungalow's two bedrooms and then paused, staring at me in shock.

About all I could do was stare back at him in response. I knew I'd never seen him before, because I would have remembered the cleanly chiseled, almost boyish features, the head of wavy brown hair…the clear blue eyes that seemed to focus on me like laser beams. He was dressed kind of oddly, in a white linen shirt and brown trousers I thought might be wool, with suspenders to hold them up. It definitely wasn't the sort of outfit I'd expect someone to be wearing in Jerome in June, not when we were right at the beginning of the hot season.

And he was a warlock. The twinge I experienced as he entered the room told me he couldn't be anything else.

"You're awake," he said, his voice a friendly baritone, and I blinked, forcing myself to focus on him and not his clothes.

"I am," I said. "Was I out for long?"

"A whole night and then some," he replied. "I'm Seth McAllister. Who are you?"

Seth McAllister. Seth McAllister. Had I met a Seth during the almost month I'd been living in Jerome?

I didn't think so. No, I couldn't pretend that I knew every single McAllister in the world, not when they were scattered all over the Verde Valley and even out in Payson or over in Prescott, but....

For some reason, my gaze slid past him to a calendar mounted on the wall, not too far away from the window. It had a black and white picture of an old-fashioned truck on it, with a fancy border that went all around the picture and down onto the section that displayed the date and year.

June 1926.

It was like a punch to my gut, and I could only be glad that I hadn't stood up yet after all.

No, that date had to be wrong.

Except....

I looked back at Seth McAllister, standing there in those clothes that made him look as if he'd raided a vintage store or something. He appeared completely natural in them, not like he was wearing a costume.

And I'd never seen him before or met anyone in town with that name.

My screwy "talent" for playing with time had messed with me before, but nothing on this scale. Somehow, though, when I'd fallen and hit my head, it had gone wild, sending me back into the past.

Well, that or I was having the mother of all nightmares.

Seth didn't seem like someone out of a nightmare, though. No, his expression was worried, even as he stood a careful distance away from the couch where I'd been lying, as if he didn't want to frighten me by getting too close.

Oh, I was frightened, all right, but not by him. It wasn't just that I'd catapulted myself back in time by more than a hundred years and had no clear idea how the hell I'd ever get back to where I came from.

The world of the Arizona witches in the 1920s was very, very different from the one I lived in. Back then, the McAllisters and the Wilcoxes had been mortal enemies. True, they seemed to have mostly stayed out of each other's territories, but that didn't mean awful things might not have happened if they'd crossed paths for whatever reason, magical duels or sideways-flung curses or God knows what else. Any public displays of magic like that would have been disastrous, considering how hard we all worked to make sure the civilian population had no idea who we really were.

I was half Wilcox.

But...I didn't really look like a Wilcox. I wasn't as dark as they usually were and instead favored my father in looks, with medium-brown hair and blue eyes.

And I didn't bear their name.

Seth McAllister was still staring at me, a certain wariness beginning to creep into his expression, and I realized I'd been sitting there without replying for way too long. Sure, most people would have excused me for being utterly gobsmacked, but I knew I needed to say something.

"Dev—" I began in answer to his question, then realized "Devynn" wasn't a common name even in my own time, and therefore definitely unheard-of back in the 1920s. "Deborah," I said quickly. "Deborah Rowe."

There. It was close enough to my real name that I was pretty sure I'd respond to it without too much hesitation, and I also guessed there wasn't any problem using my actual last name, not when it wasn't even a witch clan name. My paternal grandfather—whom I'd never met, since he'd remained in the past with the rest of my father's relatives—had been a civilian, while my witch blood on that side came from my grandmother's family, the Winfield clan. They were located on the other side of the continent in Massachusetts, and there was a good chance the McAllisters had never heard of them. There hadn't been a lot of contact between the various clans back then, and even in the modern world, the friendliness among the three clans in Arizona —and the Castillos in New Mexico, where Angela McAllister's daughter Miranda was the *prima*—tended to be the exception rather than the rule.

And thank God and the goddess Brigid who the McAllisters prayed to that I'd inherited my father's gift for concealing my witch nature. For me, just as it was for my father, that talent was pretty much a "set it and forget it" kind of thing, which was probably why it had continued to function even while I was passed out after my descent into a different time, because I had to consciously turn it off.

Otherwise, Seth surely would have known right away that I was a witch.

He couldn't know. He couldn't know anything about me except my name.

"Well, Miss Rowe," he said politely, "I'm very

pleased to make your acquaintance. You gave us all a good scare."

"I did?" I replied, doing my best to look doe-eyed and utterly guileless.

"Yes," he said. "I found you in the mine yesterday evening. Do you have any idea what you were doing there?"

At once, I shook my head. Because, despite my history degree…I'd focused on medieval Europe…I knew so little about the world of 1926 that there wasn't much chance of me cooking up a plausible explanation for my sudden appearance here. About all I could do was use the only excuse available to me.

"I don't know," I said. "I don't remember anything at all."

His brows drew together. Again, I couldn't help but be struck by how handsome he was, from the way his thick brown hair waved back from his brow to those chiseled lips, not pouty at all, but still the kind a girl could easily imagine herself kissing.

Oh, no, I told myself. *You are not going to think about him that way, no matter how good-looking he is. You need to use every available brain cell you've got to figure out how to get yourself home.*

"You don't remember how you got in the mine?"

"I don't remember that," I said, "and I don't remember anything before it, either. I know my name is Deborah Rowe, and I know I'm twenty-two years old. But anything else just seems…gone."

Now he appeared downright confounded. "You mean you have amnesia?"

"I suppose so," I replied, still doing what I could to look utterly innocent and confused, rather than my true state of mind, which was a lot closer to scared shitless. "That is, that's what it's called when all your memories are gone, isn't it?"

"That's what I've read." He hesitated for a moment, as if not quite sure where he was supposed to go from here. "I suppose I should have my cousin Helen come talk to you—she's a kind of nurse," he added.

Probably the clan's healer. Obviously, he couldn't refer to her that way, not to a woman he had to believe was a civilian, but the point was clear enough.

"And she knows about amnesia?" I asked, not worried about how dubious I sounded. I had to believe pretty much anyone in the same situation would have been skeptical.

"She knows about a lot of things," Seth said. "And she had a look at you last night, but she said she couldn't find anything physically wrong. But now that we know we're working with some kind of memory loss, it's possible she might be able to offer some helpful advice."

Strangely, his words relieved me a little. If this Helen person had already examined me—no doubt looking for some sort of head trauma—and hadn't detected anything that proved I was a woman out of time, then it was probably safe to talk to her now. After all, my talent seemed to be working perfectly at concealing my witch nature, and even though I still wore my modern clothes, there really wasn't much about me that could prove I hadn't been born at the start of the twentieth century, just as Seth himself must have been.

"I'm feeling kind of sticky," I said then, which was only the truth. The little bungalow was uncomfortably warm, and I had to believe it would get even hotter as the day wore on. No sign of modern conveniences like air conditioning around here, that was for sure. I hadn't even spied a table fan or a ceiling fan, although I thought they must have been invented by 1926.

Most likely, they were still luxuries in an out-of-the-way place like Jerome, Arizona.

"Do you mind if I get cleaned up first?" I went on.

A sudden flush touched his cheeks, and I realized he was probably embarrassed at the thought of me using his bathroom.

Men in 1926 were clearly different from the guys I'd known in the mid-twenty-first century.

But he sounded steady enough as he said, "No, of course not. Let me show you where the bathroom is. My mother also put together some fresh clothes for you when I went over to the store last night."

"'Store'?" I echoed, although I'd already guessed at the answer.

"McAllister Mercantile," he replied, an obvious note of pride in his voice. "My family's owned it for generations. My mother took a few things from the stock there."

"I'll have to find a way to pay you back—" I began, but he only shook his head.

"It's the least we can do for someone stranded here in our town," he told me. "But I'll show you where the bathroom is."

Finally, I pushed myself up from the sofa… only to have the room tilt around me. I stumbled, and at once, Seth was at my side, placing a strong hand under my elbow while I tried to steady myself.

"Thanks," I said. "I must be a little woozier than I thought."

"Do you need to sit down again?" he asked, expression all worry, but I shook my head.

"No, I'm all right. I think it was standing up

that put me off balance. I'm already feeling better."

And I was. Those few seconds of dizziness had disappeared as quickly as they'd come, and now I felt much improved…or rather, I felt about as good as I could, considering my unpredictable talent had just flung me back in time more than a hundred years, and I couldn't begin to figure out how to fix the situation.

Almost as soon as Seth had taken my elbow, he let go, apparently guessing that I was all right to walk now. In a way, I almost regretted that he hadn't continued to support me.

I liked the feel of his hand on my arm.

But then he was walking me down the short hallway to the bathroom, which was in exactly the same place as it had been in my rented bungalow.

Was this really the same house?

Although the bathroom's location and basic layout were the same, with a sink and toilet and claw-foot tub, everything else was radically different. Small white hexagon tile with a dark blue border covered the floor, and although there was a bathtub with a reassuring set of faucets that told me they at least had running water here, that was about all I could say for it. No sign of a showerhead, no little curtain you pulled around yourself for some privacy.

I'd never been into baths, had always been a long, hot shower kind of girl. The thought of having to get clean by taking a bath didn't exactly entrance me.

Well, you're not taking a bath now, I reminded myself. *You're just freshening up a bit and changing your clothes. You can worry about the bathtub later.*

"You can meet me in the living room when you're done," Seth said, not quite meeting my eyes. "It's kind of a good thing you showed up on Saturday evening—since it's Sunday today, I don't have a shift at the mine."

"Do you have to go to church?" I asked. It wasn't just idle curiosity; while I knew the majority of the McAllister clan was steadfastly pagan, I somehow doubted they'd be able to put their leaning toward alternative religions as much on display in the 1920s as they had in the twenty-first century. I wanted to know how they handled things.

Seth's gaze was still directed somewhere near the floor. "Oh, we have prayer meetings at various family members' houses on Sundays. That's how we've always done it."

Meaning, I guessed, that they observed their old religion in private. It was kind of surprising the civilian population in town hadn't asked a lot of questions about that, but from what I was able to recall, the McAllisters had been some of the first settlers and town founders here, and maybe no one wanted to poke them about their religion.

Whatever. Some people in my own clan were religious, but a lot more were cheerfully agnostic. It wasn't as though I was too worried about missing church. No, after hearing how my mother had had to drag her bustled butt to the Methodist church in Flagstaff every Sunday when she was back in 1884, I was just glad to know I wouldn't have to do the same thing here.

"How interesting!" I said, which I hoped was more or less the way a woman in 1926 would have responded. "And thank you for showing me the bathroom. I'll be as quick as I can."

"Take as much time as you need," Seth replied. "Come find me in the living room when you're done."

I nodded, then stepped inside the bathroom and closed the door. He'd already laid out some clothes on top of the little wooden washstand, so I peeled off my jeans and shirt and socks and every-thing else, and put on the garments he'd provided. The undies were more like little cotton tap pants, and the bra was closer to a bralette than anything I'd ever seen, just a flimsy piece of cotton with some lace trim.

Luckily, I'd never been an underwire kind of girl.

A narrow slip went over the underwear, and I selected a dress with a demure green flowered print that buttoned up the front. It was shorter than I'd expected, hitting barely below the knees, although I didn't know whether that was the actual style or whether I was just tall for the period.

Well, not much I could do about that.

Silk hose that had to be held up by garters had been tucked into the pair of brown heeled lace-up shoes Seth had left for me, and for a moment, I balked, thinking there was no way I was going to wear those things, especially when I knew June in the Verde Valley regularly pushed into the nineties, sometimes hotter.

But I also didn't want to give the wrong impression. I knew a whole lot less about the 1920s than I would have liked, and yet I had the feeling that a woman who went around without hose would be considered "loose."

Better to suck it up and deal with those hose, even though I had no idea what I was doing.

The struggle took me a couple of minutes, and when I was done, I still had some bags at my ankles. It couldn't be helped, though.

He'd also helpfully provided a box of hairpins. One thing I did remember about the 1920s was that a lot of women wore their hair short, but there was no way in the world I was about to lop off my hair, which I'd been carefully growing ever since my senior year of high school and now hung midway down my back. Luckily, though, I'd watched enough YouTube videos to know how to put it up in a pretty bun, something that came in handy during those hot summer days.

So I finger-combed my wavy locks as best I could—I'd spied a wooden comb sitting on the washstand, but I thought it would be rude to borrow something of Seth's without asking—and then wrapped my hair around my hand to make the nautilus-style bun I'd perfected the summer before, placing it low on the nape of my neck in my best attempt to mimic the hairstyles of the period. When I was done, I thought I looked pretty much like someone you'd pass on the street in 1926 without even taking a second look.

Good thing I'd never pierced my ears more than once, and that I'd been wearing plain gold hoops when I slipped back in time. Seth didn't seem to have given them a second look, which told me that, even if they weren't quite what most women of his time wore, they also weren't odd enough to invite comment.

Ditto for the gel polish I'd abandoned right after I graduated from college, figuring that I'd be working with my hands a lot at Rachel's store and that it was probably better to keep things simple. While I thought that some women in the 1920s wore makeup and nail polish, I had a feeling the glittery purple I'd sported last before I went with naked nails would have raised a few questions.

There wasn't a clock in the bathroom, so I had no idea how long my primping had taken. However, Seth didn't seem too impatient when I returned to the living room, which made me think I hadn't made him wait more than ten or fifteen minutes.

Was that a spark of admiration in his eyes when I entered the room?

No, I was probably imagining things.

He'd been sitting on the couch but stood up right away as I entered the room. "Feeling better?" he asked, and I nodded.

"Much."

"Those clothes you were wearing—" he began, then stopped himself. Appearing to sort through his words, he went on, "I beg your pardon, but they were somewhat odd. Where did you get them?"

Sometimes, pretending to have complete amnesia could be a real plus. "I have no idea," I lied. "I didn't recognize them—but then, I don't remember very much."

"Of course," he said quickly. "I probably shouldn't have asked. Now that you're ready, do you think you could speak to my cousin Helen? I'm hoping she'll be able to unravel some of this mystery."

"Sure," I said. "Although I don't know how much I'll be able to tell her."

"That's fine," he assured me. "But I think it's better if you at least talk to her a little. Are you all right with going to her house? She lives just down the street, so it isn't much of a walk. I thought that might be better since she has small children."

I had to hope someone would be watching the kids while she held the interview, or I didn't know how much she'd be able to accomplish. The Wilcoxes—well, most witches in general, from what I'd seen—tended to marry and start families early, so it wasn't as though I hadn't had plenty of chances to babysit and be around little kids, starting with my sister Jessica's two-year-old son Duncan and ranging to any Wilcox cousins who needed some cheap babysitting so they could go out to dinner or the movies or whatever.

Maybe that had been part of the reason why moving to Jerome had been so appealing. So far, no one had asked me to watch their kids, giving me that much more free time to do what I liked.

"If you're sure it won't be too much of an imposition," I said.

Seth immediately shook his head. "It's fine,"

he replied. "Helen's husband Calum can watch the children while we're talking."

It seemed the McAllisters were a little more progressive about that sort of thing than I might have expected from people living more than a hundred years ago.

"Well, then," I said. "Let's go talk to Helen."

4

PLUMBING THE DEPTHS

SETH HOPED HE HADN'T OVERTLY STARED AT Deborah Rowe when she returned to the living room. It had been difficult, because in that simple flowered dress and with her heavy hair wound into a complicated knot at the back of her neck, she looked like some kind of goddess who'd descended from Olympus to consort with mere mortals.

Or at least, mere witches and warlocks.

But he did his best to keep his wits about him, despite how distracting she was, and after a brief discussion about going down to Helen's house for the interview, they headed out. Now that Deborah walked next to him, he noted how tall she was, almost to his jaw, something he rarely encountered. She walked freely, with her chin up and her clear gray-blue eyes scanning the landscape around them as she appeared to take in everything as though she was seeing it for the first time.

Most likely, she was. Her memories might have deserted her but his had not, and he knew she'd never been in Jerome before.

Her free strides and utter unself-consciousness surprised him a little, just because the few truly tall women he'd met had tended to do what they could to make themselves less conspicuous, as though they knew they already attracted enough attention solely because of their height. But he thought he liked that about her, liked the way she seemed unafraid of looking at the world even though she had no real idea of her place in it.

Well, with any luck, his cousin Helen would be able to fix that.

Although neither of them had a telephone—there was one at the mercantile, and another in the surgeon's house up on Hill Street—Seth knew it was no imposition for him and Deborah to show up like this unannounced. It was late enough that the children would have all been bathed and dressed, and because they would not be attending any kind of services...not even the homegrown ones he'd described to his unexpected guest in a very small lie...he knew it was safe enough to come here, as everyone in the McAllister clan tended to stay close to home on Sundays.

In fact, Helen opened the door so quickly, it was almost as though she'd been expecting them in that very same moment. She was not a seer—their last seer had passed away some five years earlier, and so far no one in the younger generation of McAllisters appeared to have that gift—but his cousin still had flashes of intuition from time to time.

"Good morning," she said, her tone cheery, and directed her next words to her visitor. "I'm Helen O'Dowd, Seth's cousin. Come inside. Have you eaten?"

With a rush of shame, Seth realized he hadn't offered Deborah any refreshment after she awoke, not even a glass of water. He had been up for hours, and had already had coffee—he rarely ate breakfast—and he supposed he'd been so flustered by her presence that he'd forgotten she might need something more than a change of clothes to refresh herself.

"No," he replied, and glanced at Deborah. She wore a cheerful smile and didn't look particularly hungry, but he knew women were often very good at putting on a public face when the situation warranted. "Helen, this is Deborah Rowe. I should have gotten her something to eat, but—"

"It's fine," she murmured, even as his cousin's expression turned immediately disapproving.

"Oh, it is most certainly not 'fine,'" Helen

said, and opened the door a little wider. "Come into the sitting room, and we can have some tea and scones."

Because Seth knew his cousin was just as good a baker as she was a healer, he thought he might overlook his propensity for skipping breakfast to have some of her delicious raisin scones.

"That would be wonderful," he said as she led him and Deborah into her sitting room, which was certainly much larger and grander than the space where the lost young woman had spent the night on his sofa. Fine furniture, some of it shipped in from New York and some made just down the hill in the workshop adjacent to the high school, filled the space, and brocade curtains had been pulled back from the tall windows to allow a view of the tree-lined street directly in front of the house…and to allow a peek of Sedona's red rocks and the Mogollon Rim far beyond.

Helen gestured for them to take a seat on the settee, then disappeared to fetch the promised tea and scones. Next to him, Deborah was looking around with the same lively interest she'd displayed on the walk down here.

Well, he had to admit that his cousin's house was very fine, probably the nicest on its street. True, on the hillside above the main thoroughfare were grand homes built late in the last century, fanciful Victorian houses with stained-glass windows and even turrets, but he thought Helen's place was homier while at the same time being quite elegant.

No sight or sound of her three children, and Seth guessed that she'd made sure Calum was keeping them occupied in their postage stamp of a backyard, most likely playing with a ball or possibly the croquet set, although he thought they were still a little young for that. However they were being kept busy, the house was much quieter than it usually was, and he wondered if he should say something to fill the silence.

Exactly what, he wasn't sure; other than his McAllister cousins, he did not have any great experience with young ladies. He knew some of the unattached men in the family frequented the bar at the Connor Hotel, where they might meet women they could kiss and do quite a bit more with, but while he'd entertained the idea from time to time, something about it had never felt right to him. When he was sixteen, his father had taken him aside and explained something of what was supposed to pass between a man and a woman when they were married, and he'd absorbed as much of that unexpected information as he could, even as he told himself he would not indulge in such activities with the women at his town's bars and hotels, the ones who made themselves freely available to anyone who had the coin to pay their prices.

Because even though he knew Helen could take care of whatever illnesses he might acquire while enjoying the company of such a woman, the thought of asking his cousin for that particular kind of help was just too awkward.

No, he supposed when the time came, his parents would help him meet a sufficiently distant cousin from Prescott or Payson or Wickenburg, and he would settle down with her and finally learn for himself exactly what passed between a man and a woman.

It occurred to him that he shouldn't be thinking about those sorts of things, not with such an exquisite creature as Deborah Rowe sitting next to him, and yet…

…and yet he was beginning to realize she affected him in a way no other woman ever had. The purely cynical might have pointed out that was most likely because she was very pretty and also a complete stranger, and therefore exotic in a way a McAllister cousin could never be, but he couldn't help thinking the attraction must involve something more than mere novelty.

To his relief, Helen re-entered the room, now carrying a silver tray laden with her rose-painted tea set and a basket piled high with her raisin scones, and therefore he didn't have to come up with something clever to say to Deborah. A few minutes were spent pouring tea for everyone and handing out plates so they might help themselves to a scone, but soon enough, the refreshments had been provided, and it was time to start getting to the bottom of the mystery surrounding Deborah Rowe.

"Have you tried thinking of anything that might have happened before you were found at the mine?" Helen asked.

Deborah had just taken a bite of scone, so she had to finish chewing before she could set down the pastry, wipe her fingers on the napkin Helen had provided, and allow herself some time to ponder the question.

"I've tried," she said. As far as Seth could tell, there wasn't a hint of doubt in her tone, so he had to believe she was telling the truth. "But I can't remember anything at all. I woke up this morning on Mr. McAllister's couch, and that's pretty much all I know. Everything before that is just…darkness."

Helen's mouth pursed, making her look more like one of the dolls his mother displayed at the mercantile than ever, and she didn't respond immediately, instead taking a sip of tea as if that might help to focus her thoughts.

"It can happen that way sometimes, especially if someone has experienced a traumatic event.

Why, some of our boys came back from the war hardly knowing who they were or where they'd been."

A sad truth, one Seth couldn't deny. Although the McAllister family would have preferred not to send any of its sons to fight overseas, they also knew that avoiding military service through excuses and lies would have only invited the kind of scrutiny no witch clan could afford. He and his brother Charles had been too young to enlist, thank the Goddess, but twenty-two men of eligible age had gone…and only twelve returned. Those survivors were tight-lipped to this day about what they had seen or done, and two of them, his cousins Ernest and Stephen, seemed to have lost their minds entirely. They spent their days in a small house at the edge of town, tended to by their families, but any hope of their coming back to themselves was long gone. A disease of the mind wasn't something that could be easily cured by a healer, the way Helen had made sure that those with the racking coughs brought on by exposure to mustard gas regained all their lung function.

For a moment, Deborah appeared almost confused by his cousin's comment, as though she wasn't sure which war Helen had been talking about, but then she nodded. "World War 1, right," she said.

Seth and his cousin exchanged a mystified look. Why in the world...pardon the expression...would Deborah have phrased her comment that way when everyone knew it had been the war to end all wars?

But then she added, "Against the Kaiser," and Seth allowed himself a nod.

"Yes," he said. "So, you remember that much?"

"I suppose I do," Deborah replied, although now it was her turn to appear confused. "Is it strange that I would remember something about the war but nothing about who I am or where I came from?"

"Not necessarily," Helen said. "Sometimes the mind can hold on to facts it sees as neutral and not specifically connected to itself. Can you tell us who the President is?"

Deborah's face went utterly blank. "Um... Teddy Roosevelt?"

"No," Helen said, her tone now gentle. "That was quite some years ago. Our current President is Calvin Coolidge."

"Oh," Deborah responded. She sounded worried, and Seth couldn't blame her.

How was it that she'd known about the Great War, but had no idea who the current President was?

However, his cousin didn't appear too

concerned. "It's not so strange that you might retain some facts and not others, Miss. Rowe. Can you tell me when Arizona became a state?"

"February 14th, 1912," Deborah responded immediately.

Well, that was something. Although her memory was gone, and it seemed as though there were large gaps in the knowledge she still retained, she clearly hadn't forgotten everything.

Helen set down her teacup. "Miss Rowe, I would like to see if you have any signs of head trauma. Only with your permission, of course."

Seth slanted a glance at his cousin, and she responded with a barely perceptible shake of her head. He would have thought she'd learned everything she needed the night before, but maybe it was possible that if she performed a more thorough laying-on of hands, she would be able to learn if anything truly traumatic had happened to Deborah Rowe before she'd been abandoned in that mineshaft.

"That's fine," Deborah said. However, her expression appeared more anxious than ever, belying her words.

What was she afraid that his cousin might find?

However, she didn't flinch when Helen came over to her and pressed gentle hands against her skull, clearly trying to see if she had any bumps or bruises that had been overlooked. Even that careful examination caused a strand of hair to come loose from the bun at the back of Deborah's neck, falling softly against her cheekbone.

In that moment, Seth wished he could reach out and push it back…and maybe, just maybe, touch her cheek as well to feel the velvet softness of her skin.

As best he could, he dismissed that entirely inappropriate thought. How was it that he'd traveled through life without ever getting distracted by a woman, and now, less than twenty-four hours after meeting Deborah Rowe, he could think of nothing more than how much he wanted to kiss her, to pull the pins from her hair and let all of its glorious masses fall free over his hands?

It was an entirely different kind of witchcraft from the one he knew.

To his relief, Helen spoke then, pulling him away from the dangerous course his mind seemed determined to take.

"I can't find any obvious signs of injury," she said. "No bumps or knots or half-healed wounds."

"That's good, isn't it?" Deborah ventured, but Helen's troubled expression didn't change.

"Normally, I would say yes," she replied. "But if you weren't knocked out by a blow to the head, then something else must be causing your amnesia. I suppose it's possible you were administered ether and it somehow scrambled your memory. I've read of that happening occasionally, and often the memories lost are the ones from immediately before a patient was etherized."

Deborah's blue-gray eyes widened. "Why on earth would anyone give me ether?"

"I have no idea," his cousin replied. "And unless your memory somehow comes back on its own, none of us may ever know."

They were all somewhat subdued after that exchange, even as Seth's thoughts kept tumbling over one another, trying to determine whether being etherized and dropped in the mine was worse than getting hit over the head, until he decided at last that both were equally unpleasant propositions. After all, they were both predicated on some unknown assailant or assailants having dark designs on Deborah Rowe, for whatever reason.

And that was a scenario he had a hard time accepting, mostly because she seemed so kind and friendly that he couldn't imagine why anyone would want to cause her harm.

Plenty of bad people existed in the world, though…or at least, that was the sort of sentiment his parents or the clan elders liked to intone whenever someone got a hankering to leave Jerome and try their luck elsewhere in McAllister territory. Seth had never heard of any harm coming to his cousins in Payson or Prescott or even Wickenburg, but he also had to admit that those weren't the places where their clan had originally settled and therefore were slightly less known.

"But," his cousin Helen said as they finished their tea, "until we can learn where you came from and why you ended up here in Jerome, Deborah, we need to get you in a more settled situation. After all, it just wouldn't look proper for you to continue sleeping on Seth's sofa."

"I have a second bedroom," he replied, and she sent him a look so stern, he wondered if she'd borrowed the expression from his mother.

"That won't do, and you know it," Helen told him. "It's entirely improper for an unmarried man to have an unmarried woman who isn't his sister or other close relative staying in his home." She turned her gaze toward Deborah, adding, "I would offer you a room here, but now that little Nicholas is out of the nursery, I'm afraid I don't have any spare bedrooms."

Deborah's mouth pursed. "I don't want to be any trouble—" she began, and immediately, Helen shook her head.

"You're not any trouble," she said. "There are

plenty of houses in this town where people do have spare rooms. We just have to determine which one would be best for you."

"Maybe a boarding house?" Deborah ventured.

Seth didn't like that idea at all. Most of the boarding houses in Jerome were occupied by miners or other mine workers, and a rough, untidy lot they were—even if many of them were on his crew, people he knew well enough. And the places that weren't filled with unattached men housed the same women who frequented the bars…and whose reputations were nothing to be proud of.

True, there was the surgeon's house, where the nurses who worked at the sanatorium lived, but as far as he knew, they didn't have any extra space available. Besides, Deborah wasn't a nurse…or rather, he didn't believe she was. He supposed a nursing background might have been just another element hidden in the black gulf that currently comprised her memory, and yet he didn't think so.

It seemed his cousin Helen was of the same mind, because she said at once, "Oh, no—the boarding houses here in Jerome wouldn't be suitable for you at all. It's much better if we put you up with one of our cousins. We McAllisters are a very large family, and I'm sure someone will have room for you."

"What about Daphne's room at Aunt Ruth and Uncle Timothy's house?" Seth suggested. Most likely, he'd thought of his cousin because she was already fresh in his mind, thanks to using her as a fit reference so his mother could choose clothing of the correct size for Deborah. "She and Jack Emory just got married and moved into that house on Holly Avenue, so her room would be empty now."

"Of course," Helen said, relief clear on her porcelain features. "I should have thought of that. Why don't you run up to Ruth and Timothy's house now to ask them if they'd be all right with taking on a guest, and I can walk Deborah over to your place while we're waiting?"

The words sounded casual enough, but because of the significant look his cousin gave him, he knew she expected him to blink himself up to their house once he was outside and safely out of Deborah's line of sight.

Which was already what he'd planned to do, so in this at least, they agreed.

He looked down at Deborah. Through all their back and forth, she'd seemed calm enough, but he noticed now the way her fingers were wrapped around the handle of her teacup a little too tightly, as though she wasn't sure what she would do once she let go.

Well, he had to admit that it was probably

uncomfortable to have to sit there and listen to them discuss her fate. Better to get this over with, just so she—and they—would know what was happening next.

Because as much as he would have liked to continue arguing that it was fine for her to stay at his house, he knew there was no point in wasting his breath. Such an arrangement would be scandalous at best, and he certainly didn't want to impair Deborah Rowe's reputation if or when her memory returned to her and she went back whence she came.

"This won't take very long," he assured her, and sent her a quick smile to, with any luck, let her know they were all trying to look out for her best interests.

She managed to smile in return, although he thought he detected something forced about her expression, that she was doing so only because she'd realized she wasn't in a position to argue. And that was the terrible thing about the whole situation, wasn't it? Left here with no resources, without even a penny to her name and only the utterly inappropriate clothing on her back, what else was she supposed to do except rely on the support of those around her?

He went out the front door and then immediately around to the side yard, where he was sheltered by several luxuriant holly bushes and could allow himself to disappear without anyone seeing him. Directly afterward, he appeared at Aunt Ruth and Uncle Timothy's house, again choosing a spot to emerge in their side yard that was hidden from the street. Their neighbors on either side and across the way were also McAllisters, and therefore, he could have probably emerged right in the middle of the front walk without any real repercussions, but he'd learned as a child at his mother's knee that members of the witch community had to be circumspect at all times.

Even though he was following Helen's advice —and even though he knew logically that it wouldn't look at all appropriate to have Deborah stay with him—he also hated the thought of fobbing her off on his relatives. He was the one who'd found her, and he believed he should have been the one to give her a place to stay until they could sort out the mystery of who she actually was and where she had come from. After all, his was probably the most familiar face in town to her.

But none of those arguments would hold up against the weight of societal disapproval, which was why he resigned himself to walking up the steps to Aunt Ruth and Uncle Timothy's house and rapping twice with the brass knocker affixed to the front door.

Aunt Ruth was the one who answered. She looked only mildly surprised to see him; the

McAllisters were always running back and forth between their clan members' various houses, whether it was to ask to borrow a cup of flour or possibly deliver some news.

"What is it, Seth?" she asked, stepping aside so he could enter the foyer. Like cousin Helen's house, this one was also large and well-appointed, although the furnishings had been purchased before the turn of the century and everything was beginning to look a bit old-fashioned. And Ruth was a little old-fashioned, too, with her graying blonde hair piled up into a pompadour rather than the low buns most women sported these days if they hadn't bobbed their long locks. Her daughter Daphne had been the youngest of her children and the last to leave the nest, and Ruth already had her first grandchild on the way.

As quickly as Seth could, he explained how he'd found Deborah Rowe in the mine the evening before, and how Helen had determined that she seemed to be just fine physically despite the loss of almost all her memories.

"It wouldn't look right for me to put her up at my place," he concluded. "So we were hoping you and Uncle Timothy might let her stay in Daphne's old bedroom."

Ruth had listened to the story with alternating surprise and worry, but she nodded at once after the true reason for his visit had been revealed.

"The poor girl," she said. "This must have all been a terrible shock for her."

"It was," he replied. "But she's handling it pretty well, despite everything. I just want to make sure she has a safe place to stay until we can try to get this figured out."

"Well, one thing we have is plenty of room," Ruth said, which was only the truth. Their big Victorian had four bedrooms, and now only one of them was probably in use. Seth had heard Timothy comment about wanting to change one of the extra bedrooms into an office, but even if he'd carried out those plans, that still left two spares, either of which should be fine for Deborah. "You just send her along whenever you like. Timothy's out working in the garden, but otherwise, we didn't have any plans for today."

It definitely didn't sound as if Deborah was going to impose on them too much. Still, Seth found himself wondering if there was some way he could keep her at his house just a little longer.

He wanted to spend as much time in her company as he could.

Ruth came to his rescue then, adding, "And why don't you come over for dinner after she's settled? That way, she can have a familiar face around her this first night. It might make things easier for her."

"That's a wonderful idea," he said, even as he

hoped he didn't sound enthusiastic to the point where his reaction might raise suspicions. "What time?"

"Oh, six as usual," she replied. "You can bring her over whenever you like, though."

Well, he thought he might as well get this over with, especially now that he knew he'd have a chance to see Deborah again soon enough. "Within the hour, probably."

"We'll be expecting her."

With the matter settled, he thanked Aunt Ruth, told her he'd be back soon enough, and then disappeared so he could meet Helen and Deborah at his own house. Everyone in his clan was used to his magical comings and goings by now, so he knew she probably hadn't even batted an eye.

Now he just had to let Deborah know where she was going.

5

ANY PORT IN A STORM

WHEN SETH REAPPEARED AFTER ABOUT A TEN-minute absence, I did my best not to show how relieved I was. Sure, his cousin Helen—who looked like a porcelain doll come to life—had been friendly enough, doing her best to keep me entertained with stories about Jerome and its various points of interest, including the store Seth's parents owned and the English Kitchen— known in later days as Bobby D's, an awesome barbecue restaurant—which served authentic Chinese cuisine.

"You'll have to try it after you're settled," Helen said. She'd sat on the sofa while I perched in a side chair. It felt a little strange to make ourselves so comfortable when he wasn't even home, but she didn't appear to have a problem with the situation. "Perhaps Seth can take you."

Was she trying to set us up?

Not that I thought I would mind too much, but still, I shouldn't be thinking about hook-ups or even having dinner with a guy while I was here. No, I needed to be figuring out how the hell I was going to get back to the twenty-first century.

I made a noncommittal sound, and luckily, Seth walked in the front door of the bungalow only a minute later, saving me from further awkward conversation.

"It's all set with my Aunt Ruth," he informed us. "You'll just need to pack up the things I brought you."

The thought of having to stay with strangers didn't appeal to me very much, but I did my best to remind myself that they were McAllisters, and even though they weren't strictly family, they were still witches, which meant we had more in common than they might think.

"Thank you so much for arranging that," I said, wearing a smile I hoped looked genuine. "But I'm not sure how I can pack when I don't have a suitcase."

"Oh, you can borrow mine," Seth replied immediately. "It's not as if I'm going to need it any time soon."

Probably not. Witches and warlocks weren't world travelers at the best of times, and I had to imagine the opportunity for travel was even more limited in a place with no interstate highways or commercial flights, just Model Ts and whatever other cars were common in the 1920s.

And railroads, I supposed, but I had absolutely no idea if there was any rail in the area other than the trains they used to transport the copper ore from the United Verde down to the smelter in Clarkdale. The only reason I knew about that at all was because there was a great brewery that called itself Smeltertown, located in Clarkdale down the hill from Jerome, and the name had intrigued me enough to prod me to look up some of the local history.

"Then it seems I'm indebted to you once again," I said, and Seth just gave an awkward hitch of his shoulders.

"Well," Helen said, rising from her seat on the couch, "it looks like you have everything in hand, so I'll be heading home. But Deborah, if you start having headaches or any other kind of odd aches and pains, please let me know. I don't think it's very likely that you have a concussion, since you don't have any sign of physical trauma, but sometimes these things can come on a person out of the blue."

"I'll do that for sure," I promised her, although I knew that wasn't the problem here. No physical trauma at all…just the mental trauma of being trapped somewhere more than a hundred years before I was born.

But I knew I had to keep it together as best I could. Freaking out wasn't going to help me, and at least it sounded as if I was going someplace safe and stable, and not too far away. Things could have been a lot worse; I knew I was very lucky that Seth McAllister was the one who'd found me, considering what I'd heard about some of the rough types who'd inhabited Jerome during its early mining days.

Helen said goodbye and headed for home, leaving Seth and me alone in the house. Still looking a little awkward, he said, "I'll go get that suitcase."

He went down the hall to his bedroom while I waited in the front room. The clothes he'd given me were still stacked on the washstand in the bathroom, but I didn't see the point in moving them out here. Maybe it would have been a little easier to pack with some more space to spread out, except for the part where I honestly didn't have much to pack, not when I was already wearing a good third of what he'd given me.

A moment later, he returned with the suitcase —a small leather case that probably wouldn't have held much more than what I planned to put in it —and handed it over to me. "Here you are," he said.

"Thank you," I replied.

What else could I say?

I took the suitcase and went into the bath-room and, with an overwhelming sense of inevitability, put the other changes of clothes he'd given me inside. While I had no idea how long I was going to be stuck here, I somehow doubted that the tiny wardrobe was going to be enough to get me through my tenure in 1920s Jerome. Would I have to wash everything every third day and hang it up on a clothesline?

Maybe. I had the vaguest of vague ideas that maybe washing machines had already been invented by now, but I also had the impression that dryers had come along a lot later.

Not to mention that I had a whole hell of a lot more to worry about than simply keeping up with my day-to-day clothing needs.

The suitcase was packed, so I headed back to the living room. Seth hadn't sat down and instead hovered sort of nervously near the sofa, as though he hadn't quite known what to do with himself while I was otherwise occupied.

Well, that made two of us.

"All packed," I said, and lifted the suitcase I'd just filled as my way of proving those words. "So I suppose we can go to your Aunt Ruth's house now."

He nodded, although his expression wasn't

exactly what I could have called enthusiastic. Was he also wishing that I might be able to stay here with him?

"Let me carry that," he said, coming over so he could take the suitcase from me. It wasn't nearly heavy enough to be any kind of a burden, but I had a feeling that he was doing his best to be chivalrous. "It's not far to Aunt Ruth's, but it's hilly, so it's something of a climb."

Although I'd only been living in Jerome for less than a month, I was already all too aware that the simplest walk could turn into a challenging hike, thanks to the steep hillsides where the town had been built. I'd always thought of myself as being in pretty good shape—I did yoga and ran several miles daily back home in Flagstaff—but I knew my calf muscles were already a lot more toned now than they'd been before I relocated to the former mining town.

Current mining town, I reminded myself as Seth and I exited the house. I noticed he didn't stop to lock the door and wondered if that was common practice around here, or whether it was only the McAllisters who could be that casual about security. True, locked doors didn't constitute any sort of a barrier to a witch or warlock, but still, enough rough types lived here, whether working at the mine or being some kind of hang-

ers-on to the mining community, that I would
have thought he'd be a little more careful.

As we walked, though, he told me a little about
Uncle Timothy and Aunt Ruth, how Timothy had
been a blacksmith who'd gradually transitioned to
working on cars. It sounded as if the mines still
used mule teams to move the ore around, so his
original skills were often called upon, but he'd
made himself invaluable by also being able to bore
out a carburetor or rebuild a transmission.

"And with Daphne married a few months ago,
all their children have moved out," Seth went on.
By that point, we'd reached Hull Avenue, and I
was really wishing I had on my hiking boots or
even a pair of sneakers rather than the heeled lace-
up shoes I was wearing now. True, the heels were
sort of chunky and therefore much sturdier than a
pair of stilettos would have been, but still, they
weren't the most practical thing in the world. "So
Ruth and Timothy have plenty of space for you."

"It's very kind of them to take me in," I said.
I'd almost said "nice," but I was doing my best to
imitate the speech patterns of the people I'd met
so far, and "kind" just seemed more like something a young woman from the 1920s would say.
"I hope I won't be too much in the way."

"Their house is big enough that I doubt you'll
be bumping into each other much," Seth

responded, reassuring me somewhat. "Although, don't be surprised if Aunt Ruth puts you to work. She's a great baker and likes to make treats for other members of the family and also for Monroe's, a café down on Main Street."

Baking wasn't anything I'd ever gotten into, but I had to hope that all Ruth McAllister would want me to do was sift flour or pit cherries for pies or something equally mindless.

"How interesting!" I said brightly, hoping I didn't sound as intimidated as I felt.

Apparently not, because Seth only nodded. "Her pies are always the star at our holiday gatherings." He paused there before adding, voice a little too casual, "Oh, and she asked me to come to dinner tonight. She thought it might be better for you to have a familiar face there on your first night at their house."

Those words relieved me more than I wanted to admit. I'd already imagined myself sitting at Ruth and Timothy's dining room table and not knowing what the hell I was supposed to say or how I was supposed to act. Having Seth there would make the situation much more bearable.

"Oh, that's good to hear," I said, then went on, "That is, if you didn't already have plans."

He chuckled then, a warm, rich sound. His voice was just as handsome as his face, not too deep, but resonant and friendly, the kind of voice

I could imagine as a radio announcer or something. That was one thing I'd noticed about the people I'd met so far in Jerome—which, I had to admit, wasn't many. They all sounded like regular people, not the stylized voices I'd heard in old black-and-white movies. Had all that been an affectation?

Maybe. I reminded myself that I was in 1926, and I vaguely recalled that movies back then didn't even have people talking at all, just those funny little frames in between the action that spelled out what the actors were saying. So maybe they started to sound odd later on when movies had real talking in them. Not being a scholar of vintage cinema, I couldn't even begin to guess.

"No plans," Seth said. "Sometimes I have dinner with my family on Sunday nights, but they understood that today I was a little busy. Otherwise, I'll eat at home, or maybe get something from the English Kitchen or one of the other restaurants here if my cupboard is bare."

From the way he talked, it sure sounded as if he led a pretty solitary life. It also seemed very obvious that he was alone, that he wasn't married or even engaged or seeing someone.

Did people date in the 1920s?

Of course they did, I thought. *They probably called it "courting," but they still went to the movies and on picnics and maybe out to eat.*

And they danced, too, something I'd never been particularly good at. I had to hope Seth wouldn't ask me to go dancing with him—assuming there was even a place for that sort of entertainment around here—because my Charleston was pretty rusty.

It was a silly thought. He was only helping out someone he'd literally stumbled over. We didn't have any real connection, and I needed to remind myself of that, no matter how good-looking he might be.

All the same, I had a hard time banishing the mental image of me in a gorgeous beaded flapper gown while he wore a tuxedo…something I wasn't sure even existed in Jerome…and he dipped me in a pretty good imitation of Fred and Ginger doing the tango.

When did Fred Astaire's film career begin, anyway?

Those crazy thoughts flew right out the window, though, as Seth paused in front of a big Victorian house painted pale blue with darker blue and white accents, and said, "Here we are."

It was a very pretty home, large without being imposing, with red and white roses blooming in front of the expansive front porch and stained-glass windows flanking the front door and also ornamenting the turret off to one side. In fact, I thought I recognized the place, since I'd walked along this street a few times while getting acquainted with the town. In my day, the house was sage green with dark green and rusty red accents, but still, the overall shape of it was the same.

As pretty as it was, though, I couldn't ignore the quiver of unease in my stomach. Everyone I'd met so far had been extremely nice, but that didn't change the fact that Seth was going to leave me here with a couple of strangers.

We went up the steps and didn't even need to knock, because the front door opened as soon as we set foot on the porch.

A woman who looked as though she was probably in her mid-fifties stepped out and beamed at us. Even I knew her high-piled blonde hair—with some silver strands showing here and there—wouldn't have been the style in this era, although her dark plum drop-waist dress and black kid shoes seemed pretty of the moment.

"This must be Miss Rowe!" she exclaimed, coming forward so she could take my hands in hers and give them a hearty squeeze. "It is so good to meet you."

"Thank you for taking me in like this—" I began, but she only released her grip on me so she could wave away my comment with her free right hand.

"Oh, it's nothing, child. I was just so sorry to

hear of your predicament. I'm Ruth McAllister, and soon you'll meet my husband Timothy. I hope Seth told you that we have plenty of room, so it'll be a pleasure to have you here."

"He did," I said, even as his mouth quirked and his dancing blue eyes told me that he knew his aunt—or maybe she was really a cousin, and only referred to the other way because of the difference in hers and Seth's ages—could be a little overwhelming. "But still, it has to be something of an imposition to have a stranger in your house."

"Not at all," she replied at once. "But where are my manners? Come inside, the both of you."

She ushered us into a foyer that was decorated with fussy-looking antiques. No, I told myself, they weren't antiques, just heavy Victorian-style furniture, something that looked antique to my eyes even though it was probably only twenty or so years old at that point.

"Did Seth tell you he was coming back for dinner?" Ruth went on, and I nodded.

"Yes."

I'd almost added that it was kind of her to invite him over, but then I wondered if she would read more into my relief at his being there for dinner than I wanted her to.

Or maybe I was overthinking the whole thing.

She didn't appear to notice my carefully neutral response, because she took the suitcase from Seth, saying, "Thank you for walking Miss Rowe over here, Seth. We'll want to get her settled, but you can come back at six, as we already discussed."

The dismissal was clear, and it was obvious enough that Seth didn't intend to argue. "Sure." Then he paused and looked over at me. "I'll see you this evening, Miss Rowe."

I inclined my head. "I'll see you then."

After all, what was I supposed to say?

Don't leave me here?

That would have been way too dramatic, and the last thing I wanted to do was call any more attention to myself than I already had.

So I lifted my hand to wave, and he waved as well, murmuring again that he'd see me soon.

"Well," Ruth McAllister said briskly. "Let me show you where you'll be staying."

I had to admit it was a very pretty room, located on the second floor of the house and in the turret, giving me a curved wall on one side of the space, set with big windows that allowed an absolutely amazing view of Jerome and the Verde Valley beyond. Seth's house, being situated much farther down the hill, hadn't offered nearly as good a vantage point, and after Ruth showed me to the space—and mercifully added that she'd allow me some alone time to unpack—she said she'd be downstairs in the kitchen and that she expected me to join her there.

To help with dinner? That seemed an odd thing to do to a guest, but then, I had to admit I wasn't exactly sure what my status was here. Houseguest? Boarder?

Putting that thought aside, I hung my two remaining outfits in the large walnut wardrobe placed on the wall opposite the windows, then headed over there to get a good look at my surroundings. This entire street, like the one in my own time, was lined with houses that clearly had been built at least twenty or thirty years earlier, mostly Victorian in style, with carefully tended front yards. The street was gravel instead of asphalt, and the colors on many of the homes had shifted over the years, but otherwise, the setting was still recognizable enough.

As was Jerome; I knew the town had been granted historic landmark status way back in the 1960s, and therefore all the buildings had been preserved rather than torn down to make way for newer, more modern structures. Now they definitely looked much fresher, but the outline of the town was basically the same as the one I'd come to know and love.

A faint haze of smoke lay over the place,

though, probably from all the various coal-fired boilers and furnaces in the town, and maybe also from the smelter down in Clarkdale, although inside, I couldn't really smell anything, thank God. No worries about environmental impacts back in the 1920s, that was for sure.

But even the smoke wasn't enough to hide the beauty of the landscape, or the blue skies overhead. From here, I could catch an even better glimpse of Sedona's red rocks and the rolling, golden contours of the Verde Valley. Once again, it didn't seem all that different from the world I knew, except I thought the road leading away from Cottonwood and toward Sedona was narrower than it was in my time, with only a single lane in either direction.

Well, back then, there hadn't been nearly the tourist presence of modern times. These were all working towns, whether mining or farming or ranching, not the sort of places people generally came to sightsee despite their natural beauty.

However, I knew I shouldn't be concentrating on the view. No, now that I was alone, I needed to try my best to end this little trip down memory lane and get back where I belonged.

Unfortunately, I was scared shitless to try.

For the past ten years, I'd done everything I could to stifle my supposed gift, to make sure I controlled it and not the other way around. It had never been as simple as just telling myself that I wanted to travel a certain distance in time. The few occasions I'd made the attempt, I'd either gone in the opposite direction from planned, or way overshot and landed where I'd never intended to be.

And I still didn't know exactly how I'd ended up here and now. Was it only that being knocked unconscious had allowed my particular brand of magic to cut loose, finally free from the constraints I'd placed on it over the past decade?

I supposed that was one theory. It made more sense than anything else.

Another unknown was why it had sent me back to June 1926, of all times. Not that I was a scholar of McAllister family history—far from it —but from everything I'd heard, it sure sounded as if the 1920s had been a quiet, prosperous time for the clan that had once been the Wilcoxes' enemies. It just didn't make much sense for me to be here.

Of course, this all could have been completely random. It wasn't as if my talent hadn't excelled at sending me to unexpected places on more than one occasion, although nothing had been as extreme as my current excursion to times before.

I let out a breath and went to sit down on the bed. It was a narrow thing with a white iron frame and a quilt in soft, pretty colors of rose and sage and mauve covering the mattress, which gave alarmingly under my weight and which I guessed was probably stuffed with feathers.

Good thing I wasn't allergic.

How to go about this?

It had been so many years since I'd consciously tried to make my talent move me around in time that I had to stop and think about it for a long, hard moment. Problem was, I knew that every time I'd made the attempt, I'd screwed up royally.

I supposed some people would argue that I'd also messed up big-time while knocked out cold, which would seem to indicate I was pretty much screwed no matter what I did.

My stomach churned uneasily at the thought, and I did my best to ignore it. Admitting defeat before I even got started didn't seem like a very good strategy.

Maybe I was wasting way too much thought on this, though. What if I didn't try to think about how many years and months and days I had to travel, and instead only imagined when I needed to go and did my best to move things along that way?

It was worth a try...even as I realized that if I was successful, I'd appear in my own time right in this very spot, and therefore would materialize in someone's bedroom.

Well, I'd deal with that situation if and when

it happened. Trying to explain away inadvertent trespassing seemed a lot less fraught than remaining stuck in 1926, no matter how nice everyone here seemed to be.

Just in case, I got up from the bed and moved over to the window seat and sat there, my hope being that even if the furniture had gotten shifted around over the years, the window seat probably would have remained in the same place. From what I'd been able to tell, the people who owned the historic houses here in Jerome were all about preserving them rather than gutting them down to the studs to make them over into their particular vision of what their home should be.

The sun was already high enough overhead that it wasn't hitting this side of the house. Even so, the temperature in this upstairs room was warmer than I would have liked, and no doubt would just get worse as the day wore on. About all I could hope was that there'd be a nice evening breeze to cool things down once the sun slipped behind Mingus Mountain in the early evening.

If, of course, I was even around to worry about sleeping in a hot room.

I closed my eyes and breathed in and breathed out, doing my best to slow everything down, to push away the anxiety that had been bubbling under the surface ever since I arrived here in 1926. While I didn't meditate, I'd done enough yoga that I was pretty good at smoothing down the rough edges and allowing myself to focus on a single thing.

In this case, my room in my childhood home in Flagstaff, which I knew my mother hadn't touched, thinking I'd be back whenever I got tired of working at the store and wanted to return to more familiar surroundings. I'd decided to visualize that room because it was much better known to me than the one in my rented house here in Jerome—and also because I worried that if I started thinking about that particular bedroom, I'd think about Seth as well, about his quick, friendly smile and the astonishing sapphire of his eyes.

And I couldn't let myself think about him. The last thing I wanted was to allow any thoughts of people and things in this time and place to trap me here. Besides, the important thing to focus on was a when, not a where. If I was successful, I'd still be here in Jerome, simply because my gift only allowed me to travel in time, not in space.

Thinking of my room just as it had looked before I packed my bags and left for McAllister territory seemed to be the smartest thing to do. With any luck, I'd get back within a few hours of when I left.

Walls painted a serene sage green, shining wood floors. Upholstered headboard and furniture that was a fun mismatch of wood and iron, things that shouldn't have gone together but somehow did anyway. I'd completely redecorated the space my first year of college, knowing I wanted to leave behind the girlish pastels that had suited me just fine when I was younger but now seemed cloying, almost silly. And because I'd chosen everything myself, I knew the room very well, right down to the seeded glass vase that sometimes held pussy-willows and sometimes cottonwood branches, depending on the time of year.

The image was so clear in my mind that it almost felt as if I was sitting there, rather than in the prim, pretty room that had once belonged to Seth's cousin Daphne. If I reached out, would I be able to feel the smooth curves of the vase that always sat on my dresser?

Better not to try. I didn't want to touch something nearby that would fling me out of my imagining.

Instead, I sat there, holding on to that mental picture, doing my best not to force anything, only to be in the moment…a moment I hoped would morph into one more than a hundred years from now.

A knock at the door. "Miss Rowe? Seth's here, and we're getting ready to sit down to dinner."

My eyes flashed open. The same turret room surrounded me, with the white iron bedstead to one side and the jewel-toned stained glass bordering the windows, although the day outside had darkened, and I could tell far more time had passed than I'd thought. Was Ruth McAllister angry with me for not appearing downstairs as I'd promised several hours earlier? Her voice didn't sound annoyed, so maybe she thought I'd taken a nap and had left me alone to sleep.

Whatever had happened, it seemed clear her arrival had broken my concentration.

So much for that.

"I'll be right down," I said.

6

DEEP, DARK SECRETS

He knew he shouldn't have been looking forward to this dinner so much. Despite that, Seth couldn't quite keep his heart from skipping a beat as Deborah entered the dining room and sent an apologetic smile toward him and his uncle Timothy, who was already seated at the head of the table.

"I'm so sorry about that," she said as she sat down in the chair directly opposite Seth's. "I was trying hard to see if I could remember anything, and it seems I got so exhausted, I ended up falling asleep."

"Did anything come back to you?" Timothy asked. Like his wife, he was in his middle fifties, although somewhere along the way, he'd lost a good deal of his hair and was now nearly bald. The straining waistband of his trousers told the tale of the multitude of good meals that had emerged from Ruth's kitchen over the years, and yet he never seemed too bothered by his girth and would always joke that perhaps it might take a few years off his life, but at least he would die happy.

Deborah shook her head in response to Timothy's question. It seemed to Seth that she'd tidied up a bit, since those few strands that had come loose from her bun earlier today were now tucked neatly back away from her face. "No, nothing. It's frustrating, but I'll keep trying."

"Of course you will," Ruth said as she came back into the dining room, now carrying a platter that displayed a fine roast. She put it down near her husband's place setting and then took the seat immediately to his right. "In the meantime, though, you should definitely eat to keep up your strength."

Seth did his best to smother a smile. Their clan had a very good healer in Helen, but that didn't stop Ruth from thinking her home cooking was really the solution to whatever might ail you.

Deborah nodded, and the next few minutes were taken up by Uncle Timothy carving the roast and giving everyone a generous helping, while the side dishes—mashed potatoes and peas and rolls and gravy—got passed around so they all had full plates by the time they were done.

Seeming to sense that Deborah didn't want to

continue discussing her memory loss, his aunt Ruth deftly turned the conversation to bits of chitchat about Jerome, whether it was the new restaurant coming in at the very top of Main Street, kitty-corner from the mercantile, or the prospect of an early monsoon season, considering they'd gotten some good rain just the weekend before.

"You do know about the monsoons, don't you?" Ruth asked, and Deborah nodded.

"The summer rains you get here in the Southwest, right?"

"Exactly," Seth's aunt replied. "Up here on the mountainside, it often feels as if they're fiercer than they are down in the valley, in Cottonwood or thereabouts." She paused for a moment as she gave her visitor a considering look. "If you know about the monsoons, then surely you must be from somewhere in Arizona."

"They have monsoons in New Mexico as well," Timothy pointed out, but Ruth only made a dismissive sound.

"I doubt very much that she's come from there," she said. "It's all Indians and artists in that colony in Santa Fe."

Once again, Seth had to keep himself from grinning. And, judging by the dancing light in Deborah's clear blue-gray eyes, she was just as amused by Ruth's declarations as he was.

"Oh, I think there are a few more people than that," he commented as he broke open his roll to butter it. "But I also have the feeling that Deborah comes from someplace a little closer than Santa Fe."

Possibly, that impression was wishful thinking and nothing more. If she came from nearby, maybe Sedona or Cottonwood, or even over the mountain in Prescott, then she wouldn't have to travel very far to get home.

If that was the case, he might still be able to see her again after she was restored to her family.

The uncomfortable thought emerged that she might have come from Flagstaff, in which case she might as well be from Timbuktu. No McAllister ventured anywhere near there, even though the bustling mountain town had plenty of residents who weren't Wilcoxes.

It just wasn't safe, not populated as it was by a witch clan that used magic to further their own ends and viewed the McAllisters as their bitter enemies. The *primuses* who ruled that clan didn't seem to care whether they slipped over to the dark side…as long as the end result was greater wealth and power.

Through all this, the subject of their conversation had remained silent, as if she was listening to their various arguments and trying to decide whether any of them had merit. She reached for her glass of tea—wine had been banished from dinner tables for six years now—and sipped from it before saying, "I suppose anything is possible."

Maybe it was. Since she didn't seem to want to pursue that subject any longer, he thought it best to steer the conversation in another direction, bringing up the possibility he'd heard bandied around a few days earlier that Jerome might be getting a movie theater in the next year or so.

Ruth openly scoffed at that suggestion, saying that the Liberty Theatre on Main Street provided all the entertainment anyone could want, and that it was much better to see a live production rather than flickering images on a screen made by people all the way off in Los Angeles. Timothy countered that it was getting more and more expensive to have real theater and some folks just couldn't afford to go, whereas they might have been able to manage the 25¢ that a movie cost.

Back and forth they went, while Seth and Deborah exchanged amused glances but mostly stayed out of the fray. He could see why she wanted to remain silent on the subject, as she was a newcomer here and knew very little about the town. And while Seth had of course been born in Jerome, he'd long ago realized it was better not to engage with his aunt unless it was strictly necessary.

Eventually, though, the meal came to its

conclusion, and at once he said, "Aunt Ruth, would you mind if I stole Deborah for a few minutes? I thought we might take a short stroll down the block."

This was something of a gamble, because he had a feeling his aunt would rather have enlisted Deborah's help in cleaning up. But then she sent him a shrewd glance, almost measuring, and said with a smile, "No, of course I don't mind. Timothy can help me clear the table. You two enjoy the evening."

During this exchange, Deborah had looked almost puzzled, but she didn't make any protests and seemed amenable enough to heading outside —after asking Ruth if she was sure she didn't need any extra help cleaning up. Of course Ruth told her briskly that she and Timothy could manage just fine, so a few minutes later, Seth and Deborah made their way down the front steps and onto the sidewalk.

It was a fine night, the air mild and gentle after the heat of the day. Off to the east, a gibbous moon had just begun to rise behind the Mogollon Rim, and a panoply of stars glittered overhead. A soft breeze rustled in the leaves of the oaks and cottonwoods and sycamores, but it wasn't quite loud enough to drown out the lively notes of a piano played with more enthusiasm than skill in the bar at the Connor Hotel, or the rough laughter of those who didn't seem to have a problem being so raucous on a Sunday night when they all had to be at work early the next morning.

He knew that most of the bars up and down Main Street served alcohol, even though doing so was enough to get them closed down and slapped with a hefty fine. Jerome was just far enough off the beaten track that most people paid little attention to what might be going on there, and therefore the owners of those establishments tended to operate with an impunity that wouldn't have been allowed in larger towns like Prescott or Flagstaff or Phoenix.

"How are you settling in?" he asked Deborah, who'd walked alongside him in silence after leaving the house.

She smiled, although he thought something about her expression seemed a little forced. "Oh, very well," she said. "I can't say how much I appreciate the way Ruth has given me a place to land. Otherwise, I'm not sure what would have happened."

You could have stayed with me, he thought, even though he knew that had never been a real possibility. If it had turned out that Ruth was unwilling or unable to give Deborah refuge, Seth knew someone else in the clan would have stepped up. Since he was the one who had found her, they would have believed the McAllisters had a responsibility to keep her safe.

"We would have worked out something," he told her. "But I'm glad that Ruth was happy to help."

Deborah nodded, and for another moment, they walked quietly while he did his best not to stare at how her skin seemed even smoother and milkier in the moonlight, or how she walked with a self-assured grace that made him think of a queen in exile.

Or at least a princess. She wasn't really old enough to be a queen.

"I wish I could think of how to jog my memory," she said as they approached the terminus of the street where it dead-ended against a spur of the mountain. "It seems so strange to me that I can recall things like the monsoon, or know that the rug in your aunt's dining room is Persian, and still not be able to remember anything about myself."

"Maybe that's just how amnesia works," Seth replied. "It sure seemed in the books I've read where someone had some kind of memory loss, they could remember a lot about the world, just not their place in it."

Deborah paused and looked up at him, her full mouth curving in a smile. "Do you read a lot of novels?"

Heat touched his cheeks, and he hoped the moonlight wasn't strong enough to show the way he'd flushed like a stupid schoolboy called to task by the teacher.

"I used to," he said. "When I was in school, I always finished my work before anyone else, so I hid books in my desk and tried to sneak reading a page here and there when the teacher wasn't looking at me. It felt like a good way to escape."

He stopped there, wondering if he should have told her about his illicit reading habits. After all, it didn't seem much like a show of strength to admit that he'd been bored with his life in Jerome and wished he could go somewhere else, to a place where he could raft down the Nile or experience a safari on Africa's great savannahs, or travel to the dark jungles of Borneo…or even to the center of the Earth, as described in the wonderful novel by Jules Verne.

Anywhere except this dusty mining town in northern Arizona.

Deborah, however, didn't appear disapproving, but rather thoughtful. "I can see that," she said. "Reading is the perfect way to allow you to be someone other than yourself, isn't it?"

She understood. She wasn't going to trot out the reproofs he'd heard through most of his youth, that reading was a waste of time and that he needed to focus on the here and now, and not the doings of people in far-off places or the distant future. The McAllisters might have been witches and warlocks, but they also tended to be extremely down-to-earth.

"I always thought so," he said. "Not that I have much time for that sort of thing these days."

"Because of your work at the mine?" she asked, and he nodded.

"It's ten hours a day, six days a week," he told her. "By the time I get home, all I want to do is eat and sleep."

Something in her expression clouded as he described his schedule.

Could it be she was unhappy that he had to be at the mine for such long hours, precluding any real chance for him to see her regularly?

No, he wasn't so puffed up over himself that he thought she would languish if she didn't get to share his company.

"It sounds hard," she said, and he had to admit, her tone sounded normal enough, albeit tinged with a note of sympathy. "Why did you decide to work there when your family owns a store here in town?"

A valid enough question, a query he'd faced on more than one occasion. The United Verde wasn't owned by the clan, which meant anyone who worked there had to be always on their guard lest their civilian co-workers or bosses might detect something strange about their McAllister employees.

"Oh, well," he said, doing his best to sound noncommittal. "Both my parents and my brother Charles take care of the store, so they didn't really need me. It just seemed better for me to strike out on my own. It's hard work at the mine, but it pays well, probably better than working at the mercantile."

Deborah seemed to absorb this information without any real judgment involved, because she inclined her head toward him without responding at first. Then she said, "I suppose it can be difficult when your family expects you to do one thing and you want to do another."

Now she sounded almost melancholy, as though she was speaking from personal experience. But how could she be, when she recalled nothing of who she was or where she'd come from?

He wanted to ask…and then decided to let it go. While they were talking quite naturally, he also knew that they'd only recently become acquainted with one another, and it would be rude to probe too deeply. "My parents made a bit of a ruckus," he admitted. "But after a while, they realized I wasn't going to change my mind and let it alone. I've been there for three years, and now

I'm a foreman, the youngest ever at the United Verde."

As soon as the words left his mouth, he wished he could take them back. They sounded far too boastful.

Deborah, though, only appeared thoughtful. "Then it definitely seems as if you made the right choice." She paused there, and again he got the impression that she was speaking of something beyond his personal situation, as though she was comparing it to her own even when she shouldn't have been able to recall anything about her past.

By that point, they'd made it almost back to Timothy and Ruth's house. Seth hated that the walk was over so soon, even as he also knew that trying to lengthen it would only let Deborah know he was all too anxious to spend as much time as possible in her company.

As if that wasn't abundantly clear.

He also wished there were more signs of her past in her appearance. Her fingers had been bare of rings when he found her, which seemed to signal she wasn't married or engaged. Or was that wishful thinking on his part? After all, she could have been wearing a ring and lost it when she was brought to the mine.

The only jewelry she'd been wearing was a small pair of gold hoops in her ears. Piercings such as that weren't very common, except among the women in the Mexican families who'd settled in Cottonwood to work the fields there. However, Deborah clearly wasn't of Mexican descent, so he wasn't sure what he should think about that particular accessory. He supposed pierced ears might have been a family tradition. Whatever the reason for her having them, he had to admit they added to her attraction, her mystery.

There was so much he didn't know about her.

So much she didn't know about herself.

When they came to the walkway that led up to Ruth and Timothy's front porch, Seth found himself blurting, "I work long hours, but I'm still almost always finished by six-thirty. Would you be interested in going to the English Kitchen with me?"

Her brows lifted slightly. "That's a restaurant, right?"

"Yes," he replied. "It's just down the hill from Main Street—Chinese food," he added, since he knew the name of the restaurant didn't give a very good indication as to the actual content of its menu.

A moment of hesitation, one that made him think for sure she was going to turn him down, and then she said, "I love Chinese food. Do you want to meet there, or come get me here?"

"Oh, I'll meet you here," he said hastily. While he supposed it would be safe enough for her to go to the restaurant by herself…especially since six-thirty was still full daylight at this time of year… he also didn't like the thought of her wandering around downtown Jerome on her own, not with so many rough types who would also be out and about around then, looking for their own food.

And drink, even though it was supposedly forbidden.

"A quarter to seven?" he ventured next, and she smiled.

"Sounds perfect."

Seth slept extremely well, better than he thought he had in a long while. Although he didn't dream of Deborah Rowe, he knew the realization upon awaking that he would see her again tonight made him smile even as he sat up and stretched and knew he needed to hurry to get to the mine on time.

They were working on a newly opened section that morning, and keeping an eye on everyone and directing traffic—in addition to perusing some new reports from the survey team—kept him busy enough that he didn't have much of a chance to break away and check on the shaft where he'd found Deborah two nights earlier. However, toward the end of the day he had a brief opening to go take a look and write up a quick memo to the superintendent as to the eventual fate of the shaft...only to find the man himself already there, with a team starting to tack up some sheets of wood across the entrance.

"Mr. Allenby," he said, doing his best not to sound surprised.

"Ah, McAllister," his supervisor returned. Lionel Allenby was a tall, thin man with fair hair that always glistened with brilliantine and close-set gray eyes. Despite the dust and the general dirt that accompanied their profession, he was always impeccably turned out, with crisp white shirts and a bewildering variety of tailored waistcoats and silk ties. "I was looking over the surveyor's reports on this shaft and decided it was time we closed it up. Too much of a liability to simply leave it open like this if we're not actually going to mine this section."

Seth had thought much the same thing, which was part of the reason why he'd returned here at the end of the day. Still, it was generally his job to oversee a small project like boarding up the mine shaft, not the superintendent's.

However, he knew better than to question the doings of his superior. "I'm sorry about the delay in getting it closed up," he said. "It was on my list of things I needed to do this week."

"It's fine, my boy," Allenby said, and clapped

an avuncular hand on the younger man's shoulder. "I know you've been busy. But as I always say, what difference who does the work as long as it gets done in the end?"

"Of course," Seth responded right away. While he wasn't afraid to stand up for himself—or his team—when the situation truly warranted it, he also knew it was foolish to jeopardize his position at the mine by making specious protests. "I'm glad to see it was so easy to take care of."

"Well, it was rather a small shaft," Allenby said. "Too bad there wasn't anything worth digging up here, but I suppose that's just how it goes sometimes. I'll let you get back to finish up with your team."

Those words were an obvious dismissal, so Seth only nodded and headed over to the open pit where his men were working to finish the final part of their quota for the day. After all, he didn't want to linger here, not when he would be meeting Deborah for dinner very soon.

Nevertheless, he couldn't quite stop himself from wondering why Lionel Allenby had been so motivated to make sure that particular mineshaft was hidden from public view.

7

A LITTLE NOODLE

IT WAS STUPID TO BE NERVOUS, WASN'T IT? After all, this was just dinner, nothing crazy.

Right. Like this planned dinner with Seth at the English Kitchen didn't have "first date" written all over it.

Ruth hadn't seemed too worried about me skipping dinner at her house to go out with her nephew—or cousin; I was still a little foggy as to their actual relationship. In fact, she'd seemed cheered by the prospect, as though she was already thinking of us as a couple. During the day, when I'd helped her by hanging up the wash in the backyard, shelled what felt like an entire mountain of peas, and stood by and acted as operating nurse, handing over carefully measured vanilla and sugar and anything else she requested as she baked what seemed like enough apple tarts to feed the entire town, she'd told me a few things about Seth.

He was the younger of two brothers—which I'd already guessed—and McAllister Mercantile had been in the family for going on three generations. Ruth didn't seem to have any problem telling me how the clan had emigrated from Scotland some fifty years earlier, although obviously, she kept out any mention of the tiny little detail about them all being witches and warlocks. Because of her, I learned that Seth wasn't married and had never even been engaged, unlike his older brother Charles.

"But she broke it off," Ruth said, looking almost indignant, as if she couldn't imagine how anyone would have the bad taste to turn down a chance at becoming a member of the McAllister clan. "Her family was always very strict. They decided that Charles wasn't suitable, and the poor girl got sent off to stay with an aunt in Prescott. That was only six months ago, so of course Charles hasn't been in any mood to start looking for a wife. I'm sure he will again soon enough, though—at twenty-five, it's high time he got married and started a family."

That was a little old for a warlock to be unattached, especially in light of the age in which he was living. I found myself feeling sorry for Charles, whom I had yet to meet, and wondered if

Seth was being wary about settling down after seeing what had happened to his brother.

Then again, a cautious man probably wouldn't have invited me out to dinner in such a public place.

I hadn't asked a lot of questions—no need to, not when Ruth McAllister seemed just fine with volunteering all sorts of information about the family. Surface-level stuff, sure…she wasn't loose-lipped enough to let slip anything too sensitive…but still, it seemed like the clan was doing just fine, and rather than feeling impinged upon because she'd taken in a nonpaying guest, she seemed happy that someone had shown up to fill a little of the gap left behind after the youngest of her children married and moved out to start her own life.

That meant I was armed with a lot more facts now than I'd been the day before, and yet I still couldn't quite ignore the fluttery sensation in my stomach when someone knocked at the door.

I'd been sitting in the front room, pretending to read a copy of *The Ladies Home Journal*—something that probably would have brought a pretty penny if sold in a vintage shop in my own time—when Seth knocked on the door. At once, I set down the magazine and went to answer it. Ruth had already told me I could let him in when he came, since she and her husband always sat down to dinner at six-thirty and Seth would be arriving a little after that.

He'd clearly gone home and washed up, since his face was clean and shiny, hair slightly damp and combed back from his brow.

How could someone be so adorable and so drop-dead gorgeous at the same time?

"Evening," he said, and I smiled.

"Evening. Did you want to come in?"

He sent a glance past me, presumably toward the dining room where Ruth and Timothy were sharing their meal, and shook his head. "No, that's all right. We can just head down to the restaurant."

Fine by me. Ruth had fed me a lunch much bigger than I usually ate, of cold chicken and fruit and a leftover roll from dinner the night before, but that had been almost seven hours ago, and I was ready to eat again.

For a second, I thought Seth might offer me his arm, because he made a hesitant movement before deciding maybe that was taking too many liberties after such a short acquaintance. To be honest, I had very little idea of what was acceptable and what wasn't in the world of 1926, although I had a feeling that, while this wasn't the Victorian age any longer, people were still a lot more reserved than their counterparts in the twenty-first century.

Instead, we headed out, with the two of us walking down the porch steps and then following the curve of the street as it wended its way toward Jerome's main drag. Just like the night before, music and laughter drifted up toward us, letting me know that even on a Monday evening, the little mining town was still a pretty happening place. I'd gotten that impression from some of the bits of local history I'd read, but it was much different to witness all that activity in person.

I hadn't gotten much of a chance to explore yet, thanks to being stuck at Ruth's house all day, and I couldn't stop myself from looking side to side, trying to take in all the sights and sounds. The buildings appeared to be almost the same as they were in the twenty-first century, less worn, of course, but everything was pretty much right where it was supposed to be.

There were far more restaurants and hotels and boarding houses than I'd expected, and a lot fewer shops. I supposed that made some sense; back in 1926, Jerome had been very much a working town, not the tourist attraction it had become. These people needed to sleep and places to eat and drink, and probably couldn't have cared less about buying a copper bracelet or a piece of Navajo horsehair pottery.

The street layout was just the same as I remembered, and we turned down Jerome Avenue from Main Street so we could get to the English Kitchen. It seemed much smaller than its modern-day incarnation as Bobby D's, mostly because the big patio/deck off the back where you could sit outside and eat barbecue and smell the luscious pecan wood smoke from the smokers they had going all day hadn't yet made its appearance.

No, it was just a small stucco building that occupied the space right where Hull Avenue curved up the hill, not very prepossessing at all. When Seth opened the door for me, though, the interior wasn't as changed as I'd thought, and still had the big oak bar to one side with the mirrors above and a row of booths directly opposite.

All of the booths but one were occupied. I reflected it was probably a good thing that we'd come here on a Monday evening and not some other night of the week, or we might have been waiting to sit down for quite a while. A pretty Asian girl gestured for us to take a seat at the booth, then pointed at the menu tacked on the wall near the bar.

Clearly, they didn't want to waste paper on printing out their bill of fare.

It all seemed pretty basic—a lot of noodle dishes, chop suey. Not a single Szechuan item that I could see, but I told myself to go with the flow and not worry whether the offerings were what I might normally order.

"What's your favorite dish here?" I asked Seth, who definitely looked more relaxed now that he was seated across from me in a booth and not walking by my side down Main Street.

"It's all good," he replied. "But you can't go wrong with the chop suey. It's my favorite thing on the menu."

Since I knew it would be insufferably rude to point out that chop suey wasn't even traditionally Chinese but rather a dish invented by Chinese immigrants after they came to America and started adapting their recipes to American tastes, I only nodded.

"Then that's what I'll have, too."

He got up and went to the counter to place our orders, and then settled himself in the booth immediately afterward.

"They'll bring us some tea in a minute."

Fans worked away overhead, telling me they did exist in Jerome, at least in the commercial spaces. Even so, it was stuffier in the restaurant than I'd been expecting, despite the way all the windows stood open, and I hoped the hot tea and chop suey wouldn't make me too warm.

But the dress I wore was lightweight, cool cotton, and even though I could have happily ripped off those damn hose and shoved them in the nearest trashcan, I was still a lot more comfortable than I would have been if I'd slipped back in time to the 1880s or something. My mother's stories about having to wear a corset and bustle and complicated dresses that weighed upwards of ten pounds each were enough to make me very glad that I'd landed in 1926.

True, she'd gone to Flagstaff in the late autumn, when she didn't need to worry about the heat, but still.

Sure enough, the same girl—the daughter of the restaurant's owner?—brought us a little pot of blue willow ware filled with steaming tea, along with a pair of matching cups with no handles. She smiled at us and said our food would be out shortly...her English was very good, telling me she'd either lived in the U.S. for most of her life or had been born here...and then left us alone again.

Seth reached for the teapot and poured some of the fragrant, gently steaming liquid into each of our cups before setting it back down again. A smile played around his mouth, and he said, "So, did Aunt Ruth put you to work today?"

"Some," I admitted. "I hung laundry on the clothesline and then helped her in the kitchen." Since I knew that was something of a misrepresentation of what had really happened, I hurried to add, "This is, I measured things and mostly stayed out of the way. What I don't know about baking would fill a book."

He picked up his cup of tea and blew on it,

then said, "Do you think that's because you've forgotten, or just because you were never much of a baker to begin with?"

There wasn't anything in his voice except simple curiosity, which led me to believe he didn't care whether I was the reincarnation of Julia Child or whomever. The realization warmed me a little. I honestly hadn't even known what I would have expected from a man of his period, except I supposed I thought they all pretty much expected their significant others to be good wives and mothers who could do everything from baking an apple pie to ensuring the house was tidy no matter how many kids they might have been looking after.

And then I wanted to shake my head at myself. Seth McAllister wasn't my significant other, and I knew I'd already probably gone too far just by allowing myself to think about how handsome he was...or how kind and thoughtful. No, what my brain really needed to do was come up with a way to get me back to my own time, even if it had failed miserably at the task so far.

"I really don't know," I said in answer to his question. "That is, I remembered basic tasks like how to measure ingredients and separate egg whites, but putting them all together definitely wasn't anything that felt familiar."

That unfamiliarity extended to the huge cast-iron oven Ruth used to cook and bake, a monstrosity that appeared to be wood-fired and would have intimidated me at the best of times. At least she had running water—and a lovely apron-front sink that wasn't too dissimilar from the big farmhouse-style version in the house where I'd grown up—but still, I thought even a *Great British Baking Show* champion might have been intimidated by trying to work with that hulking piece of metal.

"Well, I'm sure Ruth was glad of the help, even if you weren't familiar with everything," Seth told me, and I could only lift my shoulders.

"I hope so. Mostly, I tried to stay out of the way. But I figured I should do something to try to earn my keep."

At those words, his slightly arched brows pulled together. "You really shouldn't look at it that way," he said. "We're all happy to help you out. It has to be hard to be stranded in a strange place, away from everyone you know."

I made a small sound of assent and sipped some tea from my cup. It was fragrant and mild, probably oolong, with little bits of leaf floating around in it. No teabags around the English Kitchen, that was for sure.

The weird thing was, this whole situation felt oddly dissonant, just because I did know Jerome pretty well, even if I wasn't a native. I knew how the streets were laid out, recognized most of the buildings around me. And the ones I didn't, I figured they were the structures that had either burned or fallen down or—in the case of the building that had once housed the Cuban Mary brothel, which had slid down Cleopatra Hill a few years before I was born—finally succumbed to gravity. Because of all the mining that had taken place here, the hillsides weren't terribly stable, and lots of work had been expended over the years to shore up the buildings as best they could. Some simply couldn't be saved and were left unoccupied until they finally collapsed.

At any rate, it wasn't as if I'd been dropped in the middle of 1926 Paris or something. My surroundings were familiar enough; it was the people and the cars and the music and everything else that had utterly changed.

I couldn't tell Seth any of this, obviously.

No, I could only smile and say, "Well, it would have been a lot harder if I hadn't landed in McAllister territory."

At those words, his brows drew together again, and I wanted to curse myself for my clumsiness. Most people probably would have thought the phrase utterly innocuous, but witch clans always referred to their lands as their "territory," and by doing so, I'd made an obvious stumble despite my efforts to watch what I said.

I could almost see his brain working as he analyzed my statement, trying to see if it had any meaning beyond the innocent use of a phrase that wouldn't be significant to anyone outside the witch world, telling himself that of course it had to be a coincidence. His own senses would have already reassured him that I couldn't be a witch. Otherwise, he would have known I was more than an ordinary young woman the moment we met.

Of course, he could have no idea that I'd inherited a very special gift from my father, one he'd told me wasn't uncommon in his clan but which appeared to be utterly unknown to the clans here in the Southwest.

But then Seth's expression relaxed, and it seemed clear to me that he'd brushed the slight dissonance aside.

"Maybe," he allowed. "Although I'd say most folks I've met are pretty friendly and ready to lend a helping hand to those who're in a difficult situation through no fault of their own. Still," he went on, clear blue eyes meeting mine, "I can't say I'm sorry that you ended up here."

Our gazes held for just a moment, and then he looked back down at his plate of chop suey. He might have been kicking himself for being so open, even if for only a few seconds, but I was glad he'd been so unguarded right then.

That brief instant had been enough to tell me

this was a little more than just a friendly dinner, and a certain warmth kindled in the pit of my stomach, one that had very little to do with the food I was eating or the tea I'd just drunk.

No, this was the happy realization that the guy I thought I liked seemed to like me back.

Of course, reason kicked in a minute later, reminding me that the man who'd shared that soulful gaze with me across the table had lived and died decades before I was even born, and the absolute last thing I should be doing was thinking we had any kind of a future together.

I made myself look down at my meal as well, knowing it would be absolute madness to encourage him.

Even if I really did want to.

"You've all been very kind," I said, forcing a lightness to my tone that I definitely didn't feel. "I have to thank you all for that."

As I'd hoped, the polite words might as well have been a bucket of cold water thrown on the conversation. Seth mumbled something like, "I'm glad to hear it," and the two of us attended to our food for the next few minutes without saying anything else.

But then someone paused by our table, and I looked up to see a man who was probably a year or so older than Seth and very much like him in looks, with the same mid-brown hair and blue eyes. However, his features were subtly different, not quite as perfect from every angle, even though I supposed he was attractive enough.

"Is this Aunt Ruth's guest?" the newcomer asked, and Seth put down his fork, looking resigned.

"Yes, this is Deborah Rowe," he said, then glanced over at me. "Deborah, this is my older brother Charles."

No wonder they looked so much alike. I put on a smile and said, "I'm very pleased to meet you, Charles."

He inclined his head toward me. "Pleased to make your acquaintance, Miss Rowe. It seems like my brother is taking good care of you."

Innocuous enough words, but there was an undercurrent of almost condescension to them that made my hackles go up. "Oh, he is," I said calmly, knowing I should do my best to be polite. For all I knew, I was reading way more into his tone than necessary. I was probably just a little on edge from the raw moment Seth and I had shared a moment earlier. "I wanted to see more of the town," I went on, "so Seth very kindly offered to take me to his favorite restaurant."

This was a flat-out lie, of course, because it was Seth who'd invited me to dinner, not vice versa. In fact, I noticed the way his lips parted for a moment, as though he'd intended to say something, and then realized it was probably better not to contradict me in front of his brother.

Charles smiled thinly. "I'm afraid there isn't much to see. We're in quite a little corner of the world here in Jerome."

Well, that was true enough, I supposed, but I still didn't like his tone very much. "Oh, it may be small," I replied, "but I think it's fascinating."

His gaze flicked to Seth, but my dinner companion only said, "Yes, Miss Rowe has seemed interested in just about everything she's seen so far. It makes me think she must be from somewhere far away, although of course, none of us knows yet where that might be."

"Yes, Mother told me a little about Miss Rowe's amnesia." Charles stopped there—maybe wondering if he should ask me directly about my condition?—but then he must have realized that interrupting our dinner for much longer wouldn't be very polite, because he said, "I hope you're feeling better soon. It was nice to meet you."

A nod toward me, and then he headed over to the counter, where he picked up a brown paper bag of what I assumed must be a takeout order, then headed out the door.

This mystified me somewhat. Hadn't Seth said something about his brother still living at home with their parents?

My gaze must have been questioning, as he

said, "Sometimes Charles likes to fetch his own dinner. I suppose it makes him feel more independent, since he still shares the apartment over the mercantile with our parents."

Well, that seemed to explain that. "Something that's a lot easier in Jerome, considering you can walk pretty much anywhere you need to go."

While I wouldn't have said Seth seemed exactly tense, I still couldn't help noticing the way he relaxed against the back of the booth as I spoke, as though my words had helped to dissipate a little of the tension that had arisen with the arrival of his brother. "True. I don't think our mother is very happy about him fetching his own meals from time to time, but I suppose she's trying to give him a little grace."

"'Grace'?" I echoed. As far as I'd been able to tell, Charles McAllister looked like an able-bodied man in his middle twenties. He didn't seem like the sort of person who would require a lot of coddling.

For a split second, Seth appeared vaguely uncomfortable. But then he gave a hitch of his shoulders and said, "He was engaged, but his fiancée called it off. She's living in Prescott now with her great-aunt."

Right—Ruth had already told me a little about the situation. And although I supposed on the surface the story sounded innocent enough, I couldn't help thinking there was probably more here than met the eye...or the ear. While I couldn't help thinking Seth was the more handsome of the two brothers, I also couldn't deny that Charles was good-looking enough, had a job, and stood to take over the family business once his father decided it was time to retire. On paper, that didn't sound like the kind of situation a girl from the mid-1920s would usually walk away from.

Then again, I had only a tiny piece of the story. If they'd turned out to be incompatible, then good on her for recognizing she and Charles didn't have a future and that she needed to walk away.

"I'm sorry to hear that," I said, since I didn't know how else to respond.

Seth smiled—not, I believed, because he was at all amused by his brother's situation, but because I'd responded with sympathy to the small revelation. "It was hard for him," he replied. "I suppose it's good that she's far away, and so he doesn't have to worry too much about their paths crossing, but still, he'd thought they had a future and even bought a small plot down on Juarez Street to build a house. Open land is hard to come by here in Jerome, and he probably paid more for it than he should have."

Ouch. I supposed one could look rationally at the situation and say that Charles had done well to buy the land even if he now didn't have a reason to build on it anytime soon, but still, it had to sting.

I made a sympathetic sound, and Seth added, "At any rate, that's why my parents are being gentle with him right now. I know my mother keeps hoping he'll meet someone who'll take his mind off Mary, but we haven't seen any signs of that happening yet."

"How long ago did this all happen?"

"Just after the first of the year," he said. "So, I think the wound is still too fresh for Charles to even consider moving on. But you know how parents can be."

To be honest, I really didn't, because both my mother and father had seemed to be all right with me not knowing what I wanted to do next with my life. Sure, my mother hadn't been completely thrilled about me coming here to Jerome, but she appeared to have reassured herself that this was only a phase and that I'd go back to Flagstaff soon enough.

And with my older sister married and providing them with their first grandchild, my parents seemed perfectly fine with me not being involved with anyone. More than once, I'd heard my mother remark that she needed at least a three-year break before having to plan another wedding. Considering I hadn't seen anyone seriously in the past year, I figured I definitely didn't need to worry about that particular timeline.

Obviously, I couldn't tell Seth any of that. In fact, I had to remind myself that I was still supposed to be suffering from amnesia and therefore couldn't recall anything of my interactions with my parents.

"I suppose so," I said, adding, "I can't really remember."

At once, his expression turned contrite. "I'm so sorry," he replied at once. "That was insensitive of me, considering…."

The words trailed off, as though he'd also realized that remarking on my "condition" might create the wrong impression.

"It's fine," I said quickly. "No offense taken. But right now, I just don't have much context for these sorts of situations."

He was quiet for a moment, and I noted how his eyes scanned the restaurant around us. "Does any of this jog any memories?" he said. "Anything at all, like going out to eat in the place where you come from?"

Well, of course it jogged plenty, because I'd probably grown too fond of takeout from Bobby D's and had eaten quite a few brisket plates and pulled pork sandwiches during my time in Jerome. Good thing I walked everywhere and the place was so hilly, or my hips might have regretted my choices of cuisine.

I couldn't comment on that, however. Instead, I hunted around for an answer that wouldn't give anything away but might also give him some hope, then said, "I don't know about 'memories,' but something about it seems sort of familiar, as if I've probably eaten in a Chinese restaurant before. Unfortunately, that doesn't narrow things down very much."

"Maybe not," he responded. "But still, it's something. It might be a sign that your memories are starting to come back, if only in general impressions and not any particular details."

About all I could do was nod. While I knew it wasn't in my best interest to say that I was beginning to recall specifics, I thought it might not be too bad to admit to certain overall concepts and situations becoming familiar.

That couldn't get me in too much trouble, right?

We were almost done with our meals then, so we moved the conversation to simpler topics, like the new restaurant opening near the top of Main Street and the construction of a new park with a fancy gazebo down in Clarkdale. And afterward, we headed out into a night where the moon, now a little more full than it had been the day before, was now well above the Mogollon Rim to the east and would have provided enough illumination even if there weren't gas fixtures mounted to the exteriors of some of the buildings, obvious relics of an earlier era. As far as I could tell, Jerome was fully electrified, but that didn't mean they couldn't use some of the old gas lighting if it still worked.

The way back up to Ruth's house was steep, and Seth silently offered his arm to help steady me. For a moment, I almost demurred, but then I realized the last thing I needed was to stumble and fall, maybe twist an ankle. Yes, I'd climbed this hill before, but not in unfamiliar heels.

It felt good to lean on him…probably too good. True, it was the sort of polite gesture he would have made to any female companion, but still, I liked the quiet, sturdy strength that seemed to emanate from him, the sensation of his muscled forearm beneath my fingers.

Even though he came from a time a hundred years before I was born, he still felt more real to me than anyone I'd ever met.

When we reached the walkway in front of Ruth and Timothy's house, though, I lifted my hand—not too quickly, because I didn't want him to think I wasn't grateful for his help, but still fast enough that I hoped no one had seen the way I'd leaned on him all the way up here. No sign of Ruth peeking through the curtains, thank God, so I supposed it might not have mattered.

A flicker of something passed across Seth's features, clear and fine-cut in the moonlight, but he didn't protest. His tone was neutral enough as he said, "I hope the climb wasn't too taxing for you. These hills can be difficult for newcomers in our town."

"No, it was fine," I said, then went on, "Thank you for your kind assistance. I suppose I'll get used to it soon enough."

Assuming I can't get back to my own year any time in the near future, I added mentally. Since I'd failed miserably on that front so far, I wasn't about to make any promises to myself I couldn't keep.

And I couldn't quite hold back the traitorous thought that if I could have more evenings like this one with Seth, then I wasn't sure I minded being trapped in 1926 as much as I probably should have.

The corners of his eyes crinkled ever so slightly as he smiled. "I suppose you will."

A pause then as we both looked at one another. In a different time and place, this might have been the moment when we shared a kiss, standing there alone on a moonlit street.

But this was the twenties, and I knew things were very different here. Maybe they were roaring somewhere else, and people were drinking moonshine in speakeasies and dancing the night away in beaded flapper dresses or smoking cigarettes in long ebony holders, but Jerome was very far away from the wild nightlife in New York or Chicago.

"Thank you for dinner," I said, and Seth nodded.

"Oh, you're welcome. Perhaps we can do this again later in the week? We could even drive down to Cottonwood and try something there."

He was asking me out on another date. The logical thing to do would be to politely refuse and tell him I wasn't sure that was such a good idea, considering my current situation.

I didn't want to be logical, though. Not with the way he made me feel.

"Sounds wonderful," I said.

8

MOONSHINE AND MYSTERIES

SETH WALKED AWAY FROM HIS AUNT'S HOUSE, wearing what he knew was probably a huge, silly grin on his face.

Deborah had agreed to see him again.

No firm date set, but just knowing she was fine with another dinner out lightened his step as he made his way down the hill. If she hadn't been interested in him at all—if she'd only accepted his invitation to have dinner at the English Kitchen tonight out of politeness—then he doubted she would have said she would like to share another meal.

As he walked along Main Street on the way back to his bungalow, a big Dodge truck moved past him. Under most circumstances, such a thing wouldn't have been much cause for comment, as people came and went this way all the time, since this was the only route that went over Mingus Mountain and down into Prescott Valley.

Except he knew no one else in Jerome had a Dodge truck that was painted dark green and had wooden slats protecting the bed.

No, that was the McAllister Mercantile truck. And although Seth hadn't seen the driver, he somehow doubted it had been his father behind the wheel. His mother didn't drive at all, which meant the truck must have been piloted by his brother Charles.

What on earth would he be doing out and about in the family truck at this time of night? Although they made trips to Prescott on occasion, going over the mountain to pick up shipments of supplies for the store or various items that couldn't be found in either Jerome or Cottonwood, there was absolutely no reason in the world to take such a trip well past sundown, when all the warehouses and shops in the state's former capital would have been closed for the day.

Something about this didn't smell right at all. Although he would never call himself a psychic, not when he couldn't read people's minds or see the future, Seth knew he'd always possessed a gut instinct that generally steered him in the right direction.

And right now, the pricking of his thumbs

told him something wasn't right about this situation. No, not at all.

For some reason, the image of the boarded-up mine shaft popped into his mind. He hadn't wanted to question the superintendent when he'd first spied the shaft being closed off, but more and more, the whole situation felt wrong to him.

Well, it would be easy enough to find out whether his imagination was working overtime for no reason, or whether something really was strange about spotting his brother out and about after dinner like this. Most likely, he'd realize his suspicions were entirely wrong and that Charles had been sent off on his nighttime errand because a particular item was needed at the store as soon as possible.

However, Seth knew he couldn't simply let this go.

An eyeblink, and he was at the site of the closed mine shaft. Luckily, several large boulders that sat off to one side provided decent cover, and he crouched behind them as he surveyed the scene. All seemed still enough, with nothing changed about the boards that covered the gaping hole in the hill...or anything about the immediate surroundings, either.

But then a pair of headlights raked through the darkness, and Seth dropped to his knees, not wanting to risk those headlights catching the top of his head over the boulder if the angle turned out to be wrong.

A truck stopped a few feet from the shaft, and a man got out of the driver's side. Not just any man, though.

His brother Charles.

After sending a furtive look in several directions, Charles approached the boarded-up entrance and then lifted a claw-head hammer to carefully pry loose a few of the nails. Once that task was done, he pulled off one of the boards, providing just enough space for him to squeeze past.

What in the world was he doing?

For just a moment, Seth had the impulse to call out to his brother, to ask him what errand could have brought him here long after all the miners had gone home. Some instinct stopped him, though, telling him that Charles would not be very happy to learn someone had been watching his movements.

Not too long after he'd gone into the shaft, his brother emerged, holding a heavy jug in either hand. He opened the passenger door of the truck, set the jugs down—on the floor or possibly the seat; Seth couldn't tell for sure—and then went back to fetch more.

This went on for a few more minutes, until presumably there was no room left in the cab for any more of the jugs. Charles returned to the mine entrance, carefully boarded it back up, and then put the truck in reverse and drove slowly until he reached a wide spot where he could turn around. A few moments later, Seth heard the shifting of gears as his brother turned onto the highway and then drove off.

Going higher. Going up over the mountain.

Even though he knew he was now alone, Seth still waited a bit longer before he dared get to his feet. His mind didn't want to accept what it had just seen, but he knew he couldn't deny the obvious truth.

Charles was working with bootleggers, and surely Lionel Allenby, the mine superintendent, must be in on the scheme as well. Otherwise, he wouldn't have worked so quickly to get the exploratory shaft sealed up, guessing that it would make an excellent drop spot for their moonshine.

And since Charles had continued upward along the highway, that meant he must be taking the contraband to Prescott. From what Seth had heard, the town's Whiskey Row had become a bit more subdued after the passing of Prohibition, but it hadn't shut down entirely, and that meant the saloons there needed to get their alcohol from somewhere.

Who was making the stuff? Someone in

Jerome, or possibly farther down the hill in Cottonwood or Clarkdale?

Not that Seth supposed it really mattered. From the beginning, he'd thought Prohibition was a foolish idea—a sentiment shared by most people in the McAllister clan—since all it had done was create its own forms of crime, but he'd never thought he had much of a horse in that race. After all, he'd come of age several years after the law was passed and therefore hadn't missed out on much, hadn't had anything really taken away from him.

But if Charles was involved in bootlegging, then Seth was very much involved. So was their family…the entire clan.

He wanted to curse his brother's foolishness, even if he knew doing so would only be a waste of breath.

Why would Charles have done something so stupid?

Surely it couldn't all be about the money. Every person in their clan who was eighteen or older received a monthly stipend intended to bolster whatever they earned from their work. It wasn't a huge amount, just enough to cushion their circumstances, but still, between Charles's salary from the family business and his monthly allotment, he was doing quite well for himself. There shouldn't have been any need for him to risk his personal safety…and, by extension, the safety of the clan...by getting involved with boot-leggers.

Well, since Seth had already been in the mine shaft they were using as their hidey hole, it wouldn't be too difficult to go inside and see whether his brother had taken the entire stash, or whether he'd left some behind.

He blinked himself into the tunnel, which was pitch black.

Damn it. He probably should have thought of that.

But his foot clinked against something metallic, and when he reached down, his fingers closed around the handle of a lantern. Just a quick thought to set the kerosene inside alight—he assumed his brother must have done the same thing, using the same witch talents they'd all been born with—and then he was better able to get a look at his surroundings.

A few feet away stood some boulders that he knew hadn't been there the day before, and hidden behind them were several large barrels that he guessed must be full of whiskey. If anyone removed the boards from the entrance and took only a quick glance inside, they wouldn't see anything out of the ordinary.

Well, as long as they didn't know those boulders hadn't been there a few days ago.

When he went over and thumped the barrels,

one of them sounded hollow, telling him whoever had filled the jugs had emptied it all the way. Although he had no idea how such an operation even worked, he had to believe that the bootleggers would come to retrieve the barrel and fill it up again, return to hide it back here at an opportune time, and the cycle would start all over again.

How much were they paying Charles to smuggle the liquor into Prescott?

Probably a good bit, considering the risk he was taking. True, he was being careful, hiding the jugs in the truck's cab rather than putting them in the bed where anyone could see them, but still, all it would take was being stopped by the sheriff for going a little too fast and the game would be over.

Or…would Charles even have to worry about the sheriff? Seth wasn't personally acquainted with the man or the deputies in his department, but with a lot of money being thrown around, he had to guess it might not have been too difficult to pay the local authorities enough to look the other way.

What a mess. He returned the lantern to the place where he'd found it, magically snuffed it out, and then blinked himself back outside. All was quiet, which made sense. The bootleggers would do everything in their power to keep their activities hidden, and he guessed that even if they intended to come here tonight to remove the empty barrel, they'd wait until the hour was much later than eight-thirty.

Since he knew he was alone—and he knew the moonlight would be sufficient to show him what he wanted to find—he went over to the boarded-up entrance and inspected it carefully. As he'd thought, only a few nails actually held the boards in place, while the others were just for show. It would be easy enough to pull out the nails doing the actual work, remove the boards, and then close everything back up once you were done, just as he'd seen his brother do a few minutes earlier.

He had some answers…but many more questions remained.

When Seth returned to his bungalow, it was with a growing rage roiling in his belly.

How could Charles do something like this to the clan? The one rule they all lived by…the one that had been pounded into their heads from the day they were old enough to understand that the McAllisters weren't like most people…was that they needed to live modestly and quietly, to do nothing that would attract attention to their family. Even if the authorities had been paid off to look the other way, that didn't mean his brother still hadn't taken an enormous risk. Seth had read enough in the papers about bloody gun battles by bootleggers over their territories in Phoenix and Los Angeles to know getting involved in that sort of operation meant doing business with all sorts of unsavory individuals. Everything in Jerome had been quiet so far—well, except for the usual sort of drunken brawls that always seemed to take place in mining towns, even during Prohibition—but there was no guarantee the current state of affairs would continue indefinitely.

The real problem was that, although he now had possession of some extremely unwelcome information, he had no clear idea what to do with it. His immediate thought had been to go to his parents and let them know what he'd seen, but he'd dismissed that notion at once. His father's temper had always run very high, and he tended to act before he thought, never a good combination in a warlock. Otherwise, he wouldn't have seen fit to use his magic to suspend the thief Oswald Peale upside down in the center of the mercantile until the sheriff arrived, thus making an utter spectacle that had been very difficult to explain away. Although most people agreed there should be zero tolerance for those who tried to take money right out of the cash register, they also thought Henry McAllister could have come up with a less spectacular way to restrain the thief.

But then, there were also the elders. If Seth couldn't speak with his parents, then it made sense to go to the clan elders, let them know what he'd seen, and have them decide on the best course of action. Of course, Seth had seen on more than one occasion that they didn't like to meddle any more than they absolutely had to, and he worried they might say that this was a family matter and that Charles's parents should be the ones to discipline him.

Never mind that he was a grown man of twenty-five, and therefore shouldn't be under his parents' thumb at all.

Back and forth Seth went, and then finally decided he would speak with his brother first. He had no idea whether Charles would listen to reason, but it just seemed smarter to do what he could on his own before he brought his parents into this mess...or worse, had to go to the elders for help.

And the thing that made him even angrier was that Charles's escapades had all but pushed the memory of his dinner with Deborah far away. Now that he was resolved on his course of action, Seth did his best to remember what it had been like to sit across the table from her, to watch the lively play of emotions on her lovely features and listen to her speak...to feel her hand on his arm as he guided her up the hill to Aunt Ruth's house.

Yes, that was what he wanted to think about right now.

The rest of this mess could wait until morning.

When Seth awoke, he wasn't in a much-improved mood. About the best he could say about his sleep was that he hadn't suffered any nightmares, even while he tossed and turned, doing his best to find a position that would allow him to fall back into slumber and prevent his mind from continually jumping back and forth between the problem of his brother Charles and the realization that he was beginning to feel a lot more for Deborah Rowe than simple neighborly concern.

A lukewarm bath helped a little. Not that he could linger in it for more than ten minutes at most, since he had to be at work at seven, but still, he felt a bit more human as he combed his hair, then went to the kitchen to pour himself a cup of coffee. As far as he'd been able to tell, the night had been quiet enough.

Then again, what had he been expecting? Despite all those tortured thoughts he'd suffered overnight that had conjured images of Chicago-style shoot-ups on the streets of Jerome, he doubted such nightmares would actually come to pass. No, the bootleggers would be doing their level best to avoid any sort of confrontation, which meant his brother was probably safe… for now.

Maybe.

A more immediate concern would be facing Lionel Allenby at work today. Although they didn't interact on a daily basis, the chances were still greater than fifty percent that Seth would at least see Allenby in passing, even if they didn't have much to say to one another. Would he be able to hide what he knew about the mine superintendent?

If the man was even involved at all. All Seth had to go on were suspicions, and the belief deep in his gut that Lionel Allenby would have had no reason to have his team close up the exploratory shaft if he hadn't decided it was the perfect drop-off site for the local bootleggers. It was possible that one of the men who'd dug the shaft had passed the information along to the people manufacturing the whiskey, and Lionel hadn't been involved at all.

However, that didn't explain why he would have ordered it closed so quickly.

Once again, Seth's thoughts kept chasing themselves, and it didn't seem as though a second cup of coffee would do much of anything except make him even more jittery. Instead, he got out some cornbread from the pantry, cut himself a slice, and made himself eat it slowly and deliberately, doing his best to focus on the moment rather than a million possibilities he couldn't control.

The exercise of preparing even such a meager breakfast helped a little bit, as did his morning rituals of shaving and brushing his teeth. By the time he emerged from his bungalow, he thought he might be able to face the day without letting anyone know that he'd seen something troubling…and potentially dangerous…the night before.

His route to the mine took him past Paradise Lane, and Aunt Ruth and Uncle Timothy's house. Seth couldn't stop himself from wondering if Deborah was up yet, or whether she was the type of person to sleep in.

Then he had to shake his head at himself. No matter what kind of sleeper she was, night owl or early bird, he had to believe his aunt would have her guest up at nearly dawn. She was not a supporter of sloth, even in a lost young woman who couldn't recall who she was or where she'd come from.

Well, that wasn't exactly true. At least Deborah remembered her name, and if their conversation of the night before was any indication, she also retained vague recollections of visiting certain places and performing certain tasks, even if she didn't have any real context to go on. Seth had to believe this was a promising sign, and that sooner or later, she would have recovered enough of her memories to recollect something of her origins.

And while he certainly didn't want her to go wandering through life with no clear idea of where she'd come from, he also dreaded the day when those lost memories would finally resurface, like an ancient shipwreck revealed as the tide went out. Because once she knew who she was, she'd be gone forever.

Or…would she? He might have been flattering himself, but he couldn't help thinking they'd had a certain kind of connection the night before. In that moment when their eyes met… before he, like a coward, had looked down at his plate…he could have sworn he saw the same longing in her expression that he knew he felt in his soul. If it was possible that she was coming to care for him, then maybe she would want to stay here in Jerome.

Oh, sure, he mocked himself as he drew near the gates that allowed entrance to the United Verde. *A beautiful, smart woman who could have anyone she wanted is going to be fine with living in the back of beyond with a mining foreman, in a bungalow barely big enough for one person.*

Deep down, he knew that evaluation of his home wasn't entirely fair, that with its two bedrooms and nearly one thousand square feet, his little house was certainly of a size to accommodate a couple...and maybe one child. Anything more than that, and of course they'd need something bigger.

Should he be laughing at the way his thoughts had completely gone off track? He hadn't kissed Deborah, hadn't told her that he had feelings for her, and now he was imagining a future where they were married and had children?

Well, thoughts were free, he supposed, and it wasn't as if he planned to share these innocent fantasies with anyone else. It was enough that she'd excited his heart and soul, had made him believe for the first time that such a future might be possible for him. True, she was a civilian, and those pairings were always a little more fraught for the parties involved. But there were many such couples in the McAllister clan, and he had to assume they weren't uncommon in other witch clans as well, just because magical families always had to take care that they didn't become too inbred.

Obviously, he would have to be very, very sure of Deborah before he revealed that side of himself...which meant waiting to see how matters progressed, and also waiting to see what happened when and if her memories began to return. He certainly wasn't going to take such a large step until he knew for certain that she wanted to stay in Jerome with him.

Until then, he would only do his best to get through the day ahead...and hope the Goddess might offer some inspiration as to what he should do next.

9

SHOP 'TIL YOU DROP

ANY HOPES OF TREATING MY STAY IN 1926 AS A mini-vacation were dashed the next morning when Ruth McAllister knocked on my door before the world was even light outside my window and said, "Breakfast in half an hour!"

I sat up in bed, blinking, and pushed my disheveled hair away from my face. In that moment, I realized she'd allowed me to sleep in the day before because I was newly at the house and still probably in shock over losing my memories, but now I needed to conform to the household schedule.

Which apparently included getting up at o'dark thirty.

After allowing myself a small curse, I shoved back the covers and got out the day's clothes, then headed over to the bathroom. I supposed it was something of a comfort that there were two upstairs, so at least I didn't have to share with Ruth and Timothy. Still, it was a heck of a rush to get the bathtub filled enough so I could have a quick splash, and as for my hair, forget about it. Luckily, I didn't have an oily scalp and could go three or four days before it started to look kind of nasty, but I knew I'd have to wash it tomorrow, even if that meant getting up at four in the morning.

Perish the thought.

My reward for being so quick about my morning prep was a bowl full of scrambled eggs and a plate piled high with bacon, along with toast from sourdough bread I knew Ruth must have made right in this kitchen. Timothy already sat at the table by the window, a newspaper spread before him and a cup of coffee in one hand. Judging by the way he barely tilted his head at me before he returned to his paper, I got the feeling he wasn't too interested in small talk before the stimulants kicked in.

That was fine by me. I never felt fully human until I had my coffee in the morning.

But Ruth handed me a cup almost as soon as I walked into the kitchen, and I took a few sips, being careful because it was still just a bit too hot. All the same, the caffeine started doing its job, sending out happy little bursts of energy and telling me I might survive being up and dressed by 6 a.m. after all.

"How did you sleep?" she asked.

"Very well, thank you," I replied. "It's so quiet and peaceful up here."

She'd already appeared cheerful enough, but now her expression was openly approving. "Yes, that's one of the benefits of living on Paradise Lane. We're enough away from it all that not much of the sound from Main Street makes it up here. And we almost always get a cool breeze at night."

Something I'd experienced for myself the evening before, since I'd left the window in my bedroom open before I left for my date with Seth. By the time I got back, the space had cooled down significantly, and my worries about tossing and turning all night because I was overheated appeared to have been for nothing.

"Yes, it was lovely," I agreed, and sipped some more coffee.

Her gaze grew a little more focused. "How was your dinner with Seth?"

That was a very good question. The food had been fine, but I knew sharing the meal with him had been secondary to our conversation, to the way I somehow felt more at home with him than I had with people I'd known for years. Part of it might have been simply not having to explain myself or be awkward about my miserably back-firing time-travel gift; people in witch clans didn't generally discuss their individual magical talents at cocktail parties or anything like that, but on the other hand, their particular powers tended to be common knowledge, thanks to the way news always spread around magical families.

And I knew people felt sorry for me, that I'd been born with a gift that should have been amazing, but because I couldn't control it, the damn thing was a lot more like a curse. Sure, the one I'd inherited from my father was pretty cool on its own, but when you were surrounded by fellow witches and warlocks who already knew that you possessed magical talents, it didn't come in all that handy.

Seth didn't know about any of that, obviously, and had no idea of the awkwardness my back-firing talent had caused me over the years. In fact, he knew very little about me at all because of my supposed amnesia. And that meant when we interacted, it was just as Seth and Devynn, nothing else.

It felt a lot more real.

Well, except for the part where he didn't know I was Devynn and thought I was a civilian named Deborah Rowe. More and more, I was hating that particular lie…even as I knew there was no way in the world I could possibly tell him the truth.

No matter what, I had to make sure he never found out I was half Wilcox, not in an era when the McAllisters had viewed the *primuses* of my clan as just a step away from the Devil himself.

"Dinner was very nice," I said. "The chop suey was fun, and the tea was lovely." I paused there, wondering if I should offer any more information. But then, I supposed Ruth would hear soon enough, since she seemed to be one of those people who was fully plugged into her clan's grapevine. "Seth's older brother Charles was at the English Kitchen, getting some food to take home with him, so I got to meet him, too."

Ruth's brows pulled together ever so slightly. I had a feeling she wanted to frown more deeply but wouldn't quite allow herself to.

"Oh, Charles," she said. "He's quite indispensable at his parents' store. And he and Seth get along so well, which is not always something you see with two brothers who are so close in age. But they were never competitive, thank goodness."

"Seth didn't want to work at the store with his brother?" I asked, figuring this might be a way I could get more information about the guy without looking like I was trying to give him the third degree in person. True, he'd already told me he could earn more working at the mine, but I still thought there must have been a little bit more behind his reasons for leaving the family business behind than a simple bottom line.

Now looking somewhat guarded, Ruth said, "From what I've heard, he felt they really didn't need him to work there, and he thought he might have more opportunities working at the mine, what with the way things have been booming there lately. I have to say he's done quite well for himself—getting made foreman so young, already owning a home. Whereas Charles always appeared very invested in the family business and was happy to work at the mercantile."

On the surface, this all sounded exactly like what Seth had told me the evening before, so I wondered if I was trying to see something that wasn't there. Sometimes there really wasn't any drama to be had, and I supposed I should be glad the two brothers got along so well.

"Speaking of the store," Ruth went on, "I have a few things I needed to pick up there today. Would you mind terribly if I sent you with a list? That way, I can stay here and do all my baking instead of having to run an errand."

Since I would much rather have gone to the mercantile—I was itching to see what it looked like now, compared to the touristy store it had become—than stand by and pretend to help Ruth bake scones or cookies or whatever else was on the menu today, I immediately said, "No, I don't mind. It will give me a chance to visit the place. After hearing everyone talk so much about the mercantile, I feel as if it's a Jerome landmark I shouldn't miss."

She appeared pleased that I was so eager to take on the small task, saying, "That's perfect. And I'm not sure you could call McAllister Mercantile a landmark, although I have to admit it is an important part of our community. I'll just put together a list after we're done with breakfast, and you can go down when you're ready. They don't open until eight, so there's no point in rushing."

That seemed awfully early to open a shop—in my time, the store's hours were ten until five every day except Sunday, when we opened at noon— but things were very different in this time period. Most likely, Seth's family wanted to be available to their customers if they needed to stop in and pick up something before their day began.

And since it was barely past seven now, I knew I'd have plenty of time to finish my morning meal, brush my teeth, and make sure my hair was tidy before I headed out.

An odd little anticipation rose in me.

What would Charles be like when he wasn't around his younger brother?

I supposed I'd find out soon enough.

~

The list Ruth gave me was more extensive than I'd thought—two new packets of sewing needles, thread, soap, a tin of baking soda, new stockings. However, it wasn't such a big batch of items that I'd thought I'd have a hard time carrying them all back up the hill, even though I wasn't much looking forward to the climb without Seth there to steady me.

I did my best to remind myself that I was a fit woman of twenty-two, not an octogenarian, and even though getting up the hill was something of a workout, I could still manage it just fine, even in those damn heels I had to wear all the time.

"Oh, and see if they have any more clothes that would fit you," Ruth said as she handed over the list, written in a neat copperplate script that looked like something out of a museum. "Since it seems as if you're going to be here longer than we first thought, it would just be smart for you to have a few more things to wear."

Even though I'd already started to wonder how I was going to manage with only three daytime outfits and three sets of underthings, I couldn't help protesting, "Oh, I don't want you to be extravagant on my account."

"Nonsense," Ruth said briskly. "I'm not asking you to buy a silk dress to go and meet the King. I just think it would be more comfortable for you to have a few more dresses, and another skirt and blouse outfit if they have something that would work. Molly McAllister contracts with seamstresses in both Cottonwood and Prescott, and sometimes even gets items from Los Angeles and New York, so it's hard for me to say what she has on hand. You'll just need to ask."

I could tell there wasn't much point in arguing with Ruth, not when she had that firm set to her mouth, as if she knew she was the final word in any discussion that took place in her household. And with Timothy sitting a few feet away, obviously hearing everything but not bothering to cut in with a comment about the cost of supplying me with an adequate wardrobe, it seemed my impression was correct.

"Yes, I'll be sure to see what they have," I said, then drained the final contents of my cup of coffee and ate the last bite of the bacon sitting on my plate. "I'll go get ready now."

She nodded at me, and I headed upstairs to take care of my teeth and face—and also to redo my hair, since I'd made kind of a hash of the bun in my haste earlier this morning and didn't want to look like a total slob.

I might have been a stranger with no known past, but I still wanted to make a good impression in case Seth's parents were working at the store when I got there.

~

The sun was up, but the air still felt mild enough as I made my way down the hill. Whether it would be quite so mild on my return trip, I didn't know for sure, although I told myself the hour was early enough that I wouldn't have to worry about the heat too much.

Quite a few cars and trucks came and went, but since I'd never made a study of antique vehicles, I had no idea what models and makes they all were. For some reason—probably because any images I'd seen of the era were in black and white —I'd somehow assumed all the cars would be black. Instead, they came in a multitude of shades...dark green, deep burgundy, a handsome saddle brown, one flashy convertible in a surprising pale butter yellow...and I did my best not to stare too much.

Well, except at the convertible, which was driven by a man in a straw fedora and had a woman with equally pale yellow hair in the passenger seat, a silken scarf fluttering in the breeze as they drove past. But since I wasn't the only one gawking—clearly, the striking pair were from out of town—I figured that was probably all right.

Ruth had given me a delicate wristwatch to wear, so I knew it was about eight minutes past eight when I walked through the front door of the mercantile. The façade of the building wasn't all that different from the way it looked in my time, with two picture windows flanking the door and a transom window above it, but inside it was very much changed from what I knew. Instead of the local pottery and jewelry and touristy T-shirts and baseball caps Rachel's store had on display, there were long counters on either side, with tall shelves behind them stacked with merchandise. Along the back wall stood large bins that I guessed held staples such as flour or grain, and a table in the center was piled high with boxes of shoes and other odds and ends.

I immediately noticed Charles, who stood behind one of the counters and was showing what looked like a pickaxe of some sort to an older man who didn't appear to be a miner, maybe instead a rancher or farmer. Why he'd be shopping here rather than down in Cottonwood, I didn't know —Jerome was way too hilly for any kind of agriculture—but maybe McAllister Mercantile had a better selection of those kinds of tools.

Behind one of the other counters was a woman who looked like she might be in her middle forties, pretty, with wavy, soft brown hair pulled into a low bun similar to mine and eyes so clear and blue, I knew she had to be Seth's mother.

I walked toward her, and she smiled. "How can I help you, miss?"

She had a small dimple in her right cheek, and something about her smile reminded me of Seth as well, genuine, open, without any false friendliness. I found myself smiling back as I said, "I'm Deborah Rowe, the girl who's staying with Ruth and Timothy McAllister. Ruth gave me a list of things she needed—and she also wanted you to check to see if you had any more clothes that might work for me."

As soon as I said my name, the woman's expression lit up that much more. "Oh, how nice to meet you, Deborah! I'm Molly McAllister, Seth's mother. Let me see that list, and then I'll go through our stock and find a few things for you."

Relieved that she didn't seem to find it at all odd that her cousin wanted to pay for my expanded wardrobe, I handed over the piece of paper Ruth had given me, then waited as Molly went along the shelves, gathering the requested items. Through all this, I waited at the counter, almost feeling the moment when Charles was finished with his current customer and turned his attention toward me.

In fact, he walked over while his mother was crouched down, sorting through packets of sewing needles.

"Good morning, Miss Rowe," he said.

Nothing in his expression or his words was particularly hostile, but I found my hackles going up anyway.

Something about the guy just rubbed me the wrong way.

However, I did my best to sound pleasant as I said, "Good morning, Mr. McAllister. Ruth sent me down to pick up a few things for her."

"It was kind of you to run the errand."

"Oh," I said deprecatingly, "I'm much better suited for this sort of thing than trying to help out in the kitchen."

One of his dark brown brows lifted a fraction of an inch. "Don't tell me you're one of those 'new' women."

"'New'?" I repeated, not sure what he meant. Was that what men in the 1920s called women who wanted to vote and have their own careers?

I had a dim recollection that women definitely could vote by 1926, but I had to admit I'd sort of daydreamed my way through a lot of U.S. history, finding the history of Europe in the Middle Ages much more interesting. Now I wished I'd paid more attention.

On the other hand, I had to believe there were still quite a few men who weren't too happy with the change in women's circumstances even several years after female suffrage became a thing, so maybe the exact year didn't make that much of a difference.

"As in, new to town?" I asked innocently, and Charles's brow furrowed that much more.

"Oh, of course," he said, his tone way too casual. "I need to remember that you've forgotten a great deal. Perhaps when your memory returns, so will your cooking skills."

"Perhaps," I allowed, fighting back a smile. If he'd only known that all I was good at when it came to cooking was picking up a phone and ordering takeout—or maybe nuking something in the microwave when I was trying to be frugal.

Luckily, Molly returned right then with the sewing needles and the soap and the baking powder. "I'll just go see about those clothes," she told me before turning to her son. "Charles, could you please go into the stock room and fetch me a pair of those new flat shoes we got in yesterday? Size eight."

He didn't look too thrilled about being sent on such an errand, although I couldn't tell for sure whether it was because he didn't like having his mother deliver orders in such a way, or simply because he wasn't very happy about his family handing out more freebies to the amnesiac who'd landed in town a couple of days ago.

However, it also seemed that he knew better than to argue, since he headed toward the back of the store, threading his way past the bins of flour and seed, and disappeared into the space that was still the stock room in the twenty-first century.

With him gone, Molly headed over to the shelves on the opposite side of the store, one section of which was taken up by clothes, folded stacks of shirts and trousers and underthings. I couldn't really tell what was what, since all the individual items were wrapped up in brown paper rather than the clear plastic common in my day for sellers of shirts and underwear, but she seemed to know what she was doing, briskly pulling from a pile here and a stack there, until she had a fairly impressive collection to deposit in front of me where I waited at the counter.

"This should do it," she said, sounding pleased with herself. "Two more dresses, and three blouses and three skirts. And, of course, more stockings and underclothes. I would have gotten you a coat or at least a shawl, but I generally don't stock those sorts of things at this time of year."

"I don't think I'll need either," I replied after a glance out the large front windows, where the scene was as bright and sunny as only a June day in northern Arizona could be.

"Possibly not," Molly said. "But when the monsoons come and we have a good storm, the temperature can drop as much as twenty degrees in only a few minutes. However, I'm sure Ruth has something she can loan you if the weather should take a turn."

Probably. I'd only been at the house for three days, but I could already tell my hostess was fond of pretty clothes, since I hadn't seen her wear the same thing twice. For all I knew, that was part of the reason why she'd been so dead set on making sure I had nice things to wear. Maybe buying herself a bunch of new clothes would have seemed far too extravagant when she had so many dresses of her own, but by getting me outfitted, she could experience the thrill of shopping vicariously.

"I'm sure she must," I said.

At that moment, Charles returned, carrying a shoebox and still wearing that slightly disapproving expression on his face. "Here they are," he said, and set the shoebox down on the counter next to all the clothing his mother had gathered.

With the addition of the shoes, the pile looked worryingly large. How in the world was I supposed to get all that stuff back up the hill to Paradise Lane?

I must have looked alarmed, because Molly said in reassuring tones, "Oh, I don't expect you to carry all that. Charles, give Miss Rowe a ride up to Ruth's house, won't you? I'll keep an eye on things here while you're gone."

At once I stammered, "Oh, he doesn't need to do that—" but she shook her head.

"It will only take him away for ten minutes, probably less. And that is far too much for one woman to manage, especially when you have to carry everything up that steep hill."

Charles's expression was now so neutral that I knew he must be irritated with his mother, even if he had no intention of contradicting her. "It's not a problem," he said, sounding almost wooden. "I'll need to pull the truck around to the front. You can wait here."

Without further comment, he turned away from us and walked toward the back of the store for a second time. I guessed he must be headed to the rear door of the building, which opened up on a small parking area for the shop owners' and residents' use. In the present day, those spaces were so in demand that Rachel had finally paid for an electronic gate and key card access to keep the tourists out, but I had a feeling that wasn't as much of a problem in 1926, when far fewer people had cars.

"Let me get a bag for all this," Molly said, then stepped away to retrieve a large crochet-looking contraption that unfolded to hold a lot more of my goodies than I'd thought it possibly could. The only thing that wouldn't fit was the shoebox, but I knew it would be easy enough to carry now that the rest of my new wardrobe and Ruth's purchases had been safely contained.

Just as Molly was handing everything over to me, Charles came back into the store. "Ready to go?" he asked.

"Yes," I replied. He still wore that far too neutral expression, which sure seemed like a signal to me that he wasn't happy but was far too well-mannered to get into an argument with his mother about playing chauffeur for me. I turned toward her, adding, "Thank you so much for finding all those pieces. I just realized that Ruth didn't give me anything to pay you with."

Molly waved a hand. "Oh, it will all go on her account. Don't worry—she'll take care of it at the end of the month, just as she always does. Enjoy your new clothes!"

"I will," I said, which was no more than the truth. I couldn't wait to get back to Ruth's house so I could pretend it was Christmas morning and I could open up all the packages Molly had given me.

She smiled, and I followed Charles out to the curb, where a big dark green pickup truck was parked. It was very shiny, leading me to wonder how often they washed the thing. Even I knew cars could get dusty pretty fast in Jerome, what with all the general particulates and pollen in the air. I had to imagine it must be even worse here in 1926, with the big open-pit mine farther up the hill spewing all sorts of waste into the atmosphere.

To be fair, he did open the door for me and wait until I had settled myself and the packages in the passenger seat before he went around to the driver's side and climbed in. A roar from the big engine as he turned the key, and then he shifted expertly right before pulling out onto the street.

It was about as different an experience from the self-driving cars of my own day as I could possibly imagine. The motor was so loud, I didn't think we could hold a conversation without practically yelling at each other—probably a good thing, since Charles and I both remained studiously silent—and the shock absorbers seemed to be almost nonexistent.

Then again, this was a work vehicle with an internal combustion engine from more than a hundred years before my time, not a silky electric car that you could barely even tell was running.

At least it was a short trip up the hill, only a couple of minutes. Charles stopped in front of Ruth's house and asked, "Do you need any help with those packages?"

"No," I said quickly. "I'll be fine. But thank you very much for the ride."

He only tilted his head in assent, and waited silently as I grabbed the shoebox and big string bag of other goodies before getting out of the truck. A pause of a minute or so to make sure I made it safely up the front steps, and then he pulled away, going toward the end of the cul-de-sac so he'd have a place to turn around.

When he passed Ruth's house again, I lifted a hand to wave, thinking that was the polite thing to do, but he didn't appear to acknowledge the gesture. Instead, he kept driving down the hill, until at least the rumble of the truck's engine blended with the overall background sounds of the town.

I wanted to shake my head, but what would be the point?

About all I could do right then was be very glad that Seth appeared to be nothing like his brother.

10

BOOTLEGGING BARGAIN

SETH KNEW HE HAD A STANDING INVITATION to have dinner at his parents' house whenever he liked, so he guessed he wouldn't raise any suspicions by showing up tonight. No, the real trick would be figuring out a way to talk to Charles alone.

Because that was the course of action he'd decided upon after a long day at the mine, doing his best to avoid Lionel Allenby, even while his thoughts kept chasing after one another as he tried to find a solution to what appeared to be an impossible problem. Maybe it would have been smarter to talk to the elders, or Mabel McAllister, the clan's *prima,* but Seth didn't much like the idea of going over Charles's head before he gave his brother a chance to explain himself.

At least he had let Deborah know that they

wouldn't be having dinner with each other tonight, or the night after that. As much as he hated not seeing her, he also knew it was more important to confront Charles with what he'd witnessed and give him a chance to explain himself.

And, Seth couldn't help hoping, convince his brother that he needed to stop working with the bootleggers...as long as he hadn't gotten himself dug in so deeply that there was now little way out.

"It's so good to see you again so soon," his mother said as Seth came into the apartment where he'd grown up, with its collection of family photographs in gilt frames and the sofa and love seat with the damask upholstery and carved backs, a little out of date, maybe, but something that was comfortingly familiar. "I didn't know whether you'd be entertaining Miss Rowe again. She seems like such a lovely girl."

"You've met her?" he responded, startled. True, Jerome was a small town, but....

"Oh, yes," Molly McAllister said. She'd just been setting down a platter of fried chicken when he appeared, so she left it in the place of honor next to her husband's plate and sent a bright smile at her youngest son. "She came into the store this morning with a shopping list from Ruth. I got her all the things she needed, and also sent Miss Rowe home with some more clothes. It seems Ruth thinks she might be here for a while, so she needed something more than a wardrobe that would only work for two or three days."

Well, that was something. Even with his brother's crimes hanging over his head, Seth couldn't help being relieved that Deborah clearly intended to stay in Jerome for the foreseeable future. Now all he had to do was make sure they spent as much time together as possible, no easy feat considering his work schedule.

Charles came in then, followed by their father. For just a moment, the two brothers' gazes locked, and Charles's eyes narrowed for a moment before he went to take his regular seat across from their mother and to their father's left.

Luckily, neither of their parents appeared to notice the brief few seconds of tension, and everyone took their places and settled their napkins in their laps. In civilian families, this might have been the moment when they said grace, but instead Henry murmured a quiet thank-you to Brigid for her bounty, and then they commenced passing around the fried chicken and gravy and mashed potatoes and green beans.

Once that was done, Seth's father said, "It's good to see you here tonight."

"I heard Mother was making her famous fried chicken," Seth replied, a little white lie. He'd had no idea what was on the menu, and probably would have choked down liver and onions to get a chance to talk to his brother.

However, he had to admit the fried chicken was a nice bonus.

Their talk was commonplace enough after that, with his mother jokingly offering her menu for the rest of the week in an attempt to lure him back for more family dinners, and his father talking about the new radios he'd ordered from New York, five in all, that would be proudly displayed in the mercantile.

"I know some people like to order from a catalog," he went on, "but I don't think anything beats being able to hear things in person, or to touch the cabinet and feel the fine wood. I'm hoping they'll be a good impulse buy for people fresh off a bonus."

His gaze slid toward Seth then, as if implying his son would be a good customer for that sort of luxury item. And although he had to admit he'd considered adding a radio to his living room, that sort of thing wasn't really in his budget right now despite his foreman's salary.

Or rather, he supposed he could have splurged if he hadn't been carefully saving as much spare cash as he could so he would be able to buy a bigger, grander house in a few more years.

He made a noncommittal noise, and his father seemed to realize a radio wasn't in the cards for his younger son at the moment. Molly eased the conversation toward the Fourth of July parade that was being planned for less than a month from now, saying, "And of course we'll drive in the parade again. I'll need to dig out the bunting to decorate the truck."

"It's in the attic," Seth told her. He remembered that clearly, since he'd been the one to pack it away in a box the year before and shove it up among the rafters.

"Oh, of course," she said. "Then I suppose you or Charles will be the one to get it down for me— your father never was very good with heights."

Henry, who'd just been about to take a bite of drumstick, looked more resigned than anything. "I'll go in the attic if I have to," he told her. "But it is probably better if one of the boys does it."

"I can get the bunting down for you," Charles said. "It will be easier, considering how Seth is hardly around anymore these days."

A comment about how his brother was still living at home at twenty-five rose to Seth's lips, but he swallowed it as best he could. He absolutely could not get into an argument with Charles right now, not when he needed to speak to him after dinner.

In fact, the whole question of the bunting presented a rather neat way for Seth to get his brother alone without raising anyone's suspicions.

"Why don't the two of us fetch the bunting after dinner?" he asked. "That way, it'll be out of the attic and you won't have to worry about getting it down at the last minute. You can store it in my old room until the Fourth of July."

Molly tipped her head to one side. "That's a wonderful idea, Seth," she said. "One of you can hold the ladder while the other goes up into the attic."

"I suppose that would work," Charles replied. While he didn't sound entirely enthusiastic, neither had he shot down the scheme, making Seth think this whole ploy to get him alone might work after all.

Which it did, with the two brothers dutifully trooping downstairs after dinner to fetch the ladder, and then hauling it back up to the third floor where the bedrooms—and the ceiling access to the attic—were located. The setup would help to keep their conversation private, since their parents had remained on the second floor to clean up after dinner and then retire to the living room to listen to the radio. With any luck, they wouldn't hear a single thing.

Charles positioned the ladder directly under the opening, and Seth, who'd already volunteered to be the one to go into the attic, climbed up. As he went, he had to wonder why their particular attic didn't have a drop-down ladder like he'd seen in other homes, but maybe it had been a question of space, since the attic itself was cramped and with a low ceiling barely five feet above the floor, adequate for storage but not useful for anything else.

To his relief, the box with the bunting was situated near the access point, on the opposite side from the spot where a nearly identical box filled with their Christmas ornaments sat. He reached out and got the desired box by one corner, then shimmied it closer to the place where he stood at the top of the ladder so he could grasp it with both hands. With that maneuver taken care of, he was able to slowly back his way down, bumping the box along from rung to rung until he reached solid ground once again.

He began to set the box of bunting on the floor, but Charles stopped him, saying, "Let me take that."

Even better. He could follow his brother into the spare room that had once been his and confront him there, in a place where they were the least likely to be overheard.

Charles headed into the bedroom, which, in the several years since Seth had moved out, had turned into a dumping ground for any spare odds and ends anyone in the family couldn't quite decide what to do with. More than once, his mother had made noises about clearing out the junk and turning the space into a sewing room, but so far those plans hadn't materialized—mostly because no one had time to work on the project.

After setting down the box on the table that had served as Seth's desk when he lived here, Charles turned, clearly ready to go back downstairs.

Now or never.

"I saw you up at the exploratory shaft last night," Seth said, and Charles paused almost midstep, one foot awkwardly poised a half-inch or so above the floor before he remembered to set it down.

"What the hell are you talking about?"

Well, that was his first mistake. Both brothers took care not to swear around their parents, but they also tended to toe the line around each other and do their best to be courteous. For Charles to slip like that meant Seth had caught him off guard.

"I saw you," he said calmly. "You drove up in the truck and went in the shaft, then loaded about ten or so jugs of moonshine into the cab. After that, you went up and over the mountain—to take the liquor to Prescott, I assume."

Charles stood so still that he looked almost more like a waxwork figure than a living, breathing human. Then he spoke.

"Let it alone, Seth."

No denials, no pretensions of innocence—at least, not after that first falsely shocked exclamation.

"I will not," Seth said. Although he'd gotten into a confrontation here and there with a belligerent miner who thought it was a good idea to come to work drunk, he'd never had to face down someone he knew before. A thrill of fear went through him as he wondered what his brother might do next. Charles's magic wasn't anything too frightening, only a gift for knowing where a particular item was located at any given time—useful for managing the stock at the mercantile—but he was still tall and fit, if not quite as muscular as his younger brother.

A physical altercation was the last thing Seth wanted, if not least because his parents would be sure to hear if he and his brother started throwing punches at one another.

"Let it alone," Charles said again, and Seth crossed his arms.

"I can't do that," he replied, and now he tried to make his voice as persuasive as he could. Shouting would only attract attention…and turn his brother into even more of a stone wall than he already was. "You're not just putting yourself in danger—you're endangering the clan as well, consorting with people like that. And you don't even drink!"

Now his brother's mouth curved in a smile that bordered on contemptuous. "No, I don't," he said. "I don't see the point in losing control. But that doesn't mean I won't help other people indulge if it means getting some extra money in my pocket."

Seth stared at Charles in disbelief. "You're breaking the law and putting us all at risk, just for a little money?"

"It's more than 'just a little money,'" Charles retorted. "You'd probably be surprised by how much it actually is."

Seth's jaw set. He didn't want to hear any of his brother's terrible justifications, but he'd stirred up this hornet's nest and wasn't about to back down. "Mother and Father pay you a very good wage."

An amused chuckle. "I suppose it's good enough for survival, but I want something more than the bare minimum." He stopped there and ground his hands into his pockets, as if he hoped by doing so he could prevent himself from taking a swipe at his little brother. "I want Mary back, and the only way to do that is to have a lot of money in the bank and a big, fine house that'll make that holier-than-thou mother of hers—and the rest of her family—look the other way."

About all Seth could do was stare at his brother in horror, wondering if he'd lost some part

of his mind after his fiancée ended their engagement months earlier. "And you think she'll be just
fine with marrying a bootlegger?"

Charles's lip curled. "Do you honestly believe
she'd know anything about that? All she and her
family will have to know is that I've come into my
own and can give her the kind of life she
deserves."

Clearly, Charles was convinced that this
terrible scheme was the only way to woo back the
woman of his heart. Seth searched desperately for
any counter-arguments, anything he could say to
let his brother understand what a terrible mistake
he was making.

"You don't even know if she's already found
someone else," he said, and now Charles laughed
outright.

"She hasn't," he replied. "You see, I've been
spending more time in Prescott lately, and I've
met some people who were able to make inquiries.
Mary is living quietly with her great-aunt, and
there's absolutely no sign of any suitors sniffing
around. I know I'll be able to make her mine soon
enough."

One line of argument shot down. What else
could Seth possibly come up with to convince his
brother that his current course of action would
only end in grief?

"You want to give her a fine house," he said.

"Maybe you've bought the land, but do you have any idea how long it will take to build a new home? I doubt Mary will be quite as fancy-free a year from now."

Charles only smirked. "No need to build a house when I can buy one outright. I heard that Jeffrey Waters, who owns the boarding house down the street, wants to sell everything and move back East, since it seems his wife can't stomach life in a mining town any longer. I have no intention of running a boarding house, but Waters' home up on Paradise Lane is an entirely different story. When I can show Mary what luxury she'll be living in, then I think she'll change her mind... and so will her family."

Although this news about Mr. Waters was unexpected, Seth knew the house his brother was referring to well enough. It sat on the opposite side of the street and partway down the block from the one his aunt Ruth occupied, and was somewhat bigger than her house, with three stories and a large, flat lot, uncommon in their town. Only the home that Mabel McAllister, the clan's *prima,* occupied was more grand, and he realized with a sinking sensation somewhere in his stomach that such a residence might very well be sufficient evidence to convince Mary's intransigent relatives that Charles McAllister wasn't such a bad option after all.

"You will be lying to her," Seth said, hearing the desperation in his voice but knowing he needed to press on regardless. "You will make her entire life a falsehood."

"A pleasant one, though," Charles returned. "And it isn't as if she left me because she had fallen out of love. If that were the case, I would have let her go and tried to move on with my life. But to have her sanctimonious relatives step in and decide I wasn't a suitable match for her, just because Father lost his temper that one time and made a scene? I won't stand for it…and I'll make sure they'll all be eating their words very soon."

The jut of his jaw told Seth that his older brother wasn't making an idle boast. While it was true that the Townes, who'd been in Jerome since the late 1890s, had been very firm about making sure their only daughter was safely away from the McAllisters, he also knew that they were invested in the trappings of wealth, and probably wouldn't have encouraged the match in the first place if it hadn't been for Charles's position as the eldest son in the family, a position that assured he would inherit a thriving business and would have no problem providing for Mary. If he were to come back to her with words of love…and the deed to one of the finest houses in town…it was very possible that they might decide to reconsider their opinion of the match.

And truly, if Charles had come by the money honestly, Seth wouldn't have said one word about the situation. He might have privately wondered how much love was truly involved, since he'd thought once or twice that Mary could have put her foot down and refused to go to Prescott, maybe even encouraged his brother to elope and get married someplace like Phoenix, where they could be sure no one from her family would intervene. Yes, that was de la Paz territory, but the McAllisters and the de la Pazes had always been on friendly terms, and he thought the *prima* there would probably be sympathetic to his brother's situation.

But to have the house and the reconciliation and everything else built on money earned by illegal activity?

That, as his uncle Malcolm—who was very prone to malapropisms—might say, was an entirely different ball of worms.

"What happens if you get caught?" he asked. "Do you think Mary would be content with having a husband in prison, even if she was living in one of Jerome's finest houses?"

Charles's eyes narrowed. "I won't get caught. And neither will anyone I'm working with. All I need is for you to keep your mouth shut."

Well, there lay the rub, didn't it? Seth was all too aware of the many secrets his family kept from their neighbors and the world in general, but that was an entirely different situation. Witch clans always needed to keep their magical talents hidden or risk persecution. The Salem witch trials might have taken place hundreds of years earlier, but they still served as a stark lesson regarding the hysteria that could grip the civilian population when confronted with the unknown.

In his brother's case, though, he'd be hiding something illegal, a secret that could put the entire clan at risk if the bootlegging operation was ever discovered. Some people might have argued that smuggling liquor wasn't a crime like murder or kidnapping, and that if the laws hadn't changed, it wouldn't have been a crime at all.

Seth wasn't ready to split those sorts of semantic hairs, however. All he knew was that his brother had put him in an impossible position.

"I'll keep my mouth shut," he said slowly as an idea occurred to him. Charles's expression brightened at once, but Seth didn't let that prevent him from adding, "As long as you withdraw from the operation once you have the house and you have Mary back. After that, you won't need the money any longer, since the McAllister stipend and your salary at the store should be enough to provide for you both."

This ultimatum didn't appear to sit too well, for Charles retorted, "Do you have any idea what kind of people I'm working with? It's not like tendering your resignation from a position at a bank."

"I don't care," Seth said. While he couldn't count himself relieved, he still thought he'd come up with a handy way to handle the mess. "Tell them that Father has gotten suspicious about all the gas you're using in the truck, or the way the miles are racking up. Even they should understand this isn't the sort of thing you can keep hidden forever."

"'They,'" Charles returned, "aren't exactly the most understanding people in the world. But that may be the angle I need. I can't break it off right away, though."

"And I'm not expecting you to," Seth said. "I know you need some time to buy the house and to see if Mary's family will be willing to let her come back. At least this way you won't forever be hiding your activities from your wife. Can't you see that's a better way to live?"

No response at first, as Charles seemed to be mulling what his brother had just said. At length he replied, "I suppose so. But you can't breathe a word of this to anyone in the meantime, understand?"

"I won't," Seth said.

It was a promise he intended to keep...no matter what.

11

A WISH AND A MISS

ALTHOUGH WE'D LEFT IT OPEN-ENDED AS TO when we'd go to Cottonwood for dinner, I couldn't help wondering, as a day passed and then another, whether Seth had decided that getting any more serious about the town amnesiac wasn't such a good idea after all and that he was currently indulging in the 1920s version of ghosting a person.

In which case, it was probably better for me to try to get out of here.

This time, I sat in the back parlor, which overlooked Ruth McAllister's garden. It was a lovely little spot, not really big enough for a lawn, but with beds full of roses and old-fashioned flowers like foxgloves and hydrangeas and long spikes of hollyhocks. I felt intimately acquainted with the space at the moment, considering I'd spent all morning helping Ruth pull weeds out of the flowerbeds and spray whiteflies with a little copper sprayer full of a mixture of water and white vinegar, which she claimed was a sovereign remedy for the annoying pests, always a problem in this dry climate.

I supposed that was one thing that hadn't changed much over the past hundred years, since my mother employed a similar method to deal with the whiteflies in our yard in Flagstaff.

Anyway, both my feet and my back hurt, although at least I'd been working while wearing the new flats I'd gotten from the mercantile two days earlier and hadn't been standing in heels for the better part of three hours.

Both Ruth and Timothy were gone, saying they had an errand to run in Prescott and that they'd be back sometime in the late afternoon. Ruth had even offered for me to come along, but I'd politely excused myself. Having the run of the house for a while seemed like an appealing prospect, especially since I knew it would be easier to concentrate on using my magic if no one else was around.

A clock ticked loudly on the mantel, but it was the only real sound in the room except for the happy buzzing of bees and the faint rustle of leaves in the trees outside the open windows. It was warm, although not unpleasantly so; the weather had continued to cool from its peak the day I arrived in 1926, and some clouds forming to the east seemed to signal we might get an early monsoon storm.

Or maybe it wasn't early for this day and age. I had no idea how much the climate had shifted between then and my own now, and in the end, I supposed it really didn't matter.

Not if I wasn't planning to stay here.

I closed my eyes and breathed in and out. Visualizing my room back home hadn't seemed to help me very much in my first attempt at this, so this time I was trying a different tack, one I hoped might be successful.

Rather than narrowing my focus, I was going to take it as wide as possible.

I thought of Jerome's narrow streets filled with self-driving cars, with people taking selfies in front of the shops and restaurants or at the gorgeous overlook just a few yards from Rachel's store, where you could stand in front of the railing and get an amazing shot of the Verde Valley and Sedona's red rocks beyond. And then I made my focus expand even further, taking in the narrow stripe of Interstate 17 as it cut through the northern half of the state, ranging from my hometown in Flagstaff all the way down to Phoenix. Cars moving there, too, and jets in the air, full of people traveling with laptops and tablets and phones, all those indispensable items in a world that the residents here in 1926 couldn't even begin to imagine.

That was my world…the world of the twenty-first century. I belonged there, not more than a hundred years earlier.

For just the barest second, the room seemed to waver around me. I caught a glimpse of a space of similar dimensions, only with one wall missing and everything else painted bright white. Soft furniture entirely unlike the prim Victorian-era pieces that surrounded me now, and the faintest background hum that I thought must be coming from an air conditioning unit.

Just as quickly as it had come, though, the vision disappeared, and I was still sitting in Ruth's back parlor, with a soft breeze blowing at the curtains.

Damn it.

I'd been close, though…much closer than I'd been last time. Although I couldn't be sure, I guessed I might have been seeing what this house looked like now, in my proper century. Part of the reason why I'd attempted this exercise here rather than in my bedroom was that I'd thought it would be better to emerge in a TV room or family room, rather than someplace much more private.

And the magic had almost worked. True, I had no real way of knowing whether what I'd witnessed had been from my actual year or one even five or ten years earlier, but it definitely hadn't been 1926 or anything close, despite not catching a glimpse of any technology that might have provided better clues to the decade I was seeing.

I rubbed my palms over my pleated skirt, then got up from the sofa and went into the kitchen. Ruth had told me there was a pitcher of lemonade in the icebox, and a cool, refreshing drink felt like just what I needed right then.

After pouring myself a glass, I leaned against the butcher-block countertop and glanced around me. As always, the kitchen was spotlessly clean, with the breakfast dishes dried and put away before Ruth and Timothy left on their errand and the damp rag hanging on its hook by the door. I had to admit it was a cheerful place, what with its yellow-painted cabinets and checked curtains at the windows, but it wasn't *my* place. Even that teeny glimpse of this house in the future made me realize I didn't belong here.

Especially if Seth had decided I was a bad bet.

Just as those unhelpful thoughts were passing through my mind, someone knocked at the door. At once, I set down my glass of lemonade and went to answer it. Back in the day—or, I supposed, forward in the day—I would never have answered the door if I wasn't expecting someone, because otherwise it would have been some kind of solicitor, but I knew that wasn't how people operated here. Other McAllisters seemed to drop by Ruth's house all the time, whether to leave some flowers from their yard, or a jar of honey, or just to chat a bit.

Definitely a social bunch. But then, it wasn't as if they had phone screens to distract them. In a way, I was still kind of surprised by how much I didn't miss my cell phone, the constant pull of social media or texts from friends or just my mom sending me the latest image from her garden in bloom. Even on quiet days in this Jerome of the past, there always seemed to be enough happening right in front of me that I was just fine with focusing on the here and now.

I didn't recognize the boy standing on Ruth's front porch, although, since I didn't get the tingle I usually felt when I encountered a strange witch or warlock, I guessed he must be a civilian. He looked around thirteen or fourteen, maybe a little older, thin and wearing shabby linen pants with suspenders and a shirt that could use a good bleaching or three. Dust smudged his cheek, and that, in addition to the matching blotches of reddish dirt on his clothing, made me think he must work at the mines.

So much for child labor laws.

"Miss Rowe?" the boy asked, and I nodded.

He handed over a folded piece of paper, which also bore a few smudges. "Mr. McAllister asked me to give this to you."

"Thank you," I said, mystified…or possibly not so mystified. Maybe this was Seth's way of dumping me by proxy.

Having delivered the letter, the boy nodded at me before hurrying down the porch steps.

All right, then.

I closed the door and went back into the kitchen, thinking it might be a good idea to have a few more sips of lemonade before I opened the piece of paper from Seth.

If it was even from him. There were a whole lot of "Mr. McAllister"s in Jerome.

A silly idea, though. Why would any of the other McAllister warlocks have anything to do with me?

Well, except Charles, possibly, except I had no idea why he'd want to drop me a note. He'd made it pretty clear that he wasn't terribly thrilled with me.

Unless he was trying to warn me away from his brother.

I swallowed some more lemonade and found myself wishing it was a margarita. What a stupid idea Prohibition was, anyway. How long had this bullshit even lasted?

Due to my general disinterest in U.S. history,

I couldn't remember. Was it during the Depression? Or had they repealed the dumb thing as World War 2 broke out, figuring it probably wasn't too smart to force their soldiers to be sober when they were on leave?

Not that it mattered, I supposed. I was certainly in the heart of Prohibition now, so it wasn't as though anything about the situation was going to change any time soon.

And then I opened the letter. No envelope, not even a seal, so the contents of it could have been easily read by the boy who'd brought it here, even though I didn't see any signs of the telltale dirt smudges he would have left behind.

Dear Miss Rowe,

I apologize for my neglect over the past couple of days. Work has been very busy at the mine, so I thought it better for things to slow down a bit before we attempted another meal together. Would you be available for dinner in Cottonwood tomorrow night?

If so, you can leave me a note at my house. Just tuck it under the doormat.

Your friend,

Seth McAllister

He wasn't dumping me, or playing the ghost game. No, he was just working ten-plus hours a day so he could save up for a bigger house, maybe get another promotion.

The relief that flooded through my body was so extreme, I wanted to shake my head at myself. I knew I absolutely should not be getting so emotionally invested in Seth McAllister...and the more I tried to believe that, the more I knew I'd never be able to stay away.

Even if I'd come just that much closer to returning to my own time. Shouldn't I politely decline his invitation and tell him it seemed clear he was too busy to see anyone right now, and that I thought it better if we both went our separate ways?

Well, that would have been the logical thing to do. Too bad I was feeling anything but logical at the moment. All I knew was that I wanted to spend as much time with him here as I could. If I ended up returning to the twenty-first century, my disappearance would hurt him...and yet I had to believe it would hurt him even more to know I was here and had decided I didn't want to see him anymore.

I'd appeared mysteriously...and maybe I'd disappear the same way. In the meantime, I needed to steal these moments with Seth when I could.

It felt a little strange not to lock the door behind me as I left to go to Seth's bungalow, but as far as I could tell, Ruth and Timothy didn't seem to bother much with door locks. True, any witch or warlock worth their salt didn't need a key to get in and out of a place, and yet that wasn't what was going on here. No, it seemed as if all the neighbors on this street looked after one another, and didn't appear to worry too much about the unruly denizens of the boarding houses and hotels on Main Street making their way up here to see if the homes contained any valuables worth taking.

A subtle enchantment…or merely a simpler time?

Just as I was walking down the front path to the sidewalk, a woman about my age or maybe a little younger came closer, expression curious. She had pale blonde hair and pale blue eyes, and her skin was very fair as well, giving the impression of someone who looked as though she was beginning to fade around the edges.

"Hello," she said. She had a light, pretty voice, one that matched her appearance. Like mine, her white dress was made of cotton and reached a little below her knees, but it was much fancier, with a lot of pintucking and tone-on-tone embroidery. "Are you the girl who's staying with Ruth and Timothy McAllister?"

"I am," I replied. "I'm Deborah Rowe."

And I extended a hand—one I'd remembered at the last minute to cover in the single pair of thin kid gloves Molly McAllister had provided, along with the darlingest little cloche hat made of fine straw she had included in my latest batch of clothing.

The girl was also wearing gloves, although finely crocheted ones, and the hat that covered her head was wide-brimmed, something I thought wasn't completely in fashion in the 1920s but definitely provided much more sun protection than the one I currently had on.

"Abigail McAllister," she said. "I live just down the street."

She pointed with a gloved finger toward a Victorian that was the largest and fanciest on Paradise Lane.

In fact...wasn't that Angela's house?

All right, it couldn't be Angela's now, but it certainly was more than a hundred years in the future.

And if Abigail lived there now, that meant she must be the *prima*.

No, not the *prima*, I corrected myself hastily. The *prima's* daughter, or what most witch clans referred to as the *prima*-in-waiting. The Wilcoxes were different from pretty much every other clan in that we had a male head of the family and not a woman, but even I knew that when the girl who'd been designated as next in line turned twenty-one, she had a year to find her consort, her soul mate, so she could come into the fullness of her powers whenever the current *prima* passed on.

Up close, this girl looked barely eighteen or nineteen, so I guessed she still had a few years to go before she had to worry about finding her consort. In a way, I was relieved to see that, because otherwise, Seth would probably have been among her possible consorts. From what I'd heard, the elders—or whoever else was lining up the guys to try on the glass slipper, so to speak—did their best to avoid age gaps that were too large in these situations and almost always were looking for guys who weren't more than five or six years older than the *prima*-in-waiting. At twenty-four, Seth would certainly fall into that group…as long as he wasn't too closely related to Abigail.

Obviously, I couldn't ask her about any of that, since, thanks to the magic I'd inherited from the Rowe side of the family, Abigail must have believed I was just another civilian.

"I wondered who lived there," I said, doing my best to sound casual. "It's such a beautiful house."

"I suppose it is," Abigail replied, although her tone sounded almost absent.

The world's greatest conversationalist, she was not. I had to wonder how someone so listless and pale would make a good *prima,* but I supposed that was a problem for the 1920s McAllisters to ponder, and none of my business. I did my best to smile and say, "I'm surprised I haven't seen you before, since you're just down the street."

Abigail tugged at the edge of a crocheted glove. "Oh, I don't get out very much. But it felt a little cooler today, so I thought I'd take a short walk." She stopped there to tilt her head up at the sun, expression now almost accusing. "But it's starting to feel hot, so I'd better get back inside. It was very nice to meet you, Miss Rowe."

She turned away and began walking slowly back toward the *prima's* house. It didn't seem as if she was in too much of a hurry to get out of the sun, but maybe she was just someone who naturally dawdled.

If she didn't go outside too often, that might explain why she looked so languid and pale.

I shrugged, then continued in the opposite direction, toward Main Street and Seth's bungalow just a block or so below. In the funny little bag Ruth had given me, just big enough for a tube of lipstick and a few folded dollar bills, was my reply to his note.

Dear Mr. McAllister,

I completely understand being busy. Friday night in Cottonwood sounds like an enjoyable evening. We can meet at six-thirty at your Aunt

Ruth's house and go from there. If that time doesn't work for some reason, please just send me another note, and we can arrange for a different meeting time.

Yours,

Deborah Rowe

Of course, I wasn't Seth's, not really. And I'd had to rewrite the note three or four times, trying to get the cursive I hadn't used since grade school to look like something someone from this era would have written. Eventually, though, I thought I got it close enough to resemble handwriting that wouldn't rouse too much suspicion.

Now all I had to do was wait until Friday night.

I hadn't received a note telling me that six-thirty wouldn't work, so I went ahead and got ready for my date with Seth, brushing my hair and placing it in a fresh bun, and putting on the prettiest of the dresses Molly McAllister had given me, the one in a deep burgundy shade with a sash across the hips and lines of vertical pintucking. The color was a good one for me, if maybe a little dark for June, but I still thought it the best thing to wear out to dinner.

And sure enough, Seth pulled up to the house

promptly at six-thirty, driving a little black roadster I'd never seen before. After greeting him—and telling Ruth I wouldn't be out too late—I climbed into the convertible and jammed my cloche down on my head, hoping it would be enough to keep my hair from going completely cattywampus during our drive down the hill.

"Is this really yours?" I asked Seth as he sat down in the driver's seat.

"It is," he replied. "I bought it from one of the foremen at the mine when he got married and needed something a little more practical."

We pulled away from the curb, and I said, "I've never seen it before."

Those words might have come out a little too accusing, but Seth only smiled. "Well, I don't drive it much if I'm just here in town. My bungalow has a garage I built out back, and that's where it stays during the week. But obviously, we need a car to drive to Cottonwood."

That was for sure. Even now, we were passing through downtown Jerome, past the restaurants and bars and boarding houses, and then starting down the hill toward the high school. After that came a real hairpin curve, one that led us to the section that sloped downward for quite a ways before we once again made a ninety-degree turn and were now pointed right toward Clarkdale and Cottonwood.

It was a drive I'd made plenty of times before —even in my day, Jerome didn't have anything resembling a grocery store, so I had to go down the hill any time I needed to stock up—but it felt utterly different in Seth's convertible, with the noisy engine banging away under the hood and the warm wind doing its best to pull my hair free from underneath the close-fitting hat I wore. His car didn't seem to have a radio, but if it had, I would have asked him to turn up the tunes so I could enjoy even more of the experience.

Soon enough, though, we drove through the outskirts of Clarkdale, which did look very different from its modern-day incarnation. Gone were the suburbs that had been built in the early twenty-first century, or the scattered custom homes in the hills. The only things that appeared the same were the park and the buildings clustered along its one main street, although now they were shiny and fresh and new, obviously built to accommodate the overflow of miners from Jerome and the people who worked at the smelter just outside town.

More open land between Clarkdale and Cottonwood, since those areas wouldn't be developed for probably another fifty or sixty years, but, just like in Clarkdale and Jerome, the storefronts along Main Street in Cottonwood were recognizable enough, even if the businesses that occupied them were very different from the ones in my time.

Seth stopped in front of a building that would house a real estate office a century from now. At the moment, though, it had a sign up top that said "Copper Café," and the friendly smells that wafted out every time someone opened the front door told me it had a very different occupant in 1926 than it did in my time.

"It's nothing fancy," he said as he opened the car door for me and then offered a hand to help me out. "But the food's really good, and at least it's a change of scenery from Jerome."

"I'm not much into 'fancy,'" I told him as we walked toward the entrance to the restaurant, a statement that was as true for me now as it had been in the twenty-first century. "So I'm sure if you like it, I'll like it, too."

He ducked his head at that comment, as if a little embarrassed by my vote of confidence, although that didn't stop him from reaching out and opening the front door to let me into the small waiting area. Ceiling fans churned away overhead, making the interior comfortable enough, if not the same as having real air conditioning.

And although maybe it wasn't the Ritz or anything, the restaurant was definitely a step up from the English Kitchen, with tables rather than booths and fun mosaic tile on the floor. A cheer-ful-looking woman in her forties and wearing one of the now-familiar drop-waist dresses came up to us. Her gaze was faintly speculative as she looked me over before saying, "Evening, Seth. I have a nice table by the window, if you'd like."

"Thanks, Marie," he responded. "That would be wonderful."

She led us over to the table in question, then handed us a pair of menus made of stiff card-board. From what I could tell, this seemed to be the 1920s version of a steakhouse, with lots of beef and a few chicken and pork selections.

Not for the first time since coming here, I wished I could have had a glass of wine with all this great food. Wine wasn't as big a deal in Flagstaff as it was down here in the Verde Valley, thanks to the major differences in their climates, but because of Connor and Angela owning a vine-yard and making sure bottles got handed out as gifts at the holidays, I'd drunk a lot more wine than most people in their early twenties most likely would have. These days, it just felt weird to have a nice dinner without it.

But I knew I'd probably make Seth's head explode if I commented on the lack of a nice cab to go with our steaks, so instead I asked, "Do you have any favorites here?"

"Everything's good," he replied. Since he'd

barely glanced at the menu before setting it down, I had to believe he already knew pretty much everything on it. "I suppose it depends on what you're in the mood for."

With Ruth and Timothy out of the house for most of the day, I hadn't bothered with a big lunch, just some fruit and a piece of cold chicken. Looking at everything offered at the restaurant, I had to keep my stomach from growling.

"Oh, a steak and a baked potato would be nice," I told him.

Or…was that too extravagant? The menu I'd been given didn't have any prices listed on it, so I had no idea how much any of this would even cost. Not that I had much frame of reference in a place where I'd seen a pair of pretty leather shoes in the mercantile going for the princely sum of $7.00. You couldn't even get a burger for that much where I'd come from.

"Exactly what I was going to have," Seth said, and he smiled at me from across the table.

All right, so I hadn't been too out of line with my selection. Sitting there with him, however, I thought I noted some faint shadows under his clear blue eyes, and even though his expression was pleasant enough, I couldn't shake the feeling that something was going on in his life, something that might have been a bit more stressful than merely having to work long hours.

If I'd known him better, I might have asked. As it was, I had to be glad that a waitress came along right then—wearing the same plain black dress with a white collar that Maria had had on, apparently the restaurant's uniform—and asked us if we'd like water or tea or lemonade. Tea seemed like the safest thing to have, since wine wasn't an option, and Seth requested it as well.

"I'm sorry I disappeared this week," Seth told me once we were alone. "But I had to work overtime at the mine, and I didn't have the time to stop by Ruth and Timothy's house to see you."

"It's fine," I said. Even as tired as he looked, I was still glad to be sitting across the table from him, glad to hear his voice…and, although I knew I shouldn't have felt that way, glad I'd been unsuccessful at sending myself back to the twenty-first century. "Your aunt's kept me pretty busy."

"That a fact?" he replied, an amused glint in his eyes. "Has she taught you her canning secrets yet?"

I couldn't help making a face. "Mercifully, no…but that's probably because it's not the right season for that kind of thing. But I've learned a lot more about tending a garden than I'd planned, and I think I've almost got the whole cornbread thing nailed. I suppose I'll just have to see when it comes time to make another batch."

His expression grew confused. "'Nailed'?" he repeated.

Damn it. I'd been doing my best to avoid as much slang as I could, but it hadn't even popped into my mind that people might not have used that expression in the 1920s. It wasn't as if they didn't have nails back then.

I tried my best to smile and brush it off. "Oh, it's something I heard someone say once. It just means to do well at a particular task."

"Ah, I see," he said, although he still looked a little bewildered, as if he was pretty sure he'd never heard of a single instance of someone using the word that way.

The waitress came back with our iced teas, and since Seth and I both wanted the same thing for our meals, the ordering process went smoothly. Soon enough, we were left alone again. We both picked up our drinks and had a sip—even as I wished we had some straws—and for a moment, that was all right.

But I could tell something must be going on, because we'd never been this awkward around each other before, not even that first time I'd woken up in his bungalow...my rented bungalow in the twenty-first century...with absolutely no idea how I'd gotten there.

Maybe we hadn't yet gotten to a point in our

relationship where I should be asking probing questions, but I didn't know what else to do.

"Possibly it's not my place to ask," I ventured. "But…is everything all right?"

At once, the brooding expression he'd worn vanished as if it had never been. "Oh, sure," he said, and smiled. "There's just been a lot happening at the mine this week."

"Anything you want to talk about?"

He chuckled, and the sound seemed pretty genuine to me. "I didn't ask you out to dinner so I could bore you to death. I promise I'll put work away for the evening. So, tell me about your week."

Since I could see he didn't want to talk about it, I launched into a description of my various travails at being domestic, including the cake I tried to bake that looked as though I'd stomped on it. Through all of those tales, I did my best to keep my tone light, and soon enough, he was laughing outright at Ruth's attempts to turn me into a decent baker.

And if he was at all worried that the woman he was interested in appeared to be a failure in the kitchen, he didn't show any sign of it.

The food came and was excellent, the steak perfectly marbled and accompanied by bearnaise sauce, the potato melting with butter and baked to the point where it had a sweet, nutty flavor. I asked Seth about the restaurant, and he explained it had been operating here since the turn of the century, and got its beef and all its produce from ranches and farms in the surrounding areas.

That explained why everything tasted so fresh —and also why he was on a first-name basis with the staff here. It sounded as if he'd started visiting with his family as a child, whether for special occasions or because his father had decreed that Molly needed a break from cooking, and then had continued after he moved out and was on his own.

The one thing I didn't ask was whether he'd brought any other dates here. His romantic past wasn't any of my business, and besides, I got the impression that he hadn't been seeing anyone else. Otherwise, Maria or our waitress might have seemed a little surprised for him to show up with a different girl, and I hadn't noticed a single sign of that happening.

It had cooled down enough when we went outside that Seth determined it would be better for him to put up the convertible's top. I waited on the sidewalk while he took care of that task, which was a far cry from the single button-push that kind of procedure required in my day. Eventually, though, the top was secured, and we were headed down Main Street toward Clarkdale.

"Thank you for dinner," I said. "It was lovely."

And it was. I had no idea why I'd thought restaurants in the 1920s would be some sort of primitive affairs—it wasn't as if they didn't have real appliances and gas and electricity and all the other necessities—but for some reason, I hadn't been expecting a meal that was every bit as good as anything I could have eaten at one of Sedona's fancy five-star restaurants.

"We're a quiet corner of the world, but we do have good food," Seth replied. "Most people eat at home, though. The restaurants are a special night out for most folks."

Well, I could see that. The world in 1926 was a very different place from the mid-twenty-first century, when a few taps on your phone could have all sorts of food delivered to your door. I liked the idea of a night at a restaurant as an occasional treat, however, and not something you had so often that it became commonplace.

The two of us were quiet as we zigged and zagged our way up the road leading to Jerome. Driving in the convertible with the top up was a very different experience, more intimate, and definitely not as noisy. The engine was loud enough, though, making me appreciate the electric cars of my own time that much more.

Seth pulled up in front of Ruth and Timothy's house, then shut off the engine before turning toward me. Almost shy, he said, "I had a good time."

"So did I." A pause as I pondered whether to ask him if he wanted to talk about what seemed to have been weighing on his mind at the beginning of our meal, and then I decided to put it aside for now. If he'd wanted to discuss the matter…whatever it was…then he would have brought it up, and even though we seemed comfortable enough with each other, it wasn't as if we'd reached a point in our relationship where he would be okay with divulging his deep, dark secrets. "Thank you for asking me to dinner," I added, since the silence now felt positively fraught, very different from the companionable quiet of our drive here.

He hesitated, and I wondered if he was going to lean over and kiss me.

No, scratch that—I wanted him to reach out and cup my cheek, bring me closer so he could place his lips across mine. Never mind that sharing a kiss was absolute madness. I shouldn't be allowing myself to care for him, not when I wasn't even supposed to be here at all.

But I knew I did have feelings for Seth McAllister, even after these brief moments stolen together…even when I knew so little about him.

Even though he would have been dead long, long before I was born.

"I'll come around and open your door," he

said, and hope deflated in me like a popped balloon.

Somehow, I managed to thank him, and to wait in the passenger seat while he got out and opened the car door for me, then walked me up the porch steps. I had a feeling that if he wasn't going to kiss me in the privacy of his car, then he definitely wasn't going to do so here, where we'd be in full view of anyone—namely, Ruth McAllister—who might be peeking through the curtains.

Not that I'd seen any sign of her, but still.

"Thank you again for dinner," I said.

He made a dismissive movement of one hand, then said in low tones, "I wish I could do more for you. I wish—"

The words broke off abruptly, and then he took my right hand in his and brushed his fingers across mine, very gently, before turning and hurrying back down the steps.

Even that slight touch was enough to send heat spinning through me, and I pulled in a startled gasp. If Seth could affect me like that with a simple touch of his fingers against mine, what would it be like if he actually kissed me?

I could only hope I'd find out…very soon.

12

CONSORT COMPLICATIONS

ALL DAY SATURDAY AT WORK, SETH KEPT playing over and over again in his mind moments from his dinner with Deborah—the quick flash of her smile, the way she seemed interested in every single small, silly detail he'd related to her about Cottonwood and Jerome and the Verde Valley in general.

The softness of her skin when he'd reached out to touch her as they said goodbye on Ruth's front porch.

He probably shouldn't have done that, but he hadn't quite been able to help himself. There had been a moment in his car when it truly looked as though she'd wanted him to kiss her, and he'd almost succumbed. Then reason had reasserted itself, reminding him that he hadn't known her for very long and that it was far, far too soon for a goodnight kiss.

Still.

Lionel Allenby didn't appear to be at work that day, and Seth found himself grateful for his absence. Having to continually avoid seeing the man was stress he didn't need, not when he couldn't be sure of the mine superintendent's involvement in the bootlegging operation and also didn't know whether he should try investigating further.

Probably a bad idea. Seth had to admit that he wasn't philosophically opposed to drinking, as long as it was done in moderation. But with Prohibition the law of the land, it just seemed smarter to play by the rules rather than attract any untoward attention.

At any rate, he'd made something of a bargain with Charles. Not one he was overly happy about, but it was better than nothing, and at least it had a set endpoint. His brother would buy the house on Paradise Lane, and he would woo Mary—and her family back—and then he would have no need to be part of the bootlegging operation any longer.

Problem solved.

However, when he returned to his bungalow at the end of yet another long day, Seth was surprised to see a note slipped under his doormat.

His heart began to beat a little faster as he wondered if the note was from Deborah Rowe… but as soon as he picked it up, he recognized his mother's neat, copperplate handwriting and realized the missive was from an entirely different source than the one he'd hoped.

Only a few short words.

Dinner at seven. The family needs to talk.

He didn't like the sound of that very much. Had his parents learned of his date with Deborah last night and decided to step in?

That didn't feel right, though, not when his mother seemed to think Deborah was a nice girl and definitely hadn't said anything that showed she disapproved of him seeing her.

And he somehow doubted she would have gotten all those clothes together for Deborah if she harbored any fears about her younger son showing too much interest in the pretty newcomer.

Worried thoughts churned in his brain as he washed up and changed into clothes that weren't covered in rock dust. His wardrobe wasn't extensive, but he figured he could wear the same outfit tomorrow, a day when he wouldn't be expected to do anything too taxing. A while back, he'd hired one of the maids from a local hotel to come in and clean the house every Monday, so it wasn't as though he needed to worry about tidying up.

Doing his best to look as though he didn't have a care in the world, he left his bungalow and began heading toward Main Street, passing Edgar and Denise Emory and their little boy Ralph as he went. An exchange of waves, and then he was past them and walking up Hull Avenue before turning so he could come in through the rear entrance of the mercantile. At this hour, the front door would be locked, and the family always came and went via the back door when they weren't there on store business.

The rich smell of beef stew and freshly baked bread drifted down the stairs as he made his way up to the second-floor apartment. Seth breathed it in, knowing his stomach gurgled a little as he inhaled the delicious aroma. It had been a long while since lunch.

He was the last one to get there, since his brother and his father were already seated at the dining table, and his mother was just setting down a basket of bread as he approached.

"Oh, Seth," she said. "I'm so glad you got my note. We're just about ready to eat."

No comment about his almost-tardiness, for which he was relieved. And no one seemed particularly tense, making him think this family meeting was about something other than Deborah Rowe entirely, like the ongoing discussion about whether they should get awnings for the mercantile's front windows, or whether it was time to retire the Dodge and buy a new truck.

He took his regular seat next to his brother, then put his napkin in his lap and waited for his mother to sit down as well. A glass of water had already been poured for him, so there was no need to ask for something to drink.

Henry McAllister gave his usual brief thanks to Brigid, and then he and Charles passed their plates down so their mother could give them each a large portion of stew, thick with carrots and potatoes and slices of onion, sweet from being cooked at a low simmer on the stovetop for a good part of the day. After that, they all helped themselves to some fresh-baked bread.

During all this, Charles had sent Seth a borderline warning glance from time to time, as if warning him of their agreement and letting him know he would most certainly cut him off if he attempted to bring up the subject at all. Those looks only made him that much more tense, since he'd told Charles he would keep silent until this thing with Mary was settled one way or another.

His brother should have known he would never break his word.

"We wanted to have you here for dinner tonight for two reasons," their mother said. "Some happy news this afternoon—your cousin Louise just had a baby daughter!"

A new addition to the McAllister clan was always something to celebrate, although Seth wasn't sure why his parents had seen the need to invite him over to hear the news. He would have gotten the story from his cousin Helen soon enough, since he assumed she would have presided over the child's birth. Luckily, none of Jerome's civilian population thought it too strange that a McAllister midwife would be in charge of such operations, not when women often still turned toward female help when giving birth rather than seeing a doctor.

"I thought Louise wasn't due until later in the month," Charles remarked, then put a chunk of beef in his mouth.

Molly shrugged. "Well, babies come when they want, no matter what anyone else might have to say on the subject. But little Ruby is perfectly healthy, and it doesn't seem to have been a problem that she was a few weeks early."

"That's not the only reason why we wanted to talk to you, though," Henry McAllister said. "Mabel called earlier today to specifically remind us that Abigail's twenty-first birthday is tomorrow, and very soon afterward, her consort search will begin."

Oh, Goddess. With everything that had happened over the past week—Deborah's arrival, the discovery of Charles's connection to a local bootlegging operation—Seth had completely forgotten that his cousin Abigail's all-important birthday was rapidly approaching...and that, as an unattached, not-too-distant cousin of the proper age, he would be forced to participate in the quest to find her consort.

Even before he'd met Deborah Rowe, Seth hadn't been terribly thrilled by the prospect of possibly being his cousin's future match. He supposed it wasn't Abigail's fault that she had always been so wan and languid, since he knew she'd battled one childhood disease after another. True, Helen had done her best to attend to Abigail while she fought whooping cough and diphtheria and mumps and Goddess knows what else, but even so, it seemed as though the parade of illnesses had taken its toll regardless of all the magical cures his cousin had been given.

And although no one in the clan talked about it openly, he also knew that the elders had had reservations about designating Abigail as the *prima*-in-waiting precisely because she hadn't seemed strong enough to take over the management of the McAllister clan once her mother passed away, and had even gone so far to suggest that they should find someone else of the proper age. This sort of situation cropped up from time to time exactly because of this sort of reason, or simply because the current *prima* had the misfortune to have only sons.

But Mabel had been adamant that Abigail's magic was very strong, even if her body seemed somewhat frail, and that it just made sense to designate her as the *prima*-in-waiting.

Despite all those protestations as to his cousin's fitness for her future position, Seth hadn't found the prospect of being Abigail's consort very appealing, even back before he'd known his heart was given to someone else. She was so very languid and retiring, not the sort of person he could imagine kissing, let alone sharing the sort of activities his father had explained to him when he turned sixteen, spelling out how men had these urges but that it wasn't safe to indulge them with certain loose women in the town who would be more than happy to take care of his needs…for a certain price.

Seated next to him, Charles looked less than happy as well. A few months ago, he wouldn't have even been considered for the consort search, since he'd been engaged. Now, though, he was just as much of a free agent as his brother—or at least, that was what their parents must have believed, as they would have no idea that their oldest son was fully determined to get Mary back, no matter what.

Charles was the first to speak. "I'm afraid I

can't participate. I've recently begun corre-
sponding with Mary Towne, and I think she and
her family are beginning to soften toward me. I
won't jeopardize the current situation by partici-
pating in the consort search. If word ever got back
to Mary that I'd kissed another woman, my
chances would be utterly ruined."

Both Molly and Henry looked understandably
startled by this announcement, since Seth guessed
that Charles hadn't uttered even a hint to them
that he was doing his best to reconcile with his
former fiancée. In fact, he had a strong feeling
that his older brother hadn't written to Mary at
all, and had only attempted such a gambit as a
way of delaying the inevitable.

"You didn't say anything to us about that,"
their mother said, confirming Seth's suspicions.

"Because I didn't want to mention it until I
knew the engagement was back on," Charles
replied, his chin taut. "Before then, there wouldn't
have been much point, would there? But because
of that, I absolutely cannot be part of the search
for Abigail's consort."

His parents exchanged a glance, and Seth
watched his father's mouth thin.

"If you had reconciled," he said, "then of
course your mother and I would make your
excuses to Mabel and her daughter. However,
since it doesn't sound as though it's a settled

matter, you will need to participate, just like any other eligible cousin."

"It's not anything that either you can avoid," Molly put in. Although her voice was firm, Seth couldn't miss the compassion in her clear blue eyes, telling him she knew this was difficult for everyone involved.

He found himself saying, "If that was the case, then I'm surprised you haven't done more to stop me from seeing Miss Rowe."

His mother's gaze softened even further. "Oh, Seth, you know that's not how these things work. It has never been our way to tell the young men who might be a future consort that they can't have their own lives and seek out their own wives. We trust the Goddess to guide us to the right place in this, as in all other things. If you were meant to be Abigail's consort, then you would be utterly free when it came time to find her partner. And that goes for you as well, Charles," she added, "We have to believe that if you weren't intended to be a possible consort for our *prima*-in-waiting, then you and Mary would never have fallen out in the first place."

These reasoned arguments didn't appear to have much effect on their recipient. Lip curling, Charles retorted, "And I have to believe that if Father hadn't shown off in the store that one day, then Mary and I wouldn't have had our 'falling out,' as you put it. I don't think the Goddess had anything to do with it. Just...bad luck."

Their father's eyes narrowed. "It wasn't 'showing off,' Charles," he said, tone flat. "It was stopping a thief from stealing our hard-earned money."

"Of course, Henry," Molly said, laying a placating hand on her husband's arm. "We all know why you did what you did. But we also can't deny that if your use of magic hadn't been witnessed by everyone in the store, then Mary's family would have had much less reason to make her break off the engagement. At any rate," she continued briskly, "that is neither here nor there. We are all where the Goddess wants us to be, and that means you will respond to the summons to be Abigail's possible consort, whenever that happens."

Seth couldn't quite stop himself as he reached for his glass of water to soothe his suddenly dry throat. Unlike his brother, he wouldn't offer any further protests, since he knew they would fall on deaf ears. For uncounted generations, the sons of witch families had always answered the call when it came time to find a consort for the *prima*-in-waiting. He might rail inwardly against what he thought was a ridiculous custom, and he might privately think that if the Goddess's hand was behind all this, then She had very bad timing, but he would hold his tongue. While he had absolutely no interest in becoming his sickly cousin's consort, he would have been far more resigned to the situation if he had never met Deborah Rowe and had no idea what it felt like to be truly attracted to someone.

Charles, on the other hand, didn't seem willing to let it go. "And if I don't respond to the summons? If I refuse?"

"You will not refuse," Henry McAllister replied, his voice implacable.

Their mother's expression had also hardened, although when she spoke, it was in the same soft, persuasive tones she'd used a moment earlier. "Oh, Charles, that's impossible. Don't you know the elders and the *prima* can compel you to go to Abigail and share the consort's kiss? Just because they don't rule this clan with an iron fist doesn't mean they won't bring their powers to bear if they believe that's what's required."

Seth slipped a sideways glance at his brother. Charles's jaw was still taut, but there was also a certain fear in his eyes, a clear worry about what the elders might do if he angered them enough.

Before either of them could speak, though, their mother went on, "Besides, the chances that one of you would be Abigail's consort aren't so very high. You're second cousins, and I've found that a *prima's* consort tends to be someone more distantly related. I wouldn't be surprised if our *prima*-in-waiting found her match among our relations in Prescott or Payson."

That would be the best possible outcome for everyone involved. Charles could continue in his quest to woo back Mary Towne, and Seth could continue…well, whatever he was doing with Deborah Rowe. Spending as much time as possible in her company, he supposed, knowing that her tenure in Jerome might not be a lengthy one, should her memories return to her and she go back to her people, whoever they might be.

"I suppose we'll just have to wait and see what happens," Seth said, which was the only real response he could give right then.

"Yes," Charles said, his tone far more ominous, "I suppose we shall."

That night, Seth lay awake for a long time, watching moon-cast shadows move across the ceiling. He knew the wise thing to do would be to tell Deborah they needed to spend a little time apart, just until he knew for sure whether he would be Abigail's consort or not, but he couldn't think of a single way to articulate the situation without giving far too much away about the McAllister clan's inner workings. If he was too vague, he feared he might give Deborah the wrong impression...but on the other hand, spelling things out came with its own set of issues.

Whatever happened, he knew he needed to speak to her in person. Merely sending her a note telling her they shouldn't be in contact for a while seemed too cruel.

Or maybe it was only that he wanted to spend some time alone with her, just in case his life was entirely upended in the very near future.

In a way, as much as he hated the thought of sharing the consort's kiss with his cousin Abigail...not when he'd secretly dreamed of kissing Deborah almost since the moment he met her...he also thought it might help everyone involved if he was one of the early candidates to be presented to the *prima*-in-waiting. At least if that were the case, he could get this over with as soon as possible, and would either know the worst or realize he was now free to pursue Deborah without any fear of having all his hopes of a future with her ripped away at the last minute.

And since tomorrow was Sunday and he didn't have to work, he could spend the afternoon with her...if she was free, of course, even as he guessed that whatever chores Ruth might have dreamed up for her wouldn't last the whole day...and then he could let Deborah know that family business would consume his time for the coming week or so, but that he hoped she would still want to have dinner with him once the matter was handled and he didn't have it hanging over him anymore.

What he would do if she started asking probing questions, he wasn't sure, but he had to hope he'd be able to come up with answers that sounded plausible enough but wouldn't lead to more queries.

One way or another, he should find out tomorrow.

13

COOKIES AND COURTSHIP

THE NOTE WAS DELIVERED BY A DIFFERENT kid this time, a boy who looked younger than the one who'd brought the previous message from Seth. I had a feeling this child was a McAllister, since he was much better dressed, looking more like he'd come to Ruth and Timothy's house straight from Sunday school rather than the mine...even though I doubted any McAllister child would have attended such an overtly Christian institution.

"A note for you, Miss Rowe," the boy said. He had a mop of sandy blond hair and mischievous green eyes, and looked extremely amused by his errand. "Cousin Seth told me to wait so I could bring back your answer."

Oh, really? My mouth curved in amusement

as well, and I replied, "Of course. Give me a minute to look at this."

The boy nodded, and I unfolded the piece of paper and scanned the several lines it contained.

Dear Miss Rowe,

The weather is so fine that I was hoping you might like to have a picnic lunch up on Mingus Mountain today. If that sounds agreeable, just tell Alan, and he'll bring word back to me. Then I will pick you up at 12:30.

S

He was cutting things a little close, since it was already eleven o'clock in the morning. Luckily, even though the McAllisters certainly didn't celebrate the Sabbath the way their civilian neighbors did, it seemed they were also inclined to take Sundays off from any heavy labor. That was why, after I helped Ruth with the breakfast dishes, she told me I had the rest of the day free.

Not that I had any real plans. Almost all the stores along Main Street were closed on Sunday, which meant I couldn't do any real shopping, and while I supposed I could have taken a book out to the garden and read for a while under the shade of the big maple tree there, a picnic lunch with Seth sounded like a much better use of my time.

"You can tell Seth that a picnic would be wonderful," I said to Alan, who'd been watching me the whole time, still with that glint in his eye that made me wonder if he had some mischief planned for his walk home, like stealing apples from someone's tree or skipping a few rocks at the white-winged doves that seemed to congregate along the main drag, Jerome's equivalent of a pigeon population. "And that I'll see him at twelve-thirty."

The boy gave me a salute, grinning the whole time. "Will do, miss."

He hurried down the porch steps and practically ran the length of Paradise Lane, making me wonder if Seth had promised to pay him extra if he carried out his errand within a certain amount of time. Well, if he was waiting to get this picnic together until he heard from me, I could see why Seth might treasure even an extra five minutes.

I went back inside the house, where Ruth had just emerged from the front parlor, a feather duster in her hand.

So much for not doing any household chores on Sundays.

"Who was that?"

"A boy named Alan," I said. "Seth had him bring me a note. We're going on a picnic—I assume that's all right?"

"It sounds like a lovely way to spend a Sunday afternoon," Ruth replied, allaying any fears that I might have jumped the gun by replying yes to Seth's invitation. "When is he coming to get you?"

"Twelve-thirty," I said, and she practically beamed.

"That gives me enough time to bake some cookies for your picnic. Would you like chocolate, or some macaroons?"

Since I wasn't a huge fan of coconut, I told her chocolate cookies sounded wonderful, and she hurried off to the kitchen, obviously thrilled that I'd given her some purpose on what would otherwise have been a quiet Sunday morning. I almost followed so I could ask her if she wanted any help, but I got the impression this was something she wanted to do for Seth and me.

That was why I headed up to my room instead and changed out of the floaty muslin frock I'd been wearing and into a more practical skirt and blouse, along with the flat shoes Molly McAllister had provided for me a few days earlier. Maybe it wasn't quite as elegant an outfit, but I knew it would be much better suited to climbing over rough ground or sitting on a blanket, or whatever else Seth might have planned. While in my own time there was a picnic area with tables near the top of the pass that led through the mountains, I had no idea if it even existed in 1926.

Better to be safe.

Soon enough, the warm, rich aroma of baking cookies drifted up the stairs. I headed down to find Ruth pulling them out of the oven and setting them on racks to cool.

"That's a lot of cookies for two people," I said with a smile, and she shrugged.

"Oh, I'll send a dozen with you and Seth," she responded. "The rest I'll keep here for Timothy— he does love a good chocolate cookie, even though he knows he shouldn't eat too many of them."

Probably not. Timothy stood out among the McAllisters because they generally tended to be slender, like most witches and warlocks. I had no idea why that was, although a few people had postulated that something about our witchy powers sped up our metabolisms, as though using our talents required an extra store of energy.

"Well," I said, "I'm pretty sure I can help you with those, assuming Seth and I eat all the ones you're sending with us."

"I have a feeling you will," she replied, blue eyes twinkling. "That boy can definitely eat."

Maybe he could; he didn't have much left on his plate except the bone when he was done with his steak Friday night, whereas I'd had to stop because I'd known I couldn't eat another bite. The effects of his appetite didn't show on his body, though, which was slim and well-muscled.

I probably shouldn't have been thinking about his body in front of his aunt, not when the memory of how strong his arm had felt was enough to send a not-unpleasant wash of heat through me.

"He does have something of an appetite," I agreed.

"I'll go ahead and get these cookies wrapped up," she told me. "You can wait for Seth in the front parlor, and I'll bring them to you."

This sounded like a good plan, so I headed for the room in question and sat down on one of the chairs that faced the front window, giving me an excellent vantage point for watching all the comings and goings on Paradise Lane. Of course, on that sunny Sunday morning, it was mostly quiet, except for a big, shiny black car that I thought belonged to the *prima*...Mabel...as it cruised by.

Going to Cottonwood for brunch?

Was brunch even a thing in 1926?

The car disappeared from view, and I found myself wondering whether the wan *prima*-in-waiting was accompanying her mother on this errand, or whether she had stayed home. She didn't seem like the type to get out much. Did they have some other family member who lived at the house and acted as a governess of sorts? Abigail seemed a little too old for that, but I knew that witch clans tended to be protective of their *primas*-in-waiting, even before they turned twenty-one...when they became especially vulnerable. It was during that year that they had to find their consorts and marry them so their magic couldn't be taken and controlled by someone who might wish them ill.

I only knew that because the former *primus* of the Wilcoxes, Damon, had kidnapped Angela right before her twenty-second birthday in an attempt to bind her to him. The plan had back-fired spectacularly on him, but that made me think about how that hadn't been the first time my clan had made such an underhanded attempt at seizing power. Sometime in the 1940s, the *primus* of that time, Jasper Wilcox, had tried much the same thing, only he'd been thwarted because the *prima*-in-waiting in Jerome, Ruby McAllister, had been a strong witch who'd been able to send out a mental call to her clan to save her.

Somehow I doubted that Abigail possessed those sorts of resources.

Seth hadn't talked about my clan very much, which I supposed made sense. He thought I was a civilian, and would have no reason to give me any warnings about the Wilcox family. Had there been much contact between the two witch clans during this time? I couldn't remember for sure, since anything that had happened before the 1990s felt like the Dark Ages to me.

Ruth came into the front parlor then and set a

brown paper parcel down on the coffee table. "I thought it better not to send a plate, just in case," she told me. "But I wrapped the cookies in two layers of paper, so they should be plenty secure."

"Thank you so much for that," I said. "I know the cookies will make our picnic even better."

"Oh, you can be sure of that," she replied. "As I have no idea what Seth might have rustled up for the two of you. I can only hope he went to his mother for help—she's a very fine cook."

Although I certainly didn't want Seth to impinge on his mother too much by expecting her to provide a full picnic lunch, I had to admit my interest was piqued. Maybe our meal would turn out to be a bit more than some quickie sandwiches and a couple of apples.

Seth pulled up to the curb then and got out. Because the weather was so fine, he had his convertible's top down again, and he wore a pale jacket I thought might be linen over his white shirt and brown trousers.

Just seeing him come up the front walk was enough to make my heart leap. How could he be so handsome, so absolutely wonderful, and still be interested in me? It wasn't that I hadn't dated at all in high school or college, but in general, I'd kept to myself, embarrassed and troubled by my unpredictable talent, and I knew my reticence had served to keep a lot of guys at a distance.

Seth wasn't keeping his distance, that was for sure.

"Well, I'll leave you to it," Ruth said, obviously spying her cousin's progress up the front path as well. "Dinner's at six, though, so don't be late."

"I won't," I promised as I got up from the sofa and leaned down to pick up the parcel of cookies. Her words warmed me even more; clearly, she expected me to spend the whole afternoon with Seth, and I was just fine with that.

Way more than fine, actually.

She left the parlor just as he knocked at the door, so I went to answer it.

"Good afternoon," he said.

I supposed it was afternoon…just barely. "Afternoon," I replied, and hefted the parcel I was carrying. "Ruth made us some chocolate cookies."

"Perfect," he said, taking them from me. "Shall we get going?"

"Absolutely."

We walked down the stone path to the gate, and then he opened the car door for me so I could get in. I'd been hoping he would have the top down, which was why I once again had my straw cloche hat jammed down over my ears.

Not that I thought we'd be speeding too much. Even modern cars couldn't go very fast along the switchbacks that cut their way up the face of Mingus Mountain, and I had to believe Seth would be careful, just as he'd been when he drove us to our dinner on Friday night.

He got in the driver's seat and started up the engine. "How has your day been so far?" he asked as we pulled away from the curb.

"Quiet," I said. "Yours?"

A smile tugged at a corner of his mouth. "Not as quiet, since I was busy getting our picnic together. But it was a good kind of busy."

Now I really wondered what he had planned for us. Nothing he'd said to me so far had made me think he was a gifted cook or anything like that, but people did have their way of surprising me.

I supposed I'd find out in a few minutes.

He did seem a little less weighed down by whatever had been bothering him on Friday night, although I had no way of knowing whether that was because the problem had been resolved or whether he was just doing a better job of hiding his worries. Whatever might be going on, it seemed as if he wanted this outing to be a success, so I certainly wasn't going to ask too many questions.

One of which was resolved as we pulled off the highway into a clearing I recognized well enough. True, I didn't see the small building that housed the bathrooms in my day, but otherwise, the open area under the tall ponderosa pines was familiar enough. I'd eaten a few picnics of my own here since coming to Jerome, on those days when the weather was just hot enough that I wanted to take a break in a place that reminded me of my hometown of Flagstaff. Up here, the trees and terrain were similar enough, thanks to the nearly thousand feet of elevation we'd gained since looping our way out of the little mining town.

No picnic tables, but Seth got a basket and several heavy blankets out of the car's trunk and spread them out on a patch of grass that would help to provide some cushioning. After setting down the basket, he reached out a hand.

"Do you need some help?"

I knew I could have lowered myself to the blankets on my own without any trouble, but I still took his hand anyway, happy to feel the strength of his fingers as they wrapped around mine and helped guide me to the ground. Sitting cross-legged in a skirt was out of the question, so I tucked my legs to one side and hoped the position wouldn't get too uncomfortable after a while.

Seth seated himself as well, and started to pull all sorts of yummy things out of the basket—a plate of fried chicken, some apples, a bowl of luscious-looking potato salad.

"You made all this?" I asked, and he grinned.

"Not the fried chicken," he said. "That's my

mother's specialty. But I made the potato salad, even though it's based on a recipe of hers."

"Well, it all looks wonderful."

"Here's hoping."

I shook my head to let him know I wasn't about to take that comment seriously, and then he got out a pair of speckled blue tin plates so we could load them up without having to worry about breaking anything. Had he borrowed the plates from his mother as well?

Possibly, or maybe they were on temporary "loan" from the store. Either way, they were the perfect solution for a picnic, sturdy and much better than paper plates, which I wasn't sure had even been invented yet. That was one of the crazy things about coming back to this particular decade—I knew a whole lot of modern conveniences had made their appearance in the twentieth century, but because I wasn't a student of inventions or anything close to it, there was no way in the world I'd ever be able to pinpoint when certain items made their way into the mainstream, whether they were paper plates or aluminum foil or central air conditioning.

Well, A/C definitely wasn't a thing yet in Jerome, that was for sure. I had the impression that ceiling fans, like the ones Ruth had in her parlors, were still something of a luxury, which might have been why I hadn't spotted any in

Seth's bungalow. By the time the twenty-first century had rolled around, that same home had been upgraded with air conditioning in addition to built-in fans, but they didn't seem to be a given the way they might have been in my own time.

He also poured some lemonade for us out of a flask that looked something like a Thermos, but not quite. Whatever it was, it had helped to keep the liquid cold. Although it was much cooler up here, thanks to both the elevation and the shade provided by the ponderosa pines that towered overhead, the nicely chilled lemonade still felt good on my throat, refreshing and tart and slightly sweet.

The fried chicken, although lukewarm by that point, was amazing, crisp and savory on the outside and succulent on the inside.

"This is the best fried chicken I've ever had," I said, which was the simple truth.

Take that, Colonel Sanders.

Seth had just taken a bite of a drumstick, so he needed to finish chewing before he could reply. "Thank you," he said after a moment. "I'll let my mother know you liked it."

"Like" seemed as though it was a pretty lackluster word to describe something so delicious. But I just nodded and had a bite of my own, one I followed up with some of the potato salad.

"And that's also delicious," I told him.

"My mother's recipe," he reminded me.

"Maybe," I said, "but you're the one who made it."

His shoulders lifted, although it didn't seem as if he wanted to protest further, since he also had some potato salad before returning to his half-eaten drumstick. We ate in silence for a moment, which was fine.

Actually, better than fine. Just having him seated there on the blanket a foot or so away from me made this moment feel more real, more vivid, than anything I'd ever experienced before. Maybe it was the gentle pine-scented breeze that washed over us, or the way his eyes were nearly the same color as the sapphire skies overhead, but it seemed then almost as if we'd managed to capture ourselves in a little bubble away from the world, away from time, where we could simply be and not have to worry about anything at all.

"More chicken?" he asked after I'd devoured my second drumstick.

The fried chicken was so good that I probably could have had a third piece. However, I reminded myself that we had Ruth's chocolate cookies for dessert, so it was probably a good idea for me to leave a little room.

I shook my head. "No, I'm fine for now."

"Then I'll wrap all this up."

Deftly, he gathered the oversized napkin that

had protected the plate of chicken during the drive up here, then covered the dish once again and returned it to the picnic basket. Afterward, he did much the same thing with the half-eaten bowl of potato salad before bringing out the package of cookies.

"Dessert first, or would you rather walk for a while before we have the cookies?"

"Walk," I said promptly. Although I wouldn't have said I was uncomfortably full, it just seemed better to get a little exercise first and walk off some of our meal.

"Done," Seth said as he got to his feet. "I'll put the basket back in the trunk, just to be safe. Not too many people come up here, but it's probably better not to leave the food out while we're gone." He paused there, blue eyes taking on an amused glint. "The last thing I want is someone to come along and steal Ruth's cookies."

"That would be a tragedy," I agreed with a grin. Or have them taken by a raccoon or maybe even a bear, although I didn't know for sure whether bears even roamed the pine forests here. No one had mentioned anything about them during my tenure in Jerome, but maybe that was only because they'd moved on to other areas by the time the twenty-first century rolled around.

Seth reached out a hand to help me to my feet, and I waited near the blankets—which he didn't seem to be worried about—while he secured the basket in the trunk. Afterward, he came back over to me, saying, "There's a little path that winds away from the picnic area and into the woods. It loops back around and comes out a hundred feet or so from where it starts, so you can't really get lost."

I reflected that getting lost in the woods with Seth didn't seem like such a bad idea…especially since I guessed he probably knew this land well and we wouldn't stay lost for very long. In the meantime, though, I'd be just fine with being alone with him out here, in a place where it felt as though the rest of the world was very far away.

"Lead on," I said.

He offered me his arm, and I took it. As we went, I found myself glad that I'd switched over to my flat shoes; it wasn't as though we were rock climbing or anything close to it, but still, the path was far from level and had stones and fallen branches strewn here and there, showing that, while someone might come along every once in a while to make sure the trees weren't openly encroaching on the pathway, neither were they expending too much effort to go through on a daily or even weekly basis to make sure the way was clear.

And I was okay with that. I liked the wild feel of our surroundings, and with Seth providing a steady arm to lean on, I knew I didn't have to worry about tripping and doing a face-plant in the middle of the path. Aspens grew here and there among the pines, as well as sycamores and oaks and a few other trees I didn't recognize, and the soft rustle of their leaves made me think of home, and the way my family always made an effort to go on a hike in the San Francisco Peaks wilderness when the aspens were turning in the fall.

"It's beautiful," I said.

Seth's head tilted up toward the canopy above us, and I caught a hint of a smile at the corner of his mouth. "I'm glad you like it out here. I used to come up here a lot when I was younger and just wanted a chance to walk among the trees and clear my head."

That comment made me want to smile as well. I knew he was only twenty-four, so those "younger" days must have been when he was still a schoolboy.

All the same, I understood what he meant. Although I loved my family and we got along well, I'd still had those times when I needed to get away from the noise and chaos that always seemed to come along with being the middle child of three siblings, and up to a place where I could be alone for a while and let myself breathe.

Funny how Seth and I had been born more than a hundred years apart, and yet were so alike.

"It feels as though I used to do something like this, too," I replied. Although I couldn't tell him the truth about myself, I thought maybe it would be safe to share how this walk in the trees felt familiar to me as well.

"You're remembering something?" he asked, a certain eager light showing in his eyes.

I couldn't ignore the undercurrent of excitement...of hope...in his voice. "I'm not sure 'remembering' is the right way to describe it. More like...there's something here that seems almost familiar. But it's not something I can consciously recall."

To my relief, he didn't appear too disappointed by my reply. "Still, it might mean something is waking up in your mind...that even though your memories are buried, things about your past are beginning to surface."

"I suppose it's possible," I allowed, and we walked a little further. If I hadn't known better, I would have thought we were plunging deeper and deeper into the woods, even though Seth had described this trail as one big loop, and therefore we couldn't possibly get lost as long as we stuck to the path.

A moment passed, and another. Then he said, "There's something I need to talk to you about."

"Oh?"

His steps slowed to a stop, and I paused as

well. Here, the rustle of the wind in the trees was a little louder, and from somewhere off in the distance came the impatient *tap-tap-tap* of a woodpecker, but otherwise, nothing seemed to move in the forest around us.

"There's…something happening in my family right now," he said. "It's not something I can discuss with anyone who's not a family member, not really. But because of that, I need to concentrate on being with them for a while. Not long, I hope. Maybe a week at the most. Until then, though…."

The words drifted off, caught by the breeze. Rather than look away, his gaze caught mine, pure azure, worried and somehow…ashamed?

No, that didn't make any sense.

"Until then…?" I prompted, and he released a breath.

"We won't be able to see each other."

I might have been angry, except I could tell he was under a lot of strain. Whatever was going on, he was asking for this separation…a temporary one, from the way he was talking…only because he knew it was the right thing to do.

Was one of his parents sick? As soon as the question crossed my mind, though, I promptly dismissed it. A good healer could take care of any health issues that arose in a clan, whether a broken bone or brain cancer.

Except, as with all witches, skills varied from person to person. After meeting Helen O'Dowd, I had no reason to believe she wasn't utterly competent, but what if she wasn't? What if she was fine with handling sprained ankles and childhood fevers, but fell down on the job when it came to the really big stuff?

That worry made me ask, "Is someone ill?"

"No, no," Seth said hastily. "Nothing like that. It's just...family business. I can't say more than that." He stopped there and took my hands in his. As much as I loved the strength in his fingers, I was almost annoyed with him right then.

Didn't he know how much his touch affected me? If he was trying to break things off, initiating physical contact didn't seem like a very good idea right then.

No, I was being too hard on him. Whatever might be going on with the McAllisters, I could tell it was something Seth knew he should go along with, even if he was less than happy about the situation.

"It's all right," I said gently. "I know I shouldn't pry." I hesitated, wondering if I should leave it alone...or whether I should send a clear signal that I was willing to wait as long as necessary for his family to get things straightened out.

But that wasn't a very smart stance to take, not when I knew I should be working a lot harder to get back to my own time. Instead, I'd given up after a couple of tries.

Would I have made much more of an attempt if Seth hadn't been here?

Well, I already knew the answer to that question.

His fingers tightened on mine, just for a second, and then he let go. "It's not a matter of prying. That was an honest question to ask. But I'm just not able to say anything else, except that I hope this won't take very long." A pause before he murmured, "I'm sorry."

"There's nothing to be sorry about," I assured him. If we'd kissed even once, then I might have been more comfortable going on my tiptoes so I could touch my lips to his cheek, just to reinforce the impression that I understood and wouldn't press him on the matter.

But we hadn't even hugged, and I found myself constrained by the time he lived in, by my limited understanding of interactions between men and women in this world. Somehow I knew that when we kissed, he would need to be the one to initiate the embrace, not me.

His expression cleared a little. "Thank you for being understanding."

I offered him a smile that I hoped appeared at least halfway genuine, and we resumed our walk.

~

When we got back to the picnic area, Seth fetched the chocolate cookies from the trunk—they were a little warm and melty, but not too bad—and we shared one or two. However, I guessed we both could tell the magic had gone out of the afternoon, because afterward we immediately packed up and drove down the mountain.

As always, he walked me to the door, but I knew this time there was no chance of a goodbye kiss...and I knew the bright afternoon sunlight that did nothing to conceal us wasn't the reason why.

Instead, I stood on the porch and waved as he drove off, then made myself go inside. Delicious aromas wafted through the house, telling me Ruth was cooking up something special for Sunday dinner.

Maybe by the time to sit down and eat rolled around, I'd actually have an appetite.

"I'm back," I said, sticking my head in the kitchen.

Ruth half-turned away from the stove, where she was stirring some kind of sauce, and offered me a smile. "How was your picnic?"

"It was fine." I hesitated there, wondering whether I should say anything else.

Then again, I wasn't going to get any answers if I didn't ask the questions.

"Seth is going to be busy this week with some family business," I ventured. "Do you know anything about that?"

Something in Ruth's expression went blank, almost as though she was doing her best to come up with a response that would provide some kind of answer to my question without giving too much away. "Oh," she said, sounding a little too blithe, "his cousin Abigail is turning twenty-one tomorrow. That's an important birthday for us McAllisters, so the whole family is gathering to wish her well."

Those words made a cold shock run down my spine. On the surface, they sounded innocent enough, but I knew better.

Abigail had looked much younger than that to me, maybe as young as seventeen or eighteen, so her being the *prima*-in-waiting hadn't seemed that big a deal. But if she was going to be twenty-one tomorrow, that meant…

…that meant the eligible men in the clan would have to meet with her, share the consort kiss, to see if they were the one.

And of course Seth would be eligible. He was the right age and wasn't married or engaged. Having a tenuous connection to me certainly wouldn't be enough to prevent him from doing his duty to the McAllisters.

My stomach churned. The mere thought of him kissing anyone else was bad enough, but the *prima*-in-waiting?

What if he turned out to be her consort?

"My dear, are you all right?" Ruth asked. She set her wooden spoon down on a ceramic rest near the stove and came closer to me. "You've gone terribly pale."

"I'm—I'm fine," I managed. Obviously, there was no way in the world I could tell her what was troubling me. Doing so would only let her know I possessed far more information about the McAllister clan—and witches in general—than any civilian possibly could. "I suppose being out in the sun all afternoon has caught up with me."

Her brows pulled together. "Then I think you should go upstairs and lie down for a while. I'll come fetch you when it's time for dinner."

At another time, I might have told her she didn't need to go to all that effort. Right then, however, I could only seize the opportunity to be alone with my thoughts.

"Thank you," I said faintly, then hurried out of the room.

Seth might be the next McAllister consort.

And there wasn't a goddamn thing I could do about it.

14

CONSORT'S KISS

As much of the clan as could fit gathered at Mabel McAllister's house on Monday evening. Seth wished he could bow out of the proceedings, but as one lucky—or unlucky, depending on how you looked at it—to be counted as a prospective consort, he knew his presence there was pretty much mandatory.

Because the weather was so fine, the gathering spilled out into the backyard, where festive bunting in shades of pale blue and pale pink had been hung, and a trio of musical McAllisters played flute and guitar and cello. Rather than the rollicking tunes popular on the radio, this group focused more on folksy-sounding melodies that might have harkened back to the clan's early days in Scotland, and they clearly were doing their best to provide soothing background sounds instead of playing songs that would make people want to dance.

He supposed it was a good thing that so many McAllisters had turned out for the party, since the crowd would make it much easier to avoid his cousin Abigail. Although he knew there was no way he could wriggle out of the consort's kiss, he also didn't see much point in socializing with her before then.

Somehow, he doubted he'd be able to hide his feelings from his cousin, his distraction. This party might have been fun if he could have brought Deborah with him and they could have nibbled on the various goodies and listened to the music together. Now, though, he only wanted to hide in the corner behind the *prima's* prize parlor palm until it was all over.

He'd only caught one glimpse of Abigail so far. She'd been talking to several of the elders and had worn one of her signature white frocks, although this was a fancy silk dress that looked bespoke rather than bought at his parents' mercantile or at the small JC Penney shop farther down Main Street. Since she'd been caught up in a conversation, Seth didn't think she saw him, which was all to the good.

Of course, his parents had been there, with Charles somewhat near their orbit but also just far enough away to send a clear message that, while they might have dragged him to this gathering, he had no intention of doing anything more than the bare minimum for civility. Molly McAllister had caught Seth's gaze as he went past, so at least he didn't have to worry about them thinking he'd stayed away.

A group of male cousins around his age had gathered by the punch bowl outdoors, most likely discussing their prospects for becoming the *prima*-in-waiting's consort. None of them appeared overly excited by the idea, except possibly Seth's cousin Isaac, who was the studious type, always with his nose in a book. From what Seth had heard, Isaac was taking some sort of college correspondence course, since there were no universities inside the clan's territory that he could attend.

Because Isaac was almost as shy and retiring and pale as Abigail, Seth supposed they would make a good couple. Now he could only hope that the Goddess—or fate, or whatever entity made that particular spark flare between a *prima*-in-waiting and her true consort—would also think the match made sense and would leave him and the rest of them out of it.

As good a job as he'd done in avoiding Abigail, he wasn't so lucky when it came to Mabel McAllister, the clan's formidable *prima*. She was as robust and forthright as her daughter was quiet and languid, and she quite deliberately put herself in his path as he went to refill his cup of punch.

"Oh, Seth," Mabel said, "I would like a word with you."

Whenever his mother used that phrase, Seth knew he was in some kind of trouble. In this case, though, he could guess what was coming next.

Maybe an entirely different kind of trouble, but trouble nonetheless.

"Yes, *prima?*" he said, hoping he sounded both polite and also so unassuming that Mabel would decide he didn't have nearly enough fire and conviction to be a suitable match for her daughter.

A pause as the *prima* looked him up and down. She'd had Abigail somewhat late in life, and so was in her middle fifties, trim and tall for a woman, with hair a much deeper gold than her daughter's and sharp gray eyes.

"I'm so glad you could come to the party," Mabel said. "Abigail and I have been talking, and she told me she wants you to be the first one to give the consort's kiss."

Even though he'd known this was coming, Seth had to resist the urge to flee...or maybe splash some of the cold punch he was carrying in his face to shake himself loose from this nightmare.

Unfortunately, he knew he was wide awake.

"She does?" he managed, which he knew wasn't exactly a scintillating reply.

"Yes," Mabel said. The corners of her mouth lifted in something that wasn't quite a smirk but skirted around the borders of one. "She feels quite comfortable with you…and I know she hopes you will be the one, and so her search won't have to extend any farther than her encounter with you. We'll want you to be here at the house at three o'clock tomorrow."

Something about the exchange seemed almost surreal. Was it really possible that in an age with new inventions and technology emerging at what felt like an almost weekly rate, they were still discussing something as positively medieval as choosing a consort for a young unmarried woman?

Actually, the practice went even farther back than the Middle Ages, as best he'd been able to determine, all the way back to the McAllisters' pagan roots long before the Normans ever set foot on the British Isles.

Not that it really mattered when it all started. What mattered was that he couldn't think of a single way to get out of this madness.

"I work until six," he said. He knew his tone was flat, bordering on rude, but it was the only excuse he could come up with that might buy him some more precious time.

"Oh, that's nothing to worry about," Mabel replied as she gave an unconcerned wave of her hand. "I'll speak to Mr. Allenby and let him know there's an important family matter you need to attend to."

This was no idle threat; while no one in the mine's management completely understood the inner workings of the McAllister family, all of them...Lionel Allenby included...knew enough to realize that Mabel was the one in charge and pretty much all of Jerome danced to her tune, whether they were a member of the clan or not.

However, Seth disliked the idea of having the *prima* put in a word for him, like a parent sending a note to school so he might be dismissed early.

"That's all right," he said. "I'll talk to Mr. Allenby when I get to work tomorrow morning. I've never asked him for any extra time off, so I know he won't mind if I leave a few hours early."

"Good boy," Mabel said, and he tried not to wince. "Then Abigail and I will see you tomorrow afternoon."

She swept off into the crowd after that, calling out to one of the clan's elders with the sort of cheer in her voice that seemed to indicate she was already imagining Seth as her daughter's consort. That would tie everything up in a neat, tidy bow, after all.

Never mind that he wanted no part of it, even

though he'd done his best to convince himself it was better to get all this over with as quickly as possible so he might go back to courting Deborah.

If that was even what he was doing. The word "courting" seemed far too bound up in ritual and tradition to describe how they'd been spending their time together over the past week.

Enjoying one another's company, then.

But because he'd now spoken with Mabel and set a time for his meeting with destiny, so to speak, Seth didn't see much point in staying here any longer. No, he'd go home and do his best to gather his courage…even as he tried with all his might to ignore the insidious little whisper in his mind that told him with everyone here at the party, this might be the best time to drop by Ruth and Timothy's house and spend a few stolen moments with Deborah Rowe.

The only reason he didn't give in to the impulse was that he'd already told her he would be occupied with family business this week, and he didn't want to give the impression of someone who couldn't stick to a thing once he'd set his mind to it. Besides, everything would be decided after tomorrow. Either he would be Abigail's consort, or he would be free to pursue Deborah without having to worry about any further obligations hanging over his head. Possibly, it still wasn't such a good idea to become involved with someone whose past wasn't merely a closed book, but one that had been locked and the key lost, and yet Seth refused to let her missing memories stand in his way. He knew how he felt about Deborah…

…and he was fairly certain he knew how she felt about him as well.

Asking to leave early the next day was harder than Seth had thought it would be, mainly because he'd spent so much time attempting to avoid his supervisor that it took some effort of will to force himself into the man's path.

Lionel Allenby had an office in one of the buildings on the mine's property, a space used by the inspectors and the secretaries and other support staff. After checking to make sure that his men had a good start that morning, Seth walked over to Allenby's office, wondering what he would do if the man wasn't there.

Come back later and try again, he supposed. It wasn't as if he could go to Mabel and inform her that he wouldn't be able to meet with Abigail for the consort's kiss because he hadn't been able to track down his supervisor.

As luck would have it—or maybe not,

depending on how one looked at the situation—
Lionel Allenby was seated behind his desk, poring
over a ledger full of notations, when Seth stepped
into his office and paused by the door.

Almost a full minute passed before Allenby
deigned to look up from his ledger. "What is it,
McAllister?"

"Some family business has come up," Seth
responded, glad he sounded steady and sure of
himself, giving no hint that the "business"
involved a meeting that might change his life
forever. A *prima's* consort didn't have a job, but
instead spent his days attending to clan business
and making sure his wife was supported in all
ways. This change in life circumstance was usually
explained away with a story about an unexpected
inheritance, so if it turned out he was Abigail's
consort after all, he would never come back to the
United Verde, except to say goodbye to his team
and gather the few belongings he kept in a locker
there. "I'll need to leave a little before three
today."

Allenby's brows drew together. Judging by that
frown, Seth got the impression the man wanted to
ask what kind of "family business" was involved
here but realized that probing into the McAllister
clan's private workings wasn't a very good idea.
Richard Clark might have owned the mine—and
most of Clarkdale as well—but the McAllisters

reigned supreme in Jerome, no matter what the deeds on the houses and the buildings there might have said.

Watching him, Seth did his best to conceal his dislike for the man. Up until the time when Charles had made his revelations about his connection to the bootlegging ring, he'd thought Lionel Allenby a tough supervisor but one who was generally fair enough. Now he knew it was all a front to cover up the much more lucrative business of manufacturing and distributing illegal alcohol.

"That shouldn't be a problem," Allenby said after a pause, one Seth knew was calculated to make it seem as if his supervisor actually had a say in the matter. "Just make sure you designate one of your men as temporary foreman for the hours involved so people know who to go to in case of a problem."

"I can do that," Seth replied. "Thank you, sir."

"Well, I'm not one to interfere with McAllister business," Allenby said. "But I'll still expect you to be here promptly at eight tomorrow."

Seth had no doubt his supervisor had made that comment because he wanted to let his underling know who was still boss here, even if he was granting a small accommodation. "Of course, sir."

He nodded and went back outside, then paused to allow himself a deep breath. Anger at the man flared, and for a second or two, he thought it might not be such a bad thing to become the consort to the *prima*-in-waiting if it meant he never had to come back here.

But that was irritation speaking, nothing more.

There was no way in the world he wanted to be paired with Abigail, not when he knew his heart was already given.

The fateful day both dragged and at the same time seemed as though it was flashing past far too quickly. While he had to admit there was always some benefit to hearing the worst and getting it over with, he also didn't want to believe that after today, he might not have any sort of a future with Deborah Rowe.

Not if he turned out to be Abigail's consort.

And even though he tried his damnedest to pay attention to his work and to make it seem as if this was just another ordinary day—except for the small matter of needing to leave early, something he never did—his mind kept working at the problem, wondering what he would say to Deborah if it ended up that he was fated to be with his cousin Abigail after all.

Something about arranged marriages, he

supposed. They weren't terribly common anymore, but enough families still followed the practice that he didn't believe Deborah would find anything too odd about the story. In a way, it wasn't even a falsehood; if he became Abigail's consort, one might say that the universe had arranged the match…although if that turned out to be the case, then he thought he might have a few choice words for the universe and its supposed wisdom.

Although his meeting with Abigail was at three, he left the mine at a little past two-thirty, thinking that, even if he dreaded the upcoming kiss with every fiber of his being, he should at least show his cousin—and the *prima*—the proper respect, and go home first and wash his face and hands, and change into his Sunday best. It definitely wouldn't do to appear at their house covered in reddish rock dust and sticky with sweat.

However, he couldn't help feeling just the slightest bit sticky anyway as he blinked himself from the living room of his bungalow to the tangle of bottlebrush and forsythia on one side of Mabel's house on Paradise Lane. It was a secluded enough spot that no one would have been able to see him appear there out of thin air, but using his magic rather than his feet to get here saved him from a long walk uphill in the heat of a June afternoon. Clouds massing far off above the Mogollon Rim told him they might have thunderstorms later today, although he knew they wouldn't arrive until much later, possibly even close to sunset.

Sheltering behind the bushes gave him a moment to make sure his tie was straight, and he took another moment to reach up and push his hair back from his forehead. Someone watching him would probably have thought he looked calm and collected enough, but inside, his heart wouldn't stop racing.

Had any other prospective consort ever approached this important moment with such overwhelming dread?

Maybe, somewhere far back in their clan's history. Much was always made of the belief that a *prima* and her consort were soul mates, and that they would never be bonded in such a manner if they weren't truly compatible in every way possible, but even before now, Seth had wondered how much truth lay in those reassuring tales, in the way some kind of overwhelming passion was supposed to flare between them the very second their lips touched. It seemed much more likely that, while a *prima* and her consort might have enough in common to rub along together fairly well, their supposed "connection" was as much a fluke of biology as anything else.

Well, he couldn't hide here in the bushes

forever, no matter how much he might like to avoid the coming kiss. A quick glance down Paradise Lane told him no one seemed to be around, so he emerged from his cover and strode over to the path that bisected the front yard's neat green lawn, then made himself climb the porch steps.

He'd barely lifted his hand to touch the knocker when the door opened, revealing a smiling Mabel. She, too, seemed to have deemed this occasion worthy of some effort, because she wore a silk dress that usually only made an appearance at various McAllister family functions, and the long string of pearls that her husband Abraham had bought her for their twenty-fifth anniversary hung around her neck.

"Right on time," she said in approving tones, then stepped aside so he could enter the foyer. "You must be eager to share the consort's kiss."

Eagerness had nothing to do with it. He knew it would have been disrespectful to be late to such an important meeting, and that was why he'd made sure to be prompt...even as he'd wanted to use his gift to send himself someplace far, far away from here.

Doing so would have disgraced his family, though, which meant he hadn't allowed such a traitorous notion to linger in his mind for more than a minute or two.

He forced a smile, saying politely, "And how are you and Abigail today?"

"Very well," Mabel replied, beaming in response. "In fact, she's waiting for you in the back sitting room. I thought you would have a little more privacy there."

Seth wasn't sure whether that was a good or a bad thing. While he'd inwardly dreaded the idea of having to kiss his cousin in the front parlor, a place that was far more public, he also didn't know how he felt about having to do such a thing in a more intimate setting.

If he truly was Abigail's consort, she might want to further prove their connection with another kiss.

No, she's shy and retiring, he reassured himself. *It will be enough for her to know that you're the one.*

He hoped.

"That was kind of you," he managed as he followed Mabel down the corridor that bisected the ground floor of the house and then into the room in question.

Abigail stood by the big window that over-looked the backyard, now a cheerful explosion of flowers in all colors of the rainbow, everything from bright yellow and red hollyhocks standing tall against the back fence to cheerful pansies dancing along the footpath that led to the rear gate. As usual, his cousin wore one of the pale colors she preferred, this one a soft rose, but a false bloom in her cheeks and on her lips seemed to signal that her mother had applied some subtle cosmetics, enough to make Abigail seem a little more grown-up than she usually appeared.

"I'll just be in the kitchen," Mabel announced. "You two come get me when it's over."

She sounded supremely confident, as if she believed that the entire universe, their beloved goddess Bridget included, had already blessed the match.

Seth wasn't nearly so certain, but he only nodded and said, "Of course, *prima,*" even as Abigail also murmured some sort of assent.

Mabel departed then, leaving the two of them alone. One awkward moment stretched into another, and he realized he needed to say something.

"You're looking very well, Abigail. That color suits you."

One hand brushed against the smooth cotton of her drop-waist dress, which he now noticed had ecru roses embroidered at the cuffs and around the neckline. Probably her finest summer frock, something she'd most likely worn in an attempt to impress him.

Seth had to admit she was looking prettier than usual, but she still couldn't hold a candle to

Deborah's vivid beauty, her full lips…a body that managed to be slim and lush at the same time.

Don't think about Deborah, he admonished himself. *Or at least, don't think about her until this is all over.*

"Some lemonade?" Abigail offered, and for the first time, he noticed the cut-glass pitcher sitting on a silver tray on the coffee table, with two matching glasses placed nearby.

Come to think of it, his throat was awfully dry.

Pouring the lemonade and having a sip would put off the fateful moment for just a bit longer.

"Yes, please," he replied.

She poured a glass for each of them, then gave one to him. As she did so, he couldn't help noticing the way her hand shook slightly.

Poor kid, he thought. *She's probably even more nervous about this whole thing than I am.*

Because although she'd told him she hoped he would be her consort, he had the feeling that the situation now felt far more real than it had even a day earlier.

Well, they would have some of Mabel's excellent lemonade, and at least when they kissed, they would both taste sweet and tangy.

He sipped from his glass while Abigail did the same. However, after a second swallow, she placed her tumbler back down on the tray.

"I'm ready now," she said softly.

His heart gave one heavy thump, but he did his best to look calm as he set his glass of lemonade on the tray next to hers.

"You're sure?"

Abigail nodded. "Yes. I just wanted to have a little lemonade to steady my nerves."

Seth didn't know how much good the lemonade would do…he had a feeling the moonshine his brother had been transporting over the hill to Prescott might be somewhat more effective…but he thought it best not to comment on that.

Somehow, his feet managed to move him a step closer to her, and then another. Now they were nearer than they'd ever been, and he noticed that a scent of roses clung to her hair, an aroma that echoed the flowers embroidered on her dress.

Usually, he enjoyed that scent. Now, though, it felt far too cloying, heavy in his nostrils, making it hard to breathe.

"Kiss me, Seth," Abigail said, her voice a shy whisper at odds with the almost command of those words.

He didn't want to.

He knew he had to.

Please, Goddess, went through his mind, but he didn't know whether Brigid was listening. Quite possibly, this was what she wanted.

Time to get this over with.

He bent his head and touched his lips to Abigail's.

A second passed, and another.

And…nothing.

She took a step back, disappointment clouding her too-big blue eyes, a pout touching her unnaturally rosy lips.

"You're not the one," she said, tone flat.

No, he wasn't. He'd felt absolutely nothing when he kissed her…and he knew Abigail must have experienced the same thing, or she wouldn't have said the words she'd just uttered.

"I suppose not," he replied, even as he tried to keep relief and joy from flooding into his voice. It was never a good idea to let a woman know how happy you were that you'd turned out to be incompatible with her.

The *prima*-in-waiting glanced down at her shoes, which were very smart, beige kid with slender straps and little kid-covered buttons. They weren't something sold at the mercantile, which meant Mabel must have purchased them from a catalog, wanting something extra special for her daughter's meeting with her future consort.

A consort that wasn't him. He had the wildest impulse to dance a jig, and told himself if he did so, he'd only succeed in making a fool of himself…and letting his cousin know how glad he was that he wouldn't have to marry her.

Probably not a very good idea.

"I'm sorry," he added.

Abigail's thin shoulders lifted in a shrug he guessed was supposed to appear nonchalant but appeared more forlorn than anything else.

"I wish it could have been you," she said. "But I know the universe doesn't always do what we want it to. I suppose we should go tell Mama. She'll be dreadfully disappointed."

Yes, the McAllisters' formidable *prima* was not someone who enjoyed being thwarted. But this was the hand of fate, and even Mabel couldn't do anything about it. They would go and tell her he wasn't Abigail's consort, and then he could leave.

He was free.

15

OVER THE HILL

So far, I thought I'd done a pretty good job of getting along in the early twentieth century. At least there was running water and food that seemed mostly familiar, even if a lot of it was heavier than what I was used to eating. Sure, the clothing was a little odd, and there were days when I thought I would have cheerfully committed some serious mayhem for central air conditioning, but overall, I wanted to give myself a mental pat on the back for acclimating as well as I had.

Right now, though, I would have killed for a single functioning computer or tablet or phone. Hell, I would have been okay with a TV and a decent lineup of streaming stations to distract myself.

There wasn't anything like that in 1926,

though. Only books and a radio, and everything I heard on there was just crackly and distorted enough that I didn't like listening to it at all.

True, Ruth gave me plenty of chores to do, nothing so horribly taxing that I might start to feel like Cinderella or anything close, but just enough to remind me I wasn't allowed to be simply a houseguest and nothing more. The work was something of a distraction.

Not enough, though.

Not nearly enough.

Yesterday had been Abigail's twenty-first birthday party. I wasn't invited, of course; I wasn't family. But Ruth and Timothy had attended, leaving me to wonder how it had gone, whether they were going to commence kissing consorts right away, or whether they were going to give it a little time so they could have a decent roster of candidates lined up.

To be honest, I wasn't sure how it all worked. The McAllisters of my time had a *prima*-in-waiting, of course, Angela's daughter Emily. She was almost five years older than me, so her all-important birthday—and the consort search—had all gone down while I was attending high school in Flagstaff, and she was happily paired off with the man fate had decreed would be her consort. And, even though Angela was married to the *primus* of my clan, none of it had seemed all that important

at the time, not when I'd been much more interested in school and friends and which kind of car
my parents were going to buy me for my sixteenth
birthday.

Now I wished I'd paid more attention to what
was going on with Emily and the search for her
consort, even as I tried to tell myself that they
might do things very differently in the 1920s than
they had in the mid-twenty-first century.

My chores done for the day, I'd retired to the
front parlor with a book, figuring I should do
what I could to lose myself in someone else's story.
The volume I'd chosen was *Sense and Sensibility,* a
novel I'd found close to tedious when I had to
read it in a college lit class.

Now, though, it felt more reassuring than I'd
expected, a piece of familiarity in a world utterly
unlike mine. And although Elinor and Marianne
Dashwood weren't witches, I found I could
relate to their predicament, to the unfortunate
necessity of relying on the kindness of others
thanks to their reduced circumstances, than I'd
thought.

After all, I would have been in a real world of
hurt if Ruth and Timothy McAllister hadn't taken
me in.

The book helped distract me a little, even
though I still found my attention caught by any
kind of movement outside the window, whether

that was a car driving past or one of the neighbors walking by with their dog on a leather leash.

And then....

I set down the book, my heart beginning to pound.

Was that Seth coming up the front walk?

Yes, it was. He wore a dark suit and tie, not the sort of thing I would have expected to see him sporting after a day at the mine.

Come to think of it, the time was barely three-thirty, far too soon for him to have gotten off work.

He wasn't at work, my mind told me. *He was off giving Abigail the consort's kiss. That's why he's all dressed up.*

And if he was here now....

I laid the attached ribbon along the page I'd been reading and set the book aside. Maybe it would have been better to keep reading until he got to the front door, but I knew I wouldn't have been able to retain a single word about the travails of the Dashwood sisters if I had made the attempt.

No, I sat on the couch, heart beating far too quickly, until there came a soft knock at the door.

Luckily, by that point Ruth and Timothy were just fine with me answering the door if they were occupied elsewhere, so I didn't even have to hesitate before responding to that fateful knock.

Sure enough, Seth stood outside on the porch, relief clear in every line of his handsome face.

"Good afternoon, Deborah," he said. "Would you like to go for a drive?"

I didn't even hesitate. "Love to," I replied.

We drove into Cottonwood, back to the restaurant where he'd taken me for dinner the week before. Maybe it would have been prettier to go up to our picnic spot on Mingus Mountain, but with him in his good clothes and me in a dress and heels, it just made more sense to return to a more civilized place.

At that hour of the afternoon, the restaurant wasn't very full. Seth asked the hostess for a quiet spot, so we sat in the back of the place, far away from the counter where people were drinking coffee or eating slices of pie.

And that was actually what we ordered—apple for him, berry for me, accompanied by a couple of tall iced teas. After our waitress dropped off the food, I felt as if it was finally time to ask the question I'd been holding back for the past fifteen minutes.

"So...you got your family business handled?" I inquired, and he nodded, looking far more cheerful than I'd seen him in a while.

"Yes, it's all taken care of," he replied. "It's nothing I'll need to worry about ever again."

That was all he said, but because I'd already read between the lines, I knew the consort kiss had been a swing and a miss for the McAllister *prima*-in-waiting. She was probably feeling as disappointed as he was relieved.

But although some part of me could be sympathetic to Abigail for missing out on having someone handsome and smart and kind as her consort, a much, much larger part was simply happy that Seth had been knocked out of the running, and the two of us could go back to the way things were.

What that meant exactly, I didn't know for sure. I hadn't spent all my time while he was waiting to audition to be the new McAllister clan consort simply moping or weeding the garden— no, when I was alone in my borrowed room, I'd tried several times to send myself back when I was supposed to be. And on each occasion, I'd utterly failed. Maybe I could have done more, made multiple attempts each day, and yet I wasn't sure whether that would have made any difference at all.

How long was I supposed to wait before I resigned myself to being here permanently? It had already been almost two weeks, and it sure felt as though two more weeks would pass, and two more after that, and....

At some point, I'd have to admit I didn't have the power to get back to the twenty-first century. I hoped Bellamy McAllister wasn't too wracked with guilt over daring me to go into the mine, and I prayed my family would someday be able to get past the strange disappearance of their middle child. After all, my father had left behind his own family and friends to make a life with my mother in the modern world, so this sort of circumstance wouldn't be quite as strange for them as it might have been for a lot of other people.

In the meantime, I reassured myself that all my tenure here in 1926 Jerome was slipping by in the past, and therefore neither I nor anyone else I knew had even been born yet, and if we hadn't been born, then they couldn't know I was missing. Or at least, I hoped that was how it worked. Not being an expert on time travel despite my dubious gift...or maybe because of it...I couldn't really say for sure.

The only thing I knew with any certainty was how much I cared for Seth McAllister, and how much it had hurt to think he might be Abigail's consort. All those worries had been for nothing, apparently, and that meant Seth was free to pursue a relationship with me.

Since it didn't look as though I was going

anywhere soon, either, how long was I going to place caution over the truth of my heart?

Judging by the thrill that went through me as our gazes met across the table, not for very long at all.

"That's good news," I said. Then I paused, wondering how bold I should be. Even though I'd been in 1926 for the greater part of two weeks, I still didn't have a completely firm handle as to how a young woman my age was supposed to act.

Then again, sometimes you just had to say, screw it.

"I know it was a couple of days," I went on. "But it felt like forever."

"You missed me?" Seth asked, face lighting up like a kid who just found out Santa was real.

"Of course I missed you," I replied. "I don't think I really understood how much I enjoyed our time together until you had to step away for a while."

He was quiet for a moment, sun-browned fingers playing with the handle of his fork. "Well, there's no need for that to happen again," he told me. "So we should do something fun to celebrate."

"Isn't this fun?" I asked, only half-joking. That pie was damn good.

Amused crinkles showed around his gentian-blue eyes as he grinned back at me. "Sure, it's fun," he said. "But I was thinking about something a little more interesting than a couple of slices of pie. How about we drive into Prescott tomorrow night and have dinner there?"

I had to admit that sounded like a fun outing. Despite living in Jerome for nearly a month in my own time, I still hadn't driven over the mountain to visit the former state capital. Sure, I'd gone there once when I was a kid, but I had to admit there hadn't been much about it that wowed me, except maybe the big park in front of the historical courthouse downtown. Well, that and the decidedly Wild West–themed restaurant where we had lunch and I'd had the best chocolate milkshake ever.

All the same, it also seemed like quite a drive to take on a weeknight, probably at least an hour each way. That might have been generous, considering I had no idea what the roads in 1926 looked like. Then again, a big part of the journey would be taken up by traveling the switchbacks on 89A—well, Highway 79 in the 1920s—and even in the newest and smartest self-driving car in the world, you could only go so fast because of all the mountainous hairpin turns.

"We won't be out too late?" I asked, knowing how dubious I sounded.

Another of those brilliant smiles. "I don't have

a curfew, Deborah. Did my aunt Ruth give you one?"

I couldn't help making a face. "Of course not. I was only worried about you being out so late when you have to get up and go to work the next morning."

He made a dismissive sound before scooping up another bite of apple pie. "It won't be late enough to make a difference. So...I can pick you up at six-thirty tomorrow?"

What would be the point in protesting further? I wanted to spend the evening with him, and he was a big boy. He knew that missing a little sleep wouldn't be a huge deal, even if we ended up coming back much later than expected.

Besides, I'd be lying if I didn't admit I was looking forward to taking that scenic drive in his convertible. My hair might be a mess by the time we were done, but it would still be a lot of fun.

"It's a date," I told him.

As promised, Seth was at the door to Ruth and Timothy's house right at six-thirty to pick me up. Any diffidence Ruth might have tried to hide over me seeing Seth was now completely gone, telling me the only reason she'd been concerned was his standing as a possible consort to Abigail. But with that fun little trial by fire now over with, it sure seemed as if we had her blessing. Not, of course, that she was the one to give said blessing—that would be Seth's parents' role—and yet I got the impression the McAllisters weren't too upset by our budding relationship.

It made sense, in a way; all witch clans needed to intermarry with civilians to avoid the dangers of inbreeding, and even though I might have been a little problematic to some of them due to my memory loss, I was still a young, healthy woman who would make a good addition to the family. Also, as time wore on and no one appeared to claim me, they were probably thinking it was clear that whoever I was, I certainly didn't have a husband or even a fiancé, or surely they would have heard of someone trying to find me.

That would never happen, of course, for the simple reason that anyone who knew of my existence wouldn't be born for decades.

We climbed into Seth's '24 Dodge—which was a sweet ride, no matter what century you were in—and headed up the highway. Because we'd be out after dark, I brought a borrowed wrap of Ruth's along, although it currently rested in my lap along with my purse.

Between the wind noise and the rumble from the car's flathead engine, there wasn't much use in talking. That was all right, though. For me, it was enough to be sitting there with Seth only a foot or so away, to see his fine profile caught by the light of the late afternoon sun whenever we moved out of the shadow of a stand of trees or a rocky outcropping.

We went past the little picnic area where we'd shared a meal nearly a week ago, but it slipped by quickly enough as we continued to climb, now surrounded by a ponderosa forest that again didn't seem all that different from how it looked in my own time. The real change I noticed was when we came down the western side of the mountain and into Prescott Valley, which didn't seem to contain anything except some widely scattered farms and ranches. In the twenty-first century, it was filled with tracts of homes and the inevitable mini-malls and shopping centers, but now all I saw was miles of dry golden grass punctuated by the occasional split-rail fence and grove of trees, all of which appeared to indicate a nearby homestead.

I had to admit this version of the landscape was a lot prettier.

Prescott itself hadn't sprawled nearly as much, either, and consisted mainly of the neighborhoods of older homes close to downtown I remembered from the time when I'd visited with my parents when I was around ten. Of course, those houses now were shiny and new, some of them so freshly built they didn't have trees planted yet.

The courthouse was the same, though, as were a lot of the buildings in the town's historic section, even if the businesses that occupied them were utterly different.

Well, except the venue where we appeared to be headed.

Seth pulled up to the curb and parked in front of the Palace Restaurant, the same place my parents had taken us kids when we visited Prescott. As far as I could tell, it didn't look much different, although I noticed the word "bar" was conspicuously missing from the signage.

Another casualty of Prohibition, I supposed.

I must have been staring, because Seth asked, "Is this place familiar to you?"

Surely it couldn't hurt to say it was. In fact, it might help to let a few details start to leak out, if only to give everyone hope that my memories might begin to come back at some point. After all, if I was going to entertain even the slight possibility of remaining here in the past, I'd have to figure out some way of telling him the truth about who I was and where I'd come from.

No matter how awkward such a conversation might turn out to be.

"Maybe," I allowed, then looked around the street, from the row of buildings to our right to the imposing courthouse and its park to our left.

"Something makes me feel as if I've seen it before, although I can't say for sure."

Even that measured response appeared to be enough to cheer him, because he was smiling as he came around to open my car door. "Well, then," he said, "let's go in and see if anything else jogs your memory."

He took me inside, which again didn't seem all that different from the restaurant I remembered. Possibly a few of the details about the enormous carved bar weren't quite the same, and the waitresses wore black dresses with white aprons rather than the replica-Victorian getups that seemed to be the restaurant uniform in my day, but still, my surroundings weren't too dissonant.

Even though it was nearly eight, the place was still busy enough. We had to wait a few minutes for a table, but soon enough, we were guided to a nice, quiet booth in a corner, a spot where I thought no one would pay too much attention to us.

"What do you think of Prescott?" Seth asked after the maitre d' left us to peruse the menus.

"It's bigger than I thought it would be," I replied.

His mouth quirked. "Is that because you're comparing it to Jerome and Cottonwood?"

"Possibly," I allowed. "Or maybe I do come

from here, but because I can't remember for sure, something about it doesn't feel quite right."

"I suppose I could see that." He stopped there, as if searching for what he should say next. Then his expression brightened and he added, "Maybe you'll see someone here who recognizes you."

Absolutely zero chance of that happening, but I wouldn't tell him that, not when he was looking so hopeful. It sure seemed as though he also believed I didn't have any kind of significant other, thanks to the way no one had shown up in Jerome in search of their missing fiancée or wife.

Which meant Seth must believe no barriers stood in the way of us pursuing a relationship. Not exactly true—this wasn't my time, even if it was sort of my place, at least in an adopted sort of way—but since it didn't seem as if my powers wanted to send me back where I belonged, why should I try to fight the connection between us?

For all I knew, I'd zapped myself to 1926 because my often wonky gift had somehow realized the only man for me was alive back then, and not in my present.

Stranger things had happened in the witch world, after all.

"Maybe," I allowed. "I suppose we'll just have to see what happens."

Seth seemed satisfied with that response,

because he nodded and then looked down at the menu.

Meaning I should probably do the same thing. Just like the restaurant where we'd eaten in Cottonwood, this place seemed to heavily favor steaks and pork chops and fried chicken. I supposed I shouldn't have expected anything else, but still, I found myself craving a salad or pizza or even some Indian food.

However, while I didn't know much about the history of dining out in America, I could guess that cuisines from other countries probably weren't too common in the western states, despite the Chinese food I'd eaten on my first date with Seth. If I ever got home, then I could stuff myself silly with curry or shawarma or pad thai.

In the meantime, the roast chicken plate seemed the best choice if I wanted to avoid anything too heavy.

Seth and I looked up from our menus at almost the same time, and a smile flickered around the edges of his mouth.

"What did you decide on?" he asked.

"The chicken," I replied.

"Their steaks are very good," he said, and for a second, I could only stare at him blankly.

Then I realized he was probably trying to hint that I didn't need to settle for chicken if I was only doing so because I was worried about the cost of the meal. Obviously, he would never come right out and say such a thing aloud.

"I'm sure they are," I said easily. "But I've been eating a lot of heavy food lately. Chicken just sounds better to me tonight."

At once, he appeared to relax. "Oh, I can understand that, especially with how warm it's been the past few days."

I smiled at him in response, and the waiter came over and took our orders. While we were waiting for our food, we chatted about the weather and about his work, how they were planning to start blasting a new open pit for the mine, and how I needed to prepare myself because it could get very loud.

"We do our best to make the pits not too visible from town," Seth went on. "But there's not much we can do about the noise."

Probably not. In my time, you could still see the terraced remnants of the pits as you were driving up toward Jerome from Clarkdale, but once you were in the little settlement itself, you barely could tell they were there. Yet another thing that hadn't changed as much as I'd thought it might.

"Thanks for the warning," I said. "And I suppose it will get dustier, too."

"Much," he replied with a grin. "I'm sure

you'll hear Ruth complaining about it—and I have a feeling she'll put you on dusting duty."

"Oh, I don't mind," I said. "I like being able to help."

While my own family had never subscribed to the "idle hands are the devil's plaything" mindset, I and my sister and brother still had our fair share of chores to do around the house. My father had been born in the mid-1800s, after all, and even though he'd adapted to modern life remarkably well, he was a little more strict than some of my friends' parents, and expected his children to do their part to keep the household going, even if the work mostly consisted of emptying the filter on our robot vacuum/mopper rather than getting down on our hands and knees to scrub the floor.

"I like that," Seth said, his gaze now admiring. "You're always willing to pitch in. Ruth says you've been a big help."

About all I could do was shrug—well, that, and hope the lighting inside the restaurant was sufficiently dim so he wouldn't notice the way I blushed. "I'm glad," I said. "I don't want to be a burden on her, not after she and Timothy have been so kind about giving me a place to stay."

Seth looked as though he was about to respond, but the waiter came back with our plates of food, and we had to pause the conversation so we could thank him and get started on our meals.

Once again, the lack of any wine to accompany those dishes stood out immediately to me. It just felt weird to eat at a fancy place like this and be drinking only water. Our waiter had offered tea, but unlike a lot of my college friends, I didn't care to drink caffeinated stuff late in the day unless I wanted to be up all night.

But eventually Seth and I resumed our discussion, not about anything earth-shattering, just more little tidbits about Jerome and the McAllister family.

"And I got a new cousin," he went on as he reached for a roll from the basket the waiter had brought over. "Little Ruby. She came a bit early, but she's healthy and happy, so everyone's excited about that."

Somehow, I managed to stop myself from startling at that piece of news. I supposed the McAllisters might have had more than one Ruby among their ranks, but some quick mental math told me that no, this had to be the same Ruby who'd been *prima* for years and years, hanging on way past the time when she would have preferred to leave this life and join her late husband, all so she could wait until Angela was ready to take over as head of the clan.

I couldn't say anything about that, though… just as I'd known I couldn't warn Seth about how the Great Depression was looming over them all, and that in a few more years, a lot of this bustling prosperity would be gone forever. The McAllisters had weathered the storm all right, just because witch clans had resources that regular people didn't, but still, that didn't mean they weren't in for some rough times, watching as the mine closed and all the people associated with it left, looking for opportunities elsewhere. In the end, Jerome had dwindled to a point where only a hundred or so McAllisters remained, with the rest of them moving to Payson or Prescott or even Wickenburg in an attempt to diversify their holdings and work in places where they could still earn a decent living.

All that had turned around starting in the late 1960s and moving on into the twenty-first century, but it had been touch-and-go there for a while.

"Ruby's a pretty name," I said as I reached for my glass of water. "Is it one you use a lot in your family?"

"Not really," Seth replied. "To be honest, I don't know where my cousin Miriam got the name from. I suppose she just thought it was pretty, too."

That made sense—my mother had chosen my name because she'd heard it on a TV show and liked it, and my father had agreed—so I supposed there wasn't as much difference in choosing baby names between then and now as I might have thought.

Still, it was extremely weird to think of Ruby McAllister, who'd always sounded to me like a somewhat terrifying old woman, as a tiny baby lying in her crib.

At least I knew she had a long, long life ahead of her, with a man she loved and two healthy sons who grew to adulthood and were prominent members of the clan. Maybe she'd been a little sad that she never had a daughter, someone who could carry on her direct line as *prima,* but according to everything Angela had said about her great-aunt, Ruby had never spoken a word about any regrets over having sons rather than daughters.

Seth and I chatted a little more, and then we were finished with our meals and he quietly handed two dollar bills over to the waiter. I'd been in 1926 long enough to begin to get used to how inexpensive everything was, but it still boggled my mind that we could effectively have a steak dinner at a four-star restaurant for only a couple of bucks.

As with so many other things in this new world, however, I didn't comment on that astonishing fact. No, I waited for Seth to come over and help me out of my chair—those gentlemanly little touches were also something I'd had to get used to, although I thought I liked them very much—and then we headed outside to the spot where we'd left the car parked at the curb partway down the block.

Just as he was opening the convertible's door for me, a green truck passed us by and turned down the alley behind the restaurant. The man driving it had hair a shade lighter than Seth's, with a remarkably similar profile.

"Was that your brother Charles?" I asked, and Seth startled, then put on a smile that didn't look terribly convincing.

"It could have been," he replied while I got into the passenger seat and he shut the door. "We often have to make deliveries here in Prescott."

At nine-thirty at night? I wanted to ask, but I held my tongue. While Charles's presence here at this hour might have seemed odd, I supposed it was possible he had to do these deliveries after the store was closed for the day. It wasn't as if they had a huge staff at the mercantile, just Charles and Molly and Henry McAllister.

Instead, I waited until Seth had gotten behind the wheel before saying, "I hope it's not too dangerous, driving up and down Mingus late at night."

Although he was in profile to me, I couldn't ignore the flicker of relief that passed over his features. Was he glad I'd made such an innocuous comment?

"Oh, it's not too bad," he replied as he pulled away from the curb. "We have to be careful in the winter because of the ice, but otherwise, there's nothing to it."

I wasn't so sure about that. Although using self-driving cars had greatly reduced overall accidents, the nav systems could still have trouble when a deer decided to run across the road or a monsoon downpour appeared out of nowhere and reduced visibility to almost nothing. And if we still had accidents despite having every modern safety device available to us, I had to believe the twisty route up and over Mingus presented even more difficulties in these noisy, rickety-feeling cars of the 1920s.

But I only nodded, and soon enough, we'd gotten up enough speed that further conversation was nearly impossible. As we drove back to Jerome, though, my intuition wanted to tell me that there was a lot more to Charles McAllister's presence in Prescott tonight than Seth had let on.

Whether I'd ever be able to find out what he'd been up to, though, was an entirely separate question.

16

CONSORT CONUNDRUM

SETH WANTED TO CURSE THE REMARKABLY BAD timing that had allowed his brother to drive past just as he and Deborah were about to get in the car, but it seemed as if she'd accepted his explanation about making deliveries and didn't need any further elaboration.

Wasn't that part of the reason why Charles had thought he could get away with all this in the first place? The mercantile often needed to pick up items in Prescott, although most of those sorts of work trips were handled during normal business hours. Still, his duties with the bootleggers offered enough opportunity for plausible deniability that Charles probably thought it wasn't too much of a risk.

All the same, the near-miss put Seth on edge.

When he'd first proposed this date, he'd thought that maybe he and Deborah could stop at the picnic area on the way home, could possibly take a moonlit walk and share their first kiss. Now, though, with his nerves jangling and his anger at Charles for pursuing such a dangerous means of making extra money resurfacing at exactly the wrong time, he thought it was probably better to take Deborah straight to Ruth and Timothy's house.

He wanted his first kiss with her to be perfect, and he knew it wouldn't be tonight.

So he drove back to Jerome and then helped her out of the car before walking her up the steps to the front door. Something about her lovely face seemed almost puzzled, as if she, too, had thought this might be the time they finally shared a kiss.

Doubt crept over him, but he pushed it away. While he wanted to take Deborah in his arms, he knew he didn't have any desire to share such intimacies on the front porch of his aunt Ruth's house.

"Dinner was lovely," Deborah said. "And so was the drive. It was fun to see Prescott."

If she was disappointed that they hadn't stopped somewhere to steal a few kisses, it didn't show in her expression or her tone. Maybe he'd imagined the puzzlement he'd noticed a moment earlier.

But no, there it was again, only a flicker in her clear gray-blue eyes, just enough to let him know she wanted this, even if she wouldn't attempt to initiate any intimacies.

"I'm glad you liked it," he replied. "We'll have to go back sometime."

Even as the words left his mouth, he hoped he wasn't being presumptuous. Possibly, he'd misinterpreted that flash of...something...in her face, and she was instead thinking of the best way to tell him that she didn't believe they should be planning any future meetings.

His worries were dispelled as soon as she replied, however.

"That would be wonderful," she said. "Or really, anything you can think of. It's fun getting to explore the area...and to spend time with you."

And before he could even begin to react, she reached over and gave his hand a quick squeeze, and placed an even quicker kiss against his cheek.

A tingle went through him at that brief touch, one that signaled he was more than happy to get even such a very small caress.

She flashed him a smile, then went inside.

Seth, on the other hand, stood outside on the porch for a moment, then placed his fingers against the spot on his cheek where her soft lips had been pressed only a moment earlier. How could he be so utterly thrilled by a simple kiss on the cheek from Deborah Rowe?

Because you love her, he realized then, with a kind of simple wonder.

As he walked down the porch steps and headed back to his car, he began to whistle.

Jerome didn't boast anything as fancy as a real florist, but Seth had already learned that it was just as easy to pay one of his cousins a nickel to gather some flowers for him—roses and snap-dragons and cheerful zinnias—and tie them with a ribbon before leaving them on the porch at his aunt Ruth and uncle Timothy's house, along with a note for Deborah.

No wild declarations of love—Seth knew he was no poet, just a hard-working man who also happened to be a warlock—but a proposal that they go to the dance hall in Cottonwood on Friday night, where a local band he knew was good would be playing. He supposed they could have gone dancing earlier than this, and yet he thought it was a better idea to have a few dinners and a picnic or so under their belt before he started waltzing with her.

Did she even remember how to dance? He

had no real idea, although it seemed as if she appeared to recall most things that required simple motor memory.

Well, if she wasn't especially keen on the idea of going to a dance hall, they could always have another picnic. Several spots along the Verde River offered smooth, sandy shores, perfect places to lay out a blanket and share a meal...places secluded enough that he knew he and Deborah would be shielded from any prying eyes.

All day he couldn't stop thinking about that impulsive kiss she'd pressed against his cheek, although he wouldn't allow the happy memory to distract him from his work. Still, he was cheered to see a note tucked under the doormat when he returned home a little after six.

Dancing on Friday would be fun, Deborah had written, *but I'm not sure I remember how. You'll have to show me.*

Which was more than fine by him. Although he would never count himself an expert, he could manage a box step and the foxtrot, although he knew better than to attempt a tango, even as tempting as the thought of lowering her into a seductive dip might be.

He went inside and laid her note on the kitchen table, then commenced washing up so he might review his options for supper. Although he still had some cold chicken in the icebox, the thought of eating it didn't seem terribly appealing. Maybe he should walk up to the English Kitchen and get some noodles to bring back here for dinner. In general, he did his best to avoid that sort of splurge, but he knew he was feeling restless and thought that maybe getting out and taking a walk up the hill to the restaurant would help him work off some of his nervous energy.

It wasn't just him, he realized as he headed out. The whole town seemed to have an odd energy to it, a shift he couldn't quite put his finger on, as if something fundamental had changed, even if it all appeared much the same to him. People smiled and waved at him as he walked up Hull Street toward the English Kitchen, although no one approached to discuss precisely what was so exciting.

At times like this, when it felt as if there was some momentous news he'd somehow missed, he wished he'd splurged and bought a telephone for his bungalow, even though at the time it had seemed like an expense he didn't need to make. In a town as small as Jerome, notes such as the one Deborah had left for him seemed to work perfectly well.

He was just leaving the restaurant, a bag of noodles in his hand, when he bumped into his mother, of all people.

"Oh, there you are," she said. "I just walked down to your house, but you weren't home."

"I decided I wanted some noodles for dinner," he replied, hefting the bag he held.

She gave it a dismissive glance. "No, family dinner tonight. We have a lot to discuss."

"We do?" Seth said, more mystified than ever. Like everyone else, his mother had that same air of barely suppressed excitement about her, as if she bubbled inside with news she was just dying to share.

"Yes," she said firmly, locking her arm with his. "Let's go."

He supposed he could have protested, although he knew when Molly McAllister got that look in her eyes, it was better to go along for the ride.

Besides, while he might have wasted some money on those noodles, he knew he would get much better at the family flat above the mercantile.

When they arrived, the table was already set, and the rich aroma of chicken à la king filled the air. This only increased Seth's puzzlement, since he knew his mother never splurged on such a meal unless it was a very special occasion.

His father and Charles stood near the table, obviously waiting for them to arrive. Exactly why Molly had gone on her mission to find Seth rather than sending Henry or Charles, he couldn't say for sure, although he knew his mother tended to have a better sixth sense about where to find him than either his father or his brother did.

"Sit down, sit down," Molly said. "I'll just bring in the chicken, and then Charles can share his news."

Charles was the source of all this excitement? Seth couldn't begin to think why. Somehow he doubted that his brother would have announced to everyone that he was quitting the bootlegging business, which was the only news Seth would have liked to hear.

Or…had Mary suddenly relented? He supposed he could see why such a change of heart would be an important reversal for his family, even though he still couldn't quite understand why so many other people in Jerome would be happy to hear such news.

Molly returned and set the large bowl full of chicken à la king near her husband's place setting, along with another bowl full of egg noodles. After she sat down, she sent an encouraging glance at her oldest son.

"We're all here, Charles, so go ahead and tell your brother the news."

Unlike their parents, Charles didn't seem very happy at all. His jaw was set, and his blue eyes glittered underneath the bright electric chandelier overhead.

"It appears I'm Abigail's consort," he said, his tone flat.

For a second or two, Seth could only stare at his brother in surprise.

Why hadn't he heard about any of this?

Because he'd been at work all day. And Charles…a man who had no problem keeping secrets…clearly hadn't seen the need to tell his younger brother that it had been his turn to share the consort kiss with the *prima*-in-waiting. Why Mabel had decided to go directly to Charles rather than someone else in the clan, Seth couldn't say for sure. It might have been as simple as Abigail announcing that if she couldn't have one brother, she might as well try for the other.

In the end, none of that really mattered. What mattered was that Charles, who seemed like the last person suited to be the next *prima's* consort, was going to assume that role after all.

Even as the thought flickered through his head, Seth knew it was a little uncharitable. No one else in the clan knew about his brother's bootlegging activities, after all, and only saw Charles as an upstanding son who had taken on an active role in the family business. If he was almost five years older than Abigail, so be it. She was so frail and unassuming that a lot of people in the clan probably thought it would be better for her to have a consort who took on more of a commanding role.

But what about Mary?

Because everyone was watching him, clearly waiting for his response, Seth quickly said, "Congratulations! This must be very exciting for you."

"Yes," Charles replied, although he still looked decidedly unenthusiastic. "Abigail's very happy. She and her mother are already planning the wedding."

Which would be lavish by Jerome standards, befitting the future *prima* of the clan and her new husband. Or at least, he assumed it would. He hadn't even been born when Mabel married her consort, but he'd seen photos of the blessed event, with the *prima's* hair in an elaborate pompadour and wearing a white silk wedding gown with ridiculously puffed sleeves.

Abigail's dress would be very different in style, of course, but Seth was fairly certain she'd make sure her day involved just as many flowers and just as much feasting.

"They both want a June wedding," Molly put in, gaze fond as she looked over at her eldest son. "That might seem fast, but you know how Mabel is when she gets an idea in her head."

Yes, Seth did. All the more reason why he was very glad she wouldn't be his mother-in-law.

"Can they really put something like that together in only a few weeks?" Henry asked, and his wife gave a philosophical shrug.

"With all the clan helping them out? Of course they can."

"Luckily, all I have to do is put on my best suit and show up," Charles remarked as he ladled some chicken and noodles onto his plate.

Molly's right eyebrow lifted. When she looked like that, both her sons knew they had better take notice.

"You will most decidedly do more than that, Charles Emerson McAllister," she said. "Whatever is asked of you, and more."

Although Charles didn't exactly deflate, his tone was much more conciliatory as he said, "Of course, Mother. I was only making a little joke."

"Some things are best not joked about," their father said mildly. "One of which is your marriage to the *prima*-in-waiting."

Charles nodded, and Molly took up the conversation there, talking about possibilities for Abigail's bride dress, which venue would be best for the reception, and the most likely places for Charles to go to purchase her a suitable ring. Seth did his best to act as though he was interested in all this, but through the entire discussion, he couldn't help wondering one thing.

What was his older brother going to do about

his ties to the bootleggers now that his life had been changed so utterly?

~

Dinner lasted a good long while, but eventually, Seth was able to take his box of stone-cold noodles and head for home. When he got there, he put it in the icebox, mainly because it seemed wasteful to throw away the food so soon. Why it would be any better after he let it sit for a day or two, he couldn't even say to himself, but somehow, waiting to deal with it seemed less extravagant.

After the noodles were taken care of, he poured himself a glass of water and sat down at the kitchen table, still feeling somewhat shell-shocked.

His brother was going to be Abigail's consort.

The idea had an air of utter unreality about it, as if it was something Seth had once read in a book and now didn't know for sure whether it was actually true. But the reactions of his parents— and the other McAllisters he'd seen on the street, who obviously had gotten the news well before he did—told him this actually was happening.

He didn't think anyone could have missed Charles's distinct lack of enthusiasm about the situation, but it seemed clear his parents had decided to brush it off. No doubt they were doing their best to tell themselves he was only startled because he hadn't expected to be chosen for the consort kiss until some of the McAllister cousins who were closer to Abigail in age had their turn… and also that they understood he still carried a torch for Mary Towne, even if everyone else involved had moved on.

But weren't a *prima*-in-waiting and her consort supposed to be rapturously in love once they'd shared their fateful kiss, the one that was supposed to spark a lifelong passion that would never burn out?

That was the story everyone had been told. Now, however, it seemed as if real life could be just a little more complicated.

Seth sincerely hoped his brother would get better at acting the role once his initial shock wore off. Having a future consort who appeared less than happy about his upcoming nuptials wasn't anything the McAllister clan would want to acknowledge.

In the end, though, this was a row Charles would have to decide on his own how to hoe. Seth knew he was only peripherally connected to the situation and could stay safely out of it for the most part.

Thank the Goddess.

He'd just bent down to start pulling off his

work boots when someone knocked at the door. At once he straightened, startled. He seldom had visitors, and even when he did, he usually had some advance notice that they would be dropping by.

Could it be that Deborah had slipped away from Ruth and Timothy's house and come down the hill to see him?

As much as Seth might have wanted that to be the case, he somehow doubted Deborah would do anything so bold. Not because she didn't possess the requisite fire or spirit to act on her own, but only because she wouldn't want to do anything that might compromise her reputation, which was already on slightly shaky ground thanks to the utter mystery of her origins.

Frowning, he went to the door and opened it. Outside stood his brother Charles, still wearing the same stony expression he'd been sporting through most of dinner.

"We need to talk," he said, and brushed past Seth almost as though he wasn't there at all.

That kind of behavior only deepened his scowl, but he didn't reply at once, and instead shut the door before turning toward his brother, who now stood in the middle of the living room, arms crossed.

"I thought I already offered you my congratulations," Seth commented dryly, but Charles only made an impatient gesture.

"I don't give a damn about that," he replied, irritation flashing in his eyes, their clear blue almost as bright as his own. "Believe me, this situation was none of my choosing, and you know that as well as I do."

Maybe a bit of hyperbole, but it also didn't require a mind reader to see that Charles was less than pleased to be Abigail's future consort.

"Because of Mary?" Seth ventured, and his brother's brow darkened.

"Mary," Charles replied, "and a whole lot more. This new wrinkle puts me in a hell of a bind."

"Your outside arrangement," Seth said. Even though they were alone here and the windows were shut tight, making the little house positively stuffy, he still wasn't sure if he wanted to utter the word "bootlegging" aloud.

Charles's mouth twisted. "As good a way as any of describing it. But yes, that. I know Mabel, and therefore I know she's going to want me involved with as much of the wedding planning as possible, even though I don't give a good damn about any of it. Then there's the house—"

"'The house'?" Seth repeated, not sure what his brother was driving at.

The answering look that Charles sent him

dripped with condescension. "You don't really think Mabel is going to let her precious Abigail live in a flat above a store, do you? No, she's already talking about buying the Waters' house—"

"The one you wanted for you and Mary?"

Angry fire flashed in his brother's eyes. "Yes, that one. I suppose the Goddess is having her little joke with me. Then again, good-sized houses aren't exactly thick on the ground around here, so it's probably not so surprising that Mabel would choose that one. At any rate, I'll be trying to juggle wedding preparations with setting up a new house so Abigail can go straight to a fancy new home as soon as we're married."

Seth wondered if he should say "sorry," even though none of this was his doing. However, he decided it was probably better to remain silent and allow his brother to speak his piece. It wouldn't change the situation, but it might help him a little to vent his frustration to someone he knew wouldn't betray his confidence.

"And of course Mabel wants me to stop working at the store," Charles continued. "I know that a consort doesn't work, but I didn't think she'd ask me to quit until closer to the wedding. Which is why I'm talking to you, Seth."

He didn't much like the sound of that. "What does any of this have to do with me?"

His brother released a disgusted breath. "It has

everything to do with you. If I'm not working at the store, then you have to."

Hell, no, rose in Seth's mind, but he kept that inner protest to himself. In the back of his mind, he'd always known that if something should happen to Charles, he'd need to step in to pick up the slack. Working at the mine was more lucrative, but family came first.

"I can do that," he said calmly. No point in letting his brother see that he was not entirely pleased with the prospect, even if Seth might allow himself a few inner grumbles.

"Good," Charles replied. "Because you'll need the cover of working at the store to take over my Prescott route for the bootleggers."

Had Charles completely lost his mind? But no, he stood there calmly enough, looking as though he hadn't just made a completely outlandish proposition.

"I can't do that," Seth said flatly, and his brother's eyes narrowed.

"Yes, you can, and you will," Charles returned. "They won't care about the change in my circumstances, and obviously, I can't tell them the whole story. The only way to prevent them from retaliating against me is to make sure their deliveries continue uninterrupted…and that means having you drive the truck to Prescott whenever they need you to. If there were any way to continue doing it myself, I would. But I can't risk having Mabel discover what I've been up to. She's going to be watching me like a hawk now that I'm her daughter's new consort."

On the surface, that excuse made some sense. However....

"What's the worst that could happen?" Seth asked, then went on without waiting for his brother to reply. "Maybe it would be better if the *prima* knew the truth. She certainly has the power to ensure the bootleggers stay far, far away from our family."

Charles's lip curled in contempt. "Don't be an idiot. Mabel might have magic, but they have guns. Do you really want to risk the safety of our clan members, merely for a chance to expose those men for what they are?"

But you're fine with risking my safety, Seth thought then. There had been times over the years when his older brother's words or actions had upset him, even angered him, but until now, he'd never experienced white-hot, burning fury over Charles's apparent disregard for anyone other than himself.

That anger left Seth at a loss for words, creating a brooding silence that his brother decided to fill.

"It won't be forever," he said. "Only until November or thereabouts, when the roads start to get icy. At that point, they'll move their operations to the south and come into Prescott through a different route that won't take them over the mountain."

"And when spring comes again?" Seth replied, not bothering to hide the anger in his voice. "Do you think they'll have conveniently forgotten about me by then?"

"Of course not," Charles said easily. "But I'll negotiate with them, make it understood that they'll need to find someone new for the Jerome run by the time the roads clear. In the meantime, you'll keep all of us safe…and make some good money on the side that you can spend on that pretty girl of yours."

Blood money, Seth thought, but again, he held his tongue, especially since he knew he was being a bit melodramatic. Running liquor was against the law, but most people saw breaking Prohibition as a victimless crime.

Well, except for those unfortunate souls who might come up against the wrong side of the bootleggers and never be heard from again.

Still, he hated the idea of being roped into that kind of activity, hated that his brother's rash actions were forcing him to participate in criminal behavior that could result in his going to jail if he ever got caught.

But Charles was right. A *prima's* consort didn't

328 | CHRISTINE POPE

work unless it was some kind of artistic pursuit that still allowed him to stay home and remain at her side. Being a shopkeeper certainly didn't fall into that category, which meant Seth had to take over his brother's position at the store.

A position that provided perfect cover for the much darker, more dangerous matters he pursued on the side.

With a looming sense of finality, he said, "When's the next run?"

"Tomorrow night," Charles replied at once. His tone had shifted to one of relief, as if he knew that by asking such a question, Seth had already agreed to take on the Prescott delivery route.

Of course it was Friday night. He didn't much like the idea of breaking off his date to go dancing in Cottonwood with Deborah, although maybe there was something else he could offer her, like going to the movies on Saturday evening. It wouldn't be quite the same, but it would be better than nothing. He'd just have to invent some sort of plausible excuse for canceling the date, although he supposed the sudden shift his career would probably be enough to explain away the change in plans.

What else could he do, now that he'd already tacitly agreed to take his brother's place at both the store and on the Prescott run?

"It's quite simple," Charles went on. "You just

need to drive the truck to the exploratory mine shaft. The barrel of moonshine will be hidden toward the back, behind some boulders we rolled in there to provide camouflage. Fill the jugs provided with moonshine, load them into the truck, and drive them to the Palace in downtown Prescott."

Seth's eyebrows lifted. A bootlegging operation was happening in the same restaurant where he'd taken Deborah to dinner only the day before?

Now his brother's expression turned almost condescending. "You mean you really didn't know there was a speakeasy under the Palace?"

"Not being in the habit of frequenting those sorts of places, no," Seth retorted.

Charles didn't even blink. "I never realized you were so holier-than-thou."

That was probably the last phrase Seth would have ever applied to himself. "I'm not," he said. "But I try to avoid situations that could bring trouble to our clan."

Maybe the slightest lift at the corner of his brother's mouth. "There won't be any trouble," he said smoothly. "As long as you do as you're told. Tomorrow, you'll go to Lionel Allenby and inform him you need to resign from your foreman's position to come work for the family business. I know he'll be understanding."

Of course he would, because by then, Charles

would have already let him know what had happened…or at least, he would have provided a heavily edited version of the events of the past day, one that would pass muster with a civilian.

Seth didn't bother to comment. His brother might have set them on this perilous course, but it sure looked as though he'd have to be the one to safely steer this ship to shore.

17

REVEALED

I was a little startled to see Seth coming up the front walk that Friday morning. We already had a date set for that night, and even though I was more than happy to be around him at every possible opportunity, I knew his schedule was busy enough that coming to see me in the middle of the day—except on a Sunday, like when we'd gone on our picnic—just wasn't in the cards.

So what was he doing away from the mine on Friday at a little past ten?

He wasn't wearing his working clothes, either, but an outfit he'd sported during one of our dates —pleated linen trousers and matching vest, a striped shirt and tie underneath. While I had to admit he looked particularly dashing in the ensemble, it wasn't exactly the sort of thing you'd put on to supervise a bunch of sweaty men at a dusty mine.

Because I'd already seen him approaching the front door, I was ready when he knocked, opening it almost as soon as he began to lower his hand.

"Hi," I said. "Come on in."

Normally, I wouldn't have been nearly as free with such an invitation while staying at someone else's house, but Ruth had already told me it was fine for me to have Seth over whenever I liked. I supposed she didn't view him exactly as a gentleman caller, since he was part of the family.

Also, she and Timothy had driven down to Cottonwood to do some shopping, so I was alone in the house and didn't need to worry about anyone listening in on our conversation.

"Thank you," Seth said, stepping inside. His gaze moved past me toward the hallway beyond, almost as though he feared his aunt Ruth might be lurking behind a door somewhere, doing her best to eavesdrop.

"They're down in Cottonwood," I said helpfully. "Would you like some lemonade, or a glass of water?"

"No, thank you," he replied, then paused. Something in his manner seemed almost nervous, a description I probably wouldn't have applied to him before now. Maybe we'd had an awkward moment here and there, but he'd never seemed truly ill at ease around me.

Might as well put it out there.

"Is something the matter?"

Those clear blue eyes met mine. "A few things have happened," he said. "My brother Charles just got engaged to our cousin Abigail."

For a second or two, I could only stare back at him as my brain did its best to accept the enormity of what he'd just told me.

Seth's brother would be the *prima*-in-waiting's consort.

I had to believe this wasn't as happy a bit of news as one might have expected, judging by the serious set to Seth's jaw, the way he hadn't smiled at all as he told me about this latest change in his brother's circumstances.

"Um…congratulations?" I offered, and now he smiled just the slightest bit.

"I'll pass those along," he said. "But the main reason I needed to tell you about what happened is that his engagement changes a lot of things. He now has his inheritance, which means he'll no longer be working at the store. I'm taking over his position."

This time, I was genuinely startled. Sure, I understood in a sort of abstract way that most consorts didn't work, and yet this was the first time I'd seen this sort of transition occur in real time.

"Has your family suffered a loss?" I said, thinking that was a natural question to ask when an inheritance was in play.

"No, no," Seth said quickly. "That is, the inheritance was left in a trust for Charles years ago when one of our great-aunts passed away. The stipulation was that he wouldn't receive any of the money until he got engaged. But with him planning to marry Abigail before the end of the month, the money will be coming to him very soon."

A clever way to explain why a man in the prime of life would suddenly stop working to play devoted house-husband. If they even had those in the 1920s, which I kind of doubted. Although the McAllisters were probably more equitable about such things than the general population, I couldn't help noticing that labor here in Jerome was definitely divided along sharp gender-defined roles.

Whereas people living off their inheritances had seemed to be around since time immemorial, so I doubted anyone would probe Charles McAllister's change in circumstances very deeply.

"What about your job at the mine?" I asked then, and Seth's shoulders lifted in a shrug that I didn't believe for a moment.

"I like it, and I'll miss it," he said, being a bit

more frank than I'd expected. "But family is more important, and my parents need me at the mercantile." A flash of real humor lit up those clear blue eyes as he added, "At least I won't get as dusty and dirty there."

No, probably not. And I'd been in Jerome long enough to know that the store opened at eight and closed at five, which meant he'd have much more relationship-friendly working hours.

Something in my gaze must have been questioning, because he went on, the words coming out a little faster than he'd probably intended, "My parents told me I could start whenever I liked this morning, since I had to tender my resignation at the mine and get a few things worked out. And that's why I wanted to stop and talk to you."

"To give me the news?" I asked, and he shook his head.

"Not exactly. Or rather, sure, I needed to let you know I would be at the store from now on, just so you wouldn't be surprised if you came by and saw me working there." He paused, and his expression grew much more sober. "No, the problem is that my parents had already planned to do inventory tonight, and they need me there. I'll have to cancel our date to go dancing in Cottonwood."

"Oh," I said. Not exactly the most brilliant

response, but I was a little startled by the wave of disappointment that washed over me. I hadn't realized how much I'd been looking forward to having Seth teach me the Charleston—or whatever was popular here in Arizona in 1926—until I heard that he wouldn't be able to make it after all. I summoned a smile and added, "That's all right. I know the family business needs to come first."

The tense set of his shoulders relaxed slightly. "That's what I keep trying to tell myself. It's just rotten timing. But," he went on, looking a little more cheerful, "I was hoping I could make it up to you somehow. I considered going to the picture show tomorrow, but then this morning, I thought maybe we could also go out for a dinner picnic this evening? My parents understand that this has all happened quickly, so while I'm not free later tonight, we could have an early meal and still get to spend some time together before I have to go help them with inventory."

That sounded like a wonderful idea. We'd had a great time during our first picnic, and I had to think one later in the day, after the sun had begun to go down behind Mingus Mountain, would be even more entrancing. True, we'd probably need to avoid walking in the woods, just because getting lost there after dark didn't seem like a very good idea, but if we got our timing right, we might be able to see the moon rise beyond the Mogollon Rim to the east.

Or maybe not, if our meal was early enough in the evening. I hadn't been keeping close enough track of moonrise and moonset to know for sure when it would be up.

"A dinner picnic would be lovely," I said, and Seth's expression brightened even further. "Do you need me to bring anything?"

"Only yourself," he replied. "I'll take care of the rest." He paused there, and the cheerful grin he wore looked much more like the man I knew. "Or rather, I'll probably have my mother help me put together something tasty."

Considering that Molly McAllister's fried chicken was the best I'd ever tasted, I wasn't about to argue with that proposition. "Then it's definitely a date," I said with a smile to match his.

"Perfect. I'll come by around five-thirty, and then we'll drive up to the picnic area." A pause before he added, "Now, though, I should probably get to the store."

"Yes, you'll want to be on your best behavior so you can get your mother to make you some more fried chicken," I joked, but he only nodded, looking earnest.

"You may be right about that."

He reached out to give my hand a quick

squeeze, and then he murmured a hasty goodbye and let himself out.

As much as I would have liked for him to linger, I knew he had somewhere to be. Even though it sounded as if his parents had told him he could take his time this morning, he probably didn't want it to seem as if he was taking advantage of the situation, especially since they were going to let him leave work a little early so he wouldn't have to completely cancel on me.

In a way, that was good. It was going to take a minute to absorb how much things had changed over the past couple of days. Seth was no longer in danger of becoming the *prima*-in-waiting's consort, and now he'd be working at the store rather than up at the mine.

I had no doubt that I'd be able to come up with all sorts of reasons to visit him.

Ruth didn't seem too surprised by the news about Charles.

"Oh, yes, the inheritance," she said as she rolled out some dough for a batch of peach tarts. Even though I'd told her that Seth planned to handle all the meal planning for our picnic this evening, she'd insisted that the tarts would be the perfect thing for our *al fresco* meal and that Seth would probably be disappointed if I didn't bring along some kind of special nibble for the two of us.

Since Ruth's baking skills were top-notch, I decided I wasn't going to argue with her.

"Their Great-Aunt Adelaide was a little eccentric," Ruth went on. "Her husband was one of the men who originally discovered copper here, and he sold his stake to Mr. Clarke, who owns everything now. Made millions, from what I've heard. But Adelaide never had children, and so she decided to leave most of her money to Charles, as her oldest great-nephew. However, she didn't want him to fritter away the money on gambling and other wild pursuits, which was why she put the stipulation in her will that he must be engaged before he inherited any of it."

I supposed the story made sense. Or rather, I knew it sounded plausible enough that no one looking in from the outside would question it too deeply. However, I had a rather unique perspective on the situation, and therefore knew it was a complete fabrication.

"Charles and Abigail are moving quickly," Ruth continued. "I hear they're just about to buy a house up here on Paradise Lane, for of course it wouldn't do for Charles to move his new bride into his parents' apartment. I'm sure Great-Aunt

Adelaide would be pleased that he's spending his new inheritance so wisely."

Yes, in most cases, real estate was always a good investment.

Jerome wasn't most cases, though. I'd heard that a good number of these stately Victorians had fallen into wrack and ruin as the civilian population left Jerome when the mine went bust, and it wasn't until much later that people began to move back and restore them.

Not the *prima's* house, of course. That particular home had been continuously occupied from the day it was built.

"That is fast," I commented. "But I can see why they'd want to start their marriage with a new house."

Ruth gave me an approving nod, her expression turning almost sly. "And of course this is good for you and Seth. He'll be much more available now that he's here in town all day."

I'd thought pretty much the same thing, but I didn't know whether it was a good idea to let Ruth know how on the nose she was in that assessment. "Well, I'm sure he'll still be very busy," I said. "I suppose we'll just have to see how things go."

"Yes," she replied, still with that twinkle in her gray eyes. "I suppose you will."

~

As promised, Seth arrived promptly at five-thirty to pick me up. An enormous wicker hamper had taken up residence in the back seat, letting me know this meal might be a little more elaborate than the lunch we'd shared the week before. Once we were walking down the porch steps, he sent an amused glance at the basket I had looped over one arm.

"Aunt Ruth strikes again, I see," he remarked, and I just had to chuckle.

"She absolutely would not let me leave the house without an offering for our picnic. Peach tarts," I added, and his eyes lit up.

"Well, I think we can make room for those."

It was a bit of a squeeze to get the basket in the back seat next to the hamper, but once that maneuver was accomplished, we both climbed into our seats up front and drove off. It was an absolutely stunning evening, the hilltop town bathed in golden light as the sun made its way slowly down in the west. Probably by the time we reached our destination and spread out what promised to be a sumptuous meal, it would have begun to slide behind the mountain and let the world slip into a purple dusk, but the day was bright enough for now, with no clouds at all as far as the eye could see.

I'd brought along a sweater, just in case, although I certainly didn't need it now, not with the warm wind blowing past as we drove down Paradise Lane and then onto Main Street, which turned back into the highway once we were past the town limits. And even though it was difficult to talk over the sound of the engine, I couldn't help asking, "How was the store today?"

"Fine," Seth replied. He had his eyes fixed on the road ahead of us, so I couldn't get a good read on his expression. "Busier than I remembered. But I suppose that's a good thing, isn't it?"

"I would think so," I said. More customers meant more revenue, after all. Still, even when you knew things were going well, a high enough level of activity with no breaks could leave you pretty beat up by the end of the day.

However, he seemed in good enough spirits, so I had to assume that what he was mostly dealing with was readjusting to work at the family mercantile after several years of being his own man at the mine, which I could totally understand. I loved my parents and my brother and sister, but I had to wonder if we'd all get along so well if we were forced to work together day in and day out.

But I didn't want to think about that too much, because then I'd also start to think about how much I missed them, missed seeing my mother's silly texts about what color she was thinking of painting the spare bedroom, or the memes my brother would send whenever he came across something he thought would make me laugh. Or how my father would leave books all over the house because my mother had tried and failed years ago to get him to read on a tablet.

The way my sister Jessica had given me all the pieces from her wardrobe that I'd loved the most after she started college and wanted to completely change her image. Maybe that gift had been a little self-serving, since it kept her from having to drag all that stuff to the local charity drop-off, but seventeen-year-old me had been ecstatic.

By that point, the road had really started to climb, and that meant the engine was laboring harder to get us up the steep incline and around those hairpin curves. I decided it was probably better to let our conversation languish until we reached our destination and didn't have to be shouting over the noise of the motor, so I instead watched the scenery as it passed, reflecting on how much it looked like what I'd see from the highway in my own time. Sure, the road signs were different, and the asphalt and the markings on it weren't quite the same, but the scrubby junipers and dry grass, the occasional spiky agave plant that leaned precariously off a cliff edge—those didn't seem to have changed a bit over the intervening hundred-plus years.

Seth slowed down as we came to the picnic area so he could turn off onto one of the gravel-paved parking spaces. I reached up to push a few windblown strands of hair back into my cloche hat, glad we were going to be outdoors the whole time so I wouldn't have to take it off and reveal whatever wreckage might lie underneath.

He took the big hamper of food and the folded blanket that had been concealed under-neath, while I grabbed the basket of tarts Ruth had given me. The two of us made our way over to the same flat piece of ground where we'd had our picnic the week before, and he set down the hamper so he could spread out the blanket.

With all that managed, we went ahead and seated ourselves, and he started pulling out all kinds of goodies—yummy little meat pies, more of his mother's amazing fried chicken, potato salad, a bowl of cut-up fruit, some cornbread muffins and darling little bitty jars of butter and honey.

"Do you really expect me to eat all this?" I asked with a grin. "I mean, I'll do my best, but—"

He only chuckled. "I told my mother she might be overdoing things, but she didn't want to hear it. I think she might still be a little giddy from the news about Charles's engagement."

I supposed I could understand that. While witch clans tended to be fairly egalitarian—some more than others, since I'd heard a few horror stories about how things were run in the Wilcox clan before Connor came along, way before I was even born—still, to have a son become the consort of the *prima*-in-waiting was no small thing. Seth's immediate family had gained a little more standing in their clan, even if no one might want to admit such a thing out loud.

"When I'm giddy, I go shopping rather than cook," I commented, and Seth only lifted his shoulders.

"I have to admit that shopping sounds like more fun," he said. "But then, I'm not my mother."

No, he wasn't. He was definitely all man—not macho beefcake man, but someone who could be strong and gentle at the same time, who ticked a whole hell of a lot of boxes I hadn't even realized I wanted on my checklist for the perfect partner.

Well, except for the part where he wasn't even from my own time, but considering all his other sterling qualities, I was just fine with putting that small detail aside, especially since it didn't seem as if I had much chance of getting back to the twenty-first century and needed to make my peace with staying here.

For a moment or two, we were both quiet as

we loaded up our plates. Seth poured some water from a bottle he'd brought along with the food. The sun melted behind Mingus, casting the picnic area in shadow, even though everything in the valley below was still bright and golden except the line of dark cottonwoods that marked the path of the Verde River as it wound through the landscape.

Despite the loss of sunlight, the air was still warm enough, and probably would be for a while, considering how long the days were right now with the solstice only a few weeks off. I wondered how the McAllisters of this time celebrated the year's longest day, whether they gathered in their robes on the promontory just east of downtown as they did in the twenty-first century, or whether they had to perform their observances in secret, surrounded as they were by people who had no idea they were witches at all.

Even if I stayed here that long, I knew I wouldn't get to see what they were doing, not when they thought I was an ordinary civilian.

"I was wrong," I said, and Seth blinked at me, a little startled. Smiling a little at his confusion, I added, "I thought your mother's fried chicken was the best thing I've ever eaten, but these meat pies just might have it beat."

An amused light flickered in his eyes. "I'll let her know," he replied. "She used to make them for me all the time when I first started at the mine—needed to make sure I was getting the proper nourishment during a hard day's work." Something of the cheeriness in his expression faded as he added, "I suppose she won't need to worry about that so much now that I'm working at the store instead."

It seemed obvious to me that he wasn't as thrilled about being back at McAllister Mercantile as he would have liked me—or anyone else—to believe. On the surface, you would have thought that working at the shop would be a lot less physically taxing than being at the mine all day, but I had a feeling that wasn't the whole story. Working for United Verde, he'd been able to be his own person, not just an extension of the family business. Things had changed, though, and he was probably trying to find his way to a new normal.

"Oh, I'm sure she'd make them for you if you asked," I said, trying to keep my tone light.

He nodded and looked a little more cheerful. "Probably. Then again, she made so many for this picnic that I'll probably be eating them for days anyway."

I couldn't help laughing at that mental image, and the tense moment seemed to fade away, replaced by his remembrances of Thanksgiving feasts past, and all the wonderful things his mother made on a regular basis. Hearing this, I couldn't help wondering if his particular branch of the McAllisters was connected to Rachel in some way. Stepping back her duties at the store hadn't meant she planned to cut back on her cooking at the same time, and I'd often been the beneficiary of one of her too-large pots of chili or soup, or an extra pan of lasagna because she'd just gotten "carried away" in the kitchen and needed someone else to help her finish it.

Problem was, I hadn't made a huge study of McAllister genealogy, so I had no real idea who in 1926 was connected to whom. All right, I knew that Ruby had just been born, and that meant her mother must have been Angela's great-great-aunt, but beyond that, it was pretty much a muddle.

The important thing, I supposed, was that I wasn't related to any of them, and therefore my relationship with Seth wasn't a problem...well, besides the part where he'd come from an entirely different time than mine.

Eventually, we were both so full we couldn't eat another bite, and we put the leftovers away in the hamper and the basket, then set them on the back seat of his convertible. By then, dusk had truly fallen, and, despite being from Flagstaff and generally comfortable with wandering around in the woods, I was glad I had Seth there with me. Somehow, this forest felt much deeper and darker than what I was used to, most likely because civilization seemed a lot farther away in 1926 than it did in my own time.

"Look," he said, and pointed eastward through a break in the trees. "The moon's just coming up."

So it was. Huge and yellow, it had begun to push its way upward from the plateau to the east. Not high enough yet to cast any real light, and yet something about it still caught my breath, made me stand there in wonder.

Seth's hand stole into mine. "I'm glad we could watch this together," he murmured.

I was glad, too. Or at least, the warmth that went through me as we stood there, fingers entwined, probably had just as much to do with his presence as the magical scene before us.

He shifted, and I did as well, and suddenly, we weren't gazing at the moon anymore. No, our gazes locked for what felt like an endless moment, until at last his head lowered to mine and I tilted my face to him, mouths growing closer, closer….

Our lips touched, and it was as if a bolt of lightning had suddenly struck me. My entire body zinged with energy that shrilled along every nerve ending, and at the same moment, Seth stopped backward, his face white with shock beneath his summer tan.

"You're a *witch?*" he exclaimed.

18

WITCHY WOMAN

SETH HAD IMAGINED THEIR FIRST KISS IN SO many ways. Maybe it would have been stolen as they walked along a secluded street in Jerome, or possibly he would have leaned over to touch his lips to hers as they got into his car after an evening of dancing or laughing. Perhaps that first embrace would have happened in the very spot where they now stood, with the dark pine forest crowding them on all sides.

What he never, ever could have imagined was the unmistakable tingle he got at the back of his neck whenever he met a strange witch or warlock —to be fair, always an unknown cousin from Payson or Wickenburg, since no other magical folk would have any reason to set foot in Jerome —only this time amplified a thousand-fold, so strong that it almost felt as though he'd stuck his finger in a light socket.

He staggered backward, reeling. "You're a witch!"

Deborah was absolutely white-faced, although she stood her ground as she stared back at him, her expression equally shocked. "I—"

"Don't try to deny it," he said, knowing he needed to cut in before she could offer any excuses. There was nothing she could say to justify the way she'd misled him—and the rest of the McAllister clan—for the past two weeks. "I felt my telltale. There's no way you could be anything other than a witch."

She swallowed. The cloche hat she'd been wearing looked as if it had been knocked askew, and she impatiently pulled it off, revealing a mess of tangled waves that might have been endearing if he hadn't been so angry with her.

How in the world could she have concealed such a thing from him? It was well known that everyone in the witch world had some kind of tell that would signal they were in the presence of an unknown witch or warlock, whether it was a ringing in the ears or a tingle at the back of their neck, or sometimes a quick flash of light or an odd blurriness in their vision. Not once had anyone ever told him it might be possible for a witch or warlock to hide their true nature.

"Who the hell are you?" he demanded, knowing even as he asked the question how angry, how rough he sounded.

Deborah didn't flinch, though. No, she continued to stand there and stare back at him, and then her chin went up and her lips pressed together, as if she knew she couldn't avoid answering the question but still didn't much look forward to it.

"You're not going to believe me," she said.

He wanted to respond that no, he probably wouldn't, not when she'd been misleading him and everyone else for the past two weeks. But he also realized saying such a thing to her wouldn't exactly invite her to share the truth.

"Tell me anyway," he said.

Her chest rose and fell as she released a breath. "My name isn't Deborah," she told him. "It's Devynn."

Bewildered, he could only stare back at her. "I've never heard a name like that before."

"No, you wouldn't have." Another of those long, heavy pauses. "And that's because I'm from the future."

His first impulse was to laugh, to tell her of all the lies she could have come up with, that one was surely the most ridiculous.

But then he noted that even though she looked much paler than she had a few minutes earlier, she didn't try to look away…and didn't try to instantly defend herself the way a woman who was trying to convince someone else that her lie was true might have.

No, she only stood there and waited to see what he intended to say.

"Is that your gift?" he asked. "Time travel?"

"Sort of," she replied. "That is, it allows me to move in time, but I can't control it at all. I don't have any idea why I ended up in 1926 when I fell and hit my head in the mine shaft."

"That's what happened?" In a way, it felt better to seize on the mechanics of how she'd gotten here rather than dwell on exactly where she'd come from.

A small nod. "I was knocked unconscious, so I don't know why my supposed gift decided to kick in right then. I just know what when I woke up the next day, I realized I was in 1926."

And then she'd decided to present herself as someone with amnesia as a way of hiding her ignorance of the current year from those around her.

Now some of those small bobbles and incon-sistencies began to make a great deal more sense. While he couldn't quite prevent himself from being angry with her for the way she'd hidden the truth from him, he also couldn't pretend to guess how he might have felt if he'd ended up decades or more from where he'd started, all without any way of knowing how he'd ever get home.

"But…you were here in Jerome when it happened," he said, and Deborah—Devynn, he reminded himself—nodded at once.

"My gift only allows me to travel in time, not space."

"Is Rowe your real last name?"

"Yes," she said promptly—so promptly he could tell she wasn't lying this time.

"Are you a member of the McAllister clan?" he asked then. After all, even though that last name was the one which dominated the clan, there were plenty of other surnames in use as well, thanks to the numerous nonmagical folk who'd joined the family over the years.

Finally, her gaze strayed away from his, but only for a second or two, as though she'd wanted to look down the hill toward the town before she responded.

"No," she replied. "I was just staying in town for a while. In my time, the people in Jerome are a lot more relaxed about letting witches who aren't members of the clan hang out for a bit."

Seth wasn't sure what "hanging out" meant, but he guessed it must simply mean to be present in a place for a time.

"Then what clan are you from?"

Possibly the barest hesitation. When she

spoke, though, she sounded forthright enough. "My clan is the Winfield clan from Massachusetts."

Well, at least she wasn't a Wilcox. Not that she looked like one—from what Seth had heard, the Wilcoxes tended to be quite dark, thanks to the Navajo blood that had been mixed into the clan over the years—but since they were the nearest clan geographically to the McAllisters, that would have been the most logical explanation.

But…Massachusetts?

"What in the world are you doing all the way out here in Jerome?"

She twisted the hat she held, creasing the delicate straw, and for a moment, she didn't look up at him, as though she was trying to decide how best to respond.

"Visiting, like I told you," she said. "In my time, it's no big deal to cross the continent. I wanted a change of scenery."

Seth could only gaze back at her, feeling as if there was a great deal she must be leaving out and wondering if she would ever tell him everything. But there was one fundamental question that needed an answer.

"When exactly are you from?"

A dark shadow moved over them, and she sucked in a gasp of air before she seemed to realize it was only an owl, rousing itself to go hunt in the gloaming.

"More than a hundred years from now," she said, her voice a little firmer than it had been a moment earlier. "But I don't think it's a good idea for me to tell you much more than that. There's always the risk that if I say too much about the future, it'll change history, and that's the last thing you want happening."

Seth had to admit he'd never had to think about the ramifications of time travel, even if he had spent one glorious Saturday afternoon a few years ago lost in H.G. Wells' *The Time Machine.* It was certainly one thing to read about such matters in a book and quite another to have them facing him down in the form of the woman he loved.

"Have you…?" He hated to ask the question, but some part of him needed to know whether she viewed their relationship as seriously as he did, or whether she'd only been amusing herself while trying to figure out a way back home. "Have you tried to travel to your own time?"

Once again, her lips pressed together. "In the beginning, yes. It never worked—like I said, I can't really control this 'gift' of mine. But after a while…."

The words trailed off, and he thought he understood why she'd stopped herself from completing the sentence. Doing so would have meant admitting that, after a while, she began to realize she had feelings for him…and wasn't quite as eager to return to her own time as she might once have been.

"How did you do it, though?" he asked. "How could you hide your witch nature from everybody? How could you hide it from me?"

Now her head went back up, although he didn't think it was out of pride. More…relief that she wouldn't have to conceal the truth anymore.

"It's my other gift, one I inherited from my father," she said. "I can hide who I am from other witches and warlocks. I suppose it's some sort of survival trait that came about as a way to protect a witch from enemy clans, but it doesn't seem as if it has ever occurred in any other family but the Rowes. At least, none that I've heard of."

No, Seth had never heard of such a thing, either. Possibly he could go to Mabel and ask her opinion on the matter, since she took great pride in studying witch history and most likely knew far more about all their various magical talents than he did.

Some inner impulse told him that wasn't a very good idea. He couldn't exactly say why, but even though he knew he was still upset with Devynn for the way she'd hidden the truth from him, he also thought it might be better if her secret remained between just the two of them for now.

"No one in my clan has a talent like that," he said. "And I don't remember ever hearing about it, so I don't know if it exists anywhere except among your people. I suppose it was helpful in your particular situation."

He knew he sounded cold, but he couldn't quite stop himself. Devynn had been lying to him for the past two weeks, and even though some people might have said she had ample reason for such concealment, he couldn't help thinking that if she liked him enough to want to kiss him, then she should have damn well been able to trust him with the truth, as implausible as it might have sounded.

"Yes, it was," she replied. Her tone had cooled as well, as though she'd had time to gauge his reaction and had decided she had better match him reaction for reaction. "I don't expect you to understand why I didn't confide in you."

"I *do* understand," he said. "Or at least, I can see why you needed some time to be sure of me before you revealed something so outrageous. And if you'd told me the truth, I would have done my best to help you, no matter how crazy your story might have sounded. Now…."

The words drifted away. Was there any point in finishing that sentence?

360 | CHRISTINE POPE

"Nothing's changed," she told him, her tone now emphatic. "I wouldn't have come here today if I hadn't wanted to spend the time with you. I wouldn't have kissed you if that hadn't been exactly what I wanted. You cared about me when you thought I was a civilian, so what does it matter that I'm a witch?"

"'What does it matter?'" he repeated, knowing how incredulous he sounded. "Being a witch or a warlock is the very basis for who we are! How can you possibly say that it doesn't matter?"

"In my case, it doesn't," Devynn said, her voice now very firm, very sure of itself. "Yes, I may be a witch, but I'm also a thousand other things. It doesn't define me. I won't allow it to, especially when one of my talents is so unpredictable—so dangerous—that I would much rather have never had it at all."

Underneath his anger, pity stirred. His own gift had always been so strong, so predictable and there for him whenever he needed it, that he had no idea what it would have felt like if it was as capricious as Devynn's. Would he have been so proud to be a McAllister warlock if his magical talent might have sent him to London one time and to the North Pole the next, all without any conscious direction from him?

That would be no way to live.

"I like you, Seth," Devynn said then. Neither

her face nor her tone were pleading as she uttered those words. No, it was more that she wanted to make sure he understood how she felt, and he could do with that information as he willed. "I like you a lot. The whole time, I've been trying to think of a way to let you know who I really was and where—*when*—I came from. But I suppose I was a coward."

Her voice faltered just the slightest bit on that last word, and Seth found himself wavering. It was all very well and good to feel righteous about the way she'd concealed her identity and her past from him…but he wasn't a woman. He had no idea what it would feel like to be thousands of miles and more than a hundred years away from everyone she knew, from anyone who might have stepped in to protect her.

No wonder she'd thought she needed to hide her witch nature—and everything else about her identity—until she was absolutely sure of him.

"It's all right," he said…even as he wondered if it actually was. He needed some time to think about what had just happened, what he'd learned. "But I should probably take you home now."

The moon had risen enough that its cool light had begun to filter through the trees. Deborah looked paler than ever as she gazed at him, expression especially troubled. "Are you going to tell them?"

Some people might have said that he needed to let the entire clan know about the witch from the future who'd been hiding in their midst. But Seth understood how precarious Deborah's position was here. The last thing he would ever do was jeopardize the shelter Ruth and Timothy had provided for her. Maybe that was being dishonest, but he knew they enjoyed having her there, now that their youngest child had married and moved on to make a life of her own.

Eventually, sure, Deborah would have to decide what to do next, since she obviously couldn't live on the McAllisters' charity forever. For now, though....

"No," he said clearly. "I'm not going to tell them."

Yet, he added mentally.

19

COVERT OPERATIONS

WHEN PUSH CAME TO SHOVE, I STILL HADN'T told him everything. I couldn't have. Bad enough that he knew I wasn't really Deborah and that I'd landed in 1926 from a time more than a hundred years in the future. But to also reveal I was half Wilcox?

That, as my father might have said, was a bridge too far.

Okay, sure, I'd been lying to Seth for the past two weeks…out of pure self-preservation. But once he discovered I was a witch—once that insanely amazing kiss we shared somehow short-circuited my one reliable power and let him know exactly what I was—my brain had gone into instant damage-control mode.

It was one thing for him to realize I was a witch.

It would be something entirely different for him to learn that I was also a Wilcox, a member of a clan all the McAllisters despised. My lies had already stretched the connection between the two of us to the breaking point. If I told him who my mother was, where I'd been raised...I honestly didn't know whether we'd recover from that revelation.

We drove back down to Jerome in silence, and although Seth was still the soul of politeness, opening my car door and walking me up the porch steps just like he always did, I could tell something was different. He didn't try to take my hand, and he didn't smile. No, he just bade me a good evening and then headed back to his convertible, even as I did my best to ignore the sinking sensation in my gut.

I didn't linger there to watch him drive away like I might have a few days earlier. Instead, I went inside, glad that the house seemed dark and still except for one crystal-accented lamp on a table in the foyer.

That way, I could get upstairs before Ruth appeared to ask me how my date had gone.

Somehow, I managed to hold it together until I was safely in my room with the door closed behind me. Then I stumbled over to the bed and fell down on it so I could let the tears come.

Not noisy sobbing, though. I didn't want to

take the smallest chance that either Ruth or Timothy could overhear me. Better to lie there and allow the tears to silently slide down my cheeks, releasing all the worry and hurt and fear that had been building for the past two weeks.

This whole time, I'd never had an endgame in mind. How could I, when I had no idea how long I might remain lost in the past, thanks to a gift I couldn't control and which appeared to have deserted me?

But some part of my mind and heart had envisioned a future with Seth McAllister. Despite the mess I was in, I knew I couldn't deny how I felt when I was around him, how I was safe and happy...and also aroused by the smallest brush of his fingers against mine, even the way those clear blue eyes of his would meet my gaze.

If I couldn't go home, I could make a life with him here.

At least, that's what I'd believed, deep down in a place I hadn't really wanted to acknowledge. Of course it hurt to think I would never see my family or friends again, to have them forever wonder what had happened to me, but I'd thought maybe I could work my way past all that if I had Seth at my side. After all, my father had done much the same thing, realizing that my mother had brought him to the twenty-first century out of love and desperation, knowing that was the only way she could keep him alive after he'd been gut shot by Samuel Wilcox, Jeremiah Wilcox's villainous younger brother. My father had made his peace with saying goodbye to that part of himself, and I'd thought I could eventually get to that place as well.

Would I have told Seth the truth?

At some point, of course. On my own terms, when I thought we were in the right place for that kind of discussion. The last thing I'd ever believed was that such a moment would be thrust on me by what appeared to be a wildly combustible chemistry.

If I ever got back to my own time, I'd need to ask someone about that. Not my father— posing such a question to him would have been way too embarrassing, even if he was the only other person I knew who possessed the same odd gift of concealing their witch heritage— but maybe Angela, whose connection to Connor Wilcox had its own quirks and unexpected side effects.

Eventually, my tears stopped flowing. Ruth had thoughtfully provided a whole box of new handkerchiefs for me, maybe fearing I had allergies that would flare up when surrounded by all these junipers and cottonwood trees. So far, I hadn't needed them, but I pulled one out now and wiped my eyes and blew my nose. The fine cotton was surprisingly soft, almost as good as a tissue from my own time would have been.

Now that I'd cried it out, I found myself calmer than I would have expected. Sure, things were still a mess between Seth and me, but I had to believe we could work through this somehow. After all, he hadn't said he would expose me, hadn't threatened to tell Ruth and Timothy, which might have endangered my somewhat shaky position as their houseguest. As far as I could tell, Seth intended to keep my secret.

And that made me feel worse than ever. He shouldn't have to lie for me and be part of this cover-up I'd concocted for myself.

It was a horribly tangled web, one that I needed to unravel piece by piece...no matter what.

You have to stop, I realized then. *You have to go to him and tell him the rest.*

While that inner voice sounded confident enough, the cowardly part of me quailed all over again. What would Seth do once he learned I wasn't just a witch from the future, but a member of the hated Wilcox clan?

I really didn't want to think about his reaction.

On the other hand, I couldn't keep lying like this. He had to know that in the world I came from, the Wilcoxes and the McAllisters were allies, were far more connected than he could even begin to imagine. He was smart enough to understand that some of what I revealed would need to be kept between the two of us, but if I ever wanted a future with him, then I'd have to tell him everything I'd been hiding.

Tomorrow, I would go and talk to Seth McAllister. It would probably be the hardest thing I'd ever done, but he needed to know everything. What happened after full disclosure…well, I supposed I'd figure that out when the time came.

Drained but also strangely light of heart, I set aside the handkerchief I'd been holding and started to get ready for bed.

Of course, getting a chance to talk to Seth was easier said than done. True, I supposed it would have been even more difficult if he'd still been working at the mine, but finding the opportunity to speak with him alone while he was manning the counter at his family's mercantile presented its own set of challenges.

I reasoned that he would have to take a lunch break at some point, and probably the best thing to do would be to see if he headed for home or whether he only went around the corner to the English Kitchen to get something quick and easy.

This wasn't the sort of conversation I wanted to have in a public place, but still, better there than at the store. Besides, I could always try to convince him that we needed to talk at his house. Considering the topic, he'd probably want to make sure no one overheard us anyway.

This all sounded like a reasonable enough plan. I told Ruth I was going for a walk down Main Street, and while she seemed a little surprised that I'd want to be away during lunch, she didn't try to stop me.

"I'll just put a sandwich aside for you, dear, and you can have that when you get back."

I thanked her and headed out. Just like almost every other day since I'd come to 1926 Jerome, the skies were brilliantly blue overhead, the sun warm, verging on hot. However, the little hat I wore helped to shade my eyes more than I'd thought it would, and the dress of fine, pale green cotton I wore was surprisingly crisp and cool.

After I started walking down the street, a few people smiled or even waved when I went by. Although I certainly hadn't been partying hearty while I was here, I'd met enough of the town's residents—McAllisters or otherwise—that we had at least a nodding acquaintance. Their acknowledgments helped to ground me a bit, making me feel as though I might have a chance at making a real life here.

If, of course, Seth ever forgave me for all my lies.

But just as I was approaching the store, a dark green truck drove past, clearly headed down the hill toward Cottonwood.

Seth was behind the wheel.

Goddamn it.

I almost pivoted on my heel and started walking back to where I'd come from, but some instinct stopped me. For one thing, Ruth might think it a little strange that I'd come right back to the house after telling her I'd be out for at least an hour or so, and besides, even if Seth wasn't here, that didn't mean I couldn't go inside and get the lay of the land, so to speak. If his mother acted cold toward me, then I'd know he must have told her at least something of what had passed between us the night before.

If not...well, maybe I'd be able to get some information out of her.

And I had two whole quarters burning a hole in my purse, thanks to Ruth telling me I should have a little cash on hand in case I saw something I wanted to buy and handing the coins over as I was about to walk out the door.

I pushed the mercantile's door inward and went inside the shop. It was much dimmer in there than outside, and I blinked as my eyes adjusted to the sudden shift in lighting.

"Oh, Miss Rowe," Molly McAllister said. She stood off to my left behind the counter, and, judging by the bolts of fabric that sat nearby, must have just finished measuring material for one of her customers. "I'm afraid you just missed Seth. He had to drive down to Cottonwood to pick up a few things."

Something I already knew, of course, but I did my best to feign dismay. "I sometimes think I have the worst timing in the world," I replied. As far as I could tell, nothing in her expression or her attitude seemed to signal that she knew anything more about me than she already had, which meant Seth must have kept our conversation to himself. "But since I'm here, I'll go ahead and look for a few things I've been needing."

Molly smiled. In her clear-cut features and bright blue eyes, I could see something of Seth, although of course, he was much taller and sturdier. "Just let me know if you need help with anything."

I nodded, then headed over to the part of the store where they kept small bibs and bobs like combs and brushes and scissors, nail files, that kind of thing. Since I'd given myself a nasty hangnail that morning, it seemed a good idea to get a file and a small pair of nail scissors.

After some deliberation, I selected the items I wanted and headed over to the cash register. As

Molly was ringing me up, I ventured, "You have so many different items here in the store that I can see why Seth needed to work late yesterday evening to help with inventory."

She blinked at me, her pretty features now a study in puzzlement. "'Inventory'?" she echoed, then shook her head. "Oh, no. I think you must have misheard him. We always do inventory on Sundays, since that's the only day we're closed. And we're not planning to do that for a little while, anyway, since we took stock of everything at the beginning of May."

Interesting. So, Seth had lied to me about why he needed to cancel our date. Although irritation flared, I told myself I was the last person to be getting on my high horse about him misrepresenting something, not when I'd been lying about pretty much everything since the moment I awakened in his bungalow and realized I wasn't in Kansas anymore.

Or even in the twenty-first century.

I put on a silly little smile, one I hoped Molly would think was my way of laughing at myself for getting things so wrong. "Oh, I suppose I did," I said. "We were talking about the store, and it seems I misinterpreted what he said about doing inventory."

She handed me my change and the little paper bag of sundries I'd just purchased. "It's fine.

Do you want me to let him know you stopped by?"

"No, that's all right," I said hastily. "I know he's busy. I'll leave him a note later."

"I'm sure he would like that," Molly replied. "You have a good day, Miss Rowe."

A hasty nod and another smile, and I made my escape. As I was walking up the hill toward Ruth and Timothy's house, though, that smile soon turned into a puzzled frown.

What exactly had Seth been doing last night that would have made him cancel our date? I knew it couldn't have been our argument, because he'd already called off our evening of dancing and fun in Cottonwood before he even discovered I was a witch.

No, something else had to be going on here… and I was determined to find out what it was.

In the end, my plan was pretty much the same one as I'd used earlier in the day—to lurk near the store and see where Seth went after he got off work. Maybe he would go straight home and I'd end up feeling like an idiot for being so suspicious, but if he hadn't told me the truth about doing inventory the night before, then I really had no idea what else he might be hiding.

I got out of dinner by telling Ruth that I was going to walk down to the mercantile and meet him once he was done for the day, and luckily, she didn't seem to detect anything suspicious about that story, instead only telling me she hoped I would have a nice time.

Well, I didn't know about nice, but I hoped it would be informative...and not leave me with some proverbial egg on my face.

Hanging around on the sidewalk in front of the store wouldn't work at all, obviously, but if Seth was going straight home, then he'd turn down Hull Avenue and walk to his bungalow along that route. At that time of year, all the trees and shrubs and flowers in Jerome were happy and full, and I was able to lurk behind a couple of exuberant-looking boxwood shrubs and be mostly hidden that way.

However, he didn't come down the steep sidewalk just beyond my hiding place. No, I heard the rumble of a truck starting up and realized the sound was Seth getting ready to drive off in the big green Dodge the family used for business.

Another errand in Cottonwood?

The truck approached, and I crouched lower, praying he wouldn't be able to see me. It was moving slowly, heading toward the street, and a wild idea sprang into my head.

I didn't stop to think. No, I bolted out from

my hiding place and jumped into the truck's bed just as Seth began to make the turn onto Hull Avenue.

The bed was composed of bare boards, and I held back a curse as my hipbone collided with the hard surface. It wasn't exactly clean back there, either, and my pretty green dress was almost immediately smudged.

Well, it wasn't anything that Ruth and her trusty Fels Naptha bar—and maybe a little magic —couldn't fix.

The truck turned right and then right again onto Main Street, heading up the hill past the fire station and the pretty little Catholic church—a near shambles in my own time—past the sanatorium that would one day become the Grand Hotel, and then rumbled its way up the mountain.

Was Seth going to Prescott? I had to admit I wasn't looking forward to crouching back here that whole time, especially since I knew it would be very cold at the top of the mountain, much chillier than the kind of temperatures my lightweight dress had been designed for.

But then the truck slowed, and we turned onto a narrow dirt road that looked as though it led to the mine.

Why would Seth be coming back here? Hadn't he quit his job?

Somehow I doubted he'd be returning to the United Verde after hours like this just to close out his locker.

I didn't dare poke my head up too far lest he realize he had a stowaway, so I couldn't see much except scrubby hillsides looming above me. This didn't look like the kind of open pit the United Verde used to extract the precious copper ore from the earth here, and I wondered again where Seth was going...and what he was up to.

Eventually, the truck came to a stop. I waited, holding my breath and thinking of what the hell I was going to say when he discovered me back here.

Footsteps crunched away from the truck and then disappeared. I poked my head above the truck's bed and saw it had been parked in an isolated spot with a partially boarded-up mine shaft a few yards away. Seth was nowhere in sight, which meant he must have already gone inside.

Something about the place felt strangely familiar, with the hillside looming above and the rocky, neglected road that dead-ended only a few yards away, and then it struck me.

This was the mine shaft where Bellamy had teased me about going inside...the one where I'd somehow slipped back in time, even if I still didn't entirely know how such a thing could have happened.

What was Seth doing in there? Had he returned to the shaft to see if there was some piece of evidence he'd missed, something I'd left behind that might corroborate my story about tripping and falling into 1926?

Something about that theory didn't feel right, but I honestly couldn't think of any other reason to come back here. The place was desolate and clearly unused, a dead end that hadn't panned out.

He still hadn't appeared, which meant it was time for me to go in search of him. While I didn't much like the idea of walking back inside that mine shaft, I had to admit that I couldn't think of a more private place to hold a conversation.

And since I'd already resolved to tell him everything, I might as well get my ass in gear.

I scooched my way out of the truck bed and did my best to smooth my skirt, although, as I'd feared, the dress was rumpled and dirty, and definitely not crisp and pretty like it had been when I first put it on this morning. The cloche hat I wore felt tight on my head, so I took it off and tossed it in the bed of the truck, then pushed a few loose strands of hair off my face.

For some reason, I just felt more like me when I was bare-headed. And I needed to be the most "me" I possibly could when I made my confession to Seth.

An uneasy sensation stirred in my stomach as

I approached the opening in the hillside. From here, I could tell that one of the boards seemed to have been attached in such a way that it was easy to be set aside as needed, just as it had been now. Everything appeared utterly dark inside, although logic told me he must be using a lantern or something to guide his way, and I just couldn't see it from where I stood.

I really didn't want to go in there.

Don't be stupid, I scolded myself. *Seth went in, so it's perfectly safe.*

Maybe. However, I couldn't quite ignore the fact that it was inside this mine shaft that I'd slipped through time.

What if I slipped again before I had a chance to explain myself to Seth?

No, that was a ridiculous idea. It was my so-called talent that had hurled me back to 1926, not the mine itself. The location had nothing to do with it.

I gritted my teeth, told myself not to be a pansy, and walked inside. The beams holding up the walls and the ceiling were fresh, raw pine, not the age-weathered wood I'd seen when I went inside the shaft on a hot summer evening that seemed as if it was from a different lifetime, but otherwise, the place looked much the same.

Well, except the lantern that had been set on the gravel-strewn ground a few feet away—and

Seth himself, who had just emerged from a little alcove sheltered by boulders toward the back of the shaft, heavy glass jugs full of amber liquid dangling from either hand.

"Deborah?" he said, his shocked voice echoing off the rock walls. "What the hell are you doing here?"

"I found out you hadn't told me the truth when you said you were doing inventory last night," I replied calmly. "And that got me thinking that I might not be the only person keeping secrets around here. So, tonight I decided to find out what you were really up to."

He shook his head. "It's not safe for you to be here."

"Why?" I asked, then nodded toward the jugs he held. "Are those what I think they are?"

Seth looked down at the bottles of moonshine, almost as if he'd forgotten he was holding them. "Yes. And we can talk about that later. Right now, you just need to get back down to Ruth and Timothy's house."

"I don't even know how to get there from here," I said, which was only partly true. Sure, I'd been crouched in the bed of the truck the whole time and therefore hadn't seen exactly where he was going, but I'd driven up here with Bellamy, so at least I had a rough idea.

That didn't mean I wanted to hike all the way

back into town, even though I'd had brains enough to put on my sensible shoes for this little spying expedition.

His mouth flattened, and I could tell he was less than thrilled with me. What had seemed like a brilliant idea back at the house now seemed not quite so brilliant.

Then again, how was I supposed to know Seth McAllister was a bootlegger?

"I don't have time to take you back into Jerome," he said. "I have to get this stuff to Prescott before nine, or there'll be hell to pay."

That I could imagine. While I hadn't done an in-depth study of bootleggers and their various activities, I had to believe they weren't the most forgiving people in the world.

"I can wait here until you get back," I said. "Or I can just ride along."

If possible, his expression grew even more pained. "There's no room," he replied. "I have to carry this stuff in the cab so it can't be seen by anyone I drive past, and I'm not about to leave you in the bed of the truck, not with night falling. It'll be way too cold for you in that dress."

Something I'd already thought about, so I wasn't going to contradict him. "Then I guess I'll wait here," I said cheerfully. "I mean, no one else knows you came to this mine shaft, right?"

"No," Seth responded, although he didn't look

very happy with my solution. "I made sure I wasn't followed. But…." He stopped there, brows drawing together. "Why did you get in the truck, anyway?"

"Because I wanted to talk to you," I said. "I wanted to tell you the truth."

Now he appeared more confused than anything else. "I thought you already did."

This was it. Even though my heart started to beat a little faster, and my stomach tightened at the thought of revealing who I really was, I knew I had to say the words. I had to leave the lies behind and let him know the real reason why I'd felt so compelled to hide my identity.

My mouth opened. "I—"

Before I could get any further than that, however, a new voice echoed through the mine shaft.

"Just what the hell is going on here?" Charles McAllister demanded.

20

A SHOT IN THE DARK

SETH BLINKED. THE SITUATION WAS ALREADY bad enough, thanks to the way Devynn Rowe had thought it a good idea to follow him here, but to have his brother turn up like this out of nowhere?

"It's all right," he said hurriedly. "We were just having a little chat."

Charles came farther into the mine shaft, and she inched closer to Seth. Her face was pale and her dress smudged with dirt—he guessed she must have hidden in the bed of the truck, and he, so preoccupied with making sure this moonshine run went off without a hitch, hadn't even noticed—but he noticed the way her chin set in defiance as she stared back at his brother.

"A private one," she said pointedly, and a corner of Charles's mouth lifted in a sneer.

"Funny place for it," he remarked, then returned his attention to his brother. "You couldn't even get this one simple thing right, could you? You had to bring her along, when you knew this place needed to be kept a secret."

The dim lantern light couldn't quite hide the flash of Devynn's eyes. "How can it be a secret from me when this was the very spot where Seth found me two weeks ago? I suppose I can see why you would want to keep your activities secret from the rest of Jerome, but it's not as if I didn't already know this mine shaft existed."

"A fair point," Charles conceded, although something in his voice told Seth he hadn't much liked acknowledging she was correct about that one particular of the situation. "However, it doesn't mean you have any reason to be here now...unless you were snooping where you shouldn't have been. Incompetent as my brother often is, I still doubt he would have brought you here on purpose."

An angry retort rose to Seth's lips, but he swallowed it before he could say the words aloud. There was no point in arguing with Charles now. The only thing he wanted to do was to get Devynn away from here as quickly as possible. He would lose precious time taking her down the hill to Ruth's house, but he absolutely couldn't leave her here, no matter how confident she'd seemed to be when she said she was fine with waiting in the mine shaft until he returned. The trip to Prescott would take at least an hour and a half even if he pushed the truck to its top speed of forty-five miles an hour, and what was she supposed to do during that time? Simply stand here and wait for him? Sit on the dirty ground, thus ensuring the ruin of her dress?

Devynn's hands went to her hips. "I don't think it's any business of yours why I'm here, Charles McAllister. That's between Seth and me. But if you're worried about me telling someone what I've seen, don't be. I can keep a secret."

That's for sure, passed through Seth's mind. However, the last thing he intended to do was let Charles know anything about all the secrets Devynn Rowe had been hiding for the past two weeks.

Charles began to open his mouth to reply, but Seth forestalled him, saying, "I'll bring her in the truck with me."

His brother didn't appear at all satisfied by that solution. "And show her where the drop-off location is? I don't think so. Besides, you'd never be able to fit the promised number of jugs in the cab if she's in there with you."

Fair point. Still, Seth wasn't about to let it go

that easily. "She can carry some," he replied. "And I'll leave her somewhere in Prescott before I get to my destination, then come back and get her. At least that way, she'll only be alone for ten or fifteen minutes, not more than an hour."

"Still unacceptable," Charles said. "I'll drive her back to Jerome, and you can go ahead with the delivery as planned."

Seth didn't like that idea very much. True, he didn't see any real reason why he shouldn't allow Devynn to be alone with his brother for the few minutes he'd be driving her down the hill—as a promised consort, it wasn't as though he would have designs on her person or anything close to it —but still, he worried that Charles might try to press her as to the real reason why she'd followed him here.

She'd been about to tell him something… something that was obviously important to her, or she wouldn't have attempted such a desperate gambit as stowing away in the truck in the first place.

What in the world could she still be hiding? Hadn't she already confessed everything to him?

On the surface, Charles's plan seemed like the most logical one. But something about the situation just didn't smell right.

"Why were you up here at all, Charles?" he

demanded. "Didn't you trust me to show up when I said I would?"

"This has nothing to do with 'trust,'" his brother replied. However, his gaze shifted away for just the barest second, and Seth realized he was lying, that he'd truly thought his younger brother couldn't manage such a simple task as gathering tonight's shipment and taking it to Prescott... something he shouldn't have had to do in the first place, since he'd already done one of these infernal runs the night before. But Charles had slipped him a note saying they needed an emergency shipment tonight as well, and Seth had known there wasn't a damn thing he could do to protest the situation. Voice taut, Charles went on, "This was about making sure that everything continues to go smoothly. Believe me, you don't want to make any mistakes with these people, and I needed to be sure that last night's shipment wasn't a fluke."

A warning Charles had made before. In that moment, though, Seth couldn't help wondering if his brother was truly concerned about his physical well-being, or whether he simply wanted to avoid the kind of messiness that might draw the eyes of the authorities toward the McAllister clan.

Or maybe it was a little of both.

Devynn had been watching the back-and-forth, a bit like someone surveying a particularly intense volley session during a tennis match. Now, though, her arched brows pulled into a frown and she said, "I can wait here, or I can go with you, Seth. But I don't want your brother to drive me back to Jerome."

"A lovely display of trust," Charles drawled, and her eyes narrowed further.

"I don't think you've given me much of a reason to trust you," she retorted, then went on before he could respond. "In fact, it's pretty clear to me that you were the one involved in bootlegging, and now that you're engaged, you want to fob it off on Seth. Tell me I'm wrong."

Had anyone ever stood up to Charles like that before? Seth somehow doubted it. The women in their clan were no shrinking violets, but as the eldest son in his immediate family and the one who would have inherited the store if he hadn't become Abigail's consort, he also held a position of some respect in the McAllister clan.

"It doesn't matter what I tell you," he replied, his tone unconcerned, "since it's fairly clear to me that you've already made up your mind on the subject. And if you think it better to stand here in this damp, chilly mine shaft for the greater part of two hours while my brother does the job he promised to do, so be it. You will not, however, accompany him to Prescott. He can't spare the time. Understood?"

For a moment, Devynn only stood there,

matching Charles stare for stare, hands placed on her hips. It wasn't as if she relented, precisely, rather that she seemed to decide the matter wasn't worth any further argument.

"Understood," she replied. "But you don't mind if I walk him to his truck, do you?"

"Not at all," Charles said smoothly. "You can help carry the rest of the cargo to the vehicle. That way, we'll make up some of the time we've lost bickering over this foolishness."

Her mouth set, but she didn't say anything, only marched over to the little alcove where the rest of the jugs he'd already prepared were waiting and scooped up several of them. Feeling resigned, Seth bent down to pick up the ones he'd originally been carrying when all of this started, and Charles did his part as well, going to retrieve his load of contraband.

They all headed out to the truck, which was now shrouded in true shadow, with the sun set well behind the mountain. Because of this, Seth didn't even notice the tall shadow that stepped out from behind a concealing boulder before it was too late.

"Quite the party here, McAllister," Lionel Allenby said, and Seth froze.

What the hell was he doing up here?

Charles startled—and then seemed to realize it was better to affect an attitude of unconcern, even as Devynn continued setting the jugs of moon-shine on the floorboard in front of the truck's passenger seat. Speaking quickly, he said, "My brother is making the new shipment as promised. Everything remains on schedule."

"Does it?" Allenby returned, moving closer. He flicked a negligent glance at his wristwatch and added, "Because it seems to me as if you're running a bit late."

"I'm leaving right after this," Seth said, knowing he needed to say whatever he could to salvage the situation, even as he prayed like hell that none of the tension gripping his body had found its way into his voice. "It's a difference of fifteen minutes at the most. I can make that time up on the road."

Lionel Allenby didn't appear moved by that argument. His mouth flattened into an ugly line, and then he said, "It seems I was right in coming here to check on you tonight, since I didn't believe you could handle two back-to-back shipments when one job was given to you at the last minute. I still wasn't convinced by your brother's argument that the transition would be seamless. He had a fire in his belly for this work, while you"—a contemptuous flare of his nostrils—"always seemed like the worst sort of Goody Two-Shoes. And to bring a woman into all this?"

Now finished with putting the moonshine in

the truck, Devynn turned back around, her expression indignant. "He didn't 'bring' me into anything," she said. "I came here without him knowing, and I offered to help to get things back on track."

The sneer never left Allenby's face. "How very Christian of you," he replied. "But you see, you've only proven how careless he is, if you could sneak up on him without him even noticing. We can't afford to have that sort of sloppiness in our operation."

"It won't happen again," Seth cut in. He definitely didn't like the way Lionel Allenby was looking at Devynn—not with desire, but with the expression of a man who needed to rid himself of an unexpected complication.

"Oh, I know it won't happen," Allenby replied. With one hand, he reached into his jacket pocket and pulled out a pearl-handled revolver.

Devynn released a startled gasp, although she didn't move, and Charles said hurriedly, "There's no need for this, Allenby. They'll keep their mouths shut."

"Yes, they will. What's that old saying? Dead men tell no tales? I suppose that goes for women as well."

The sound of the pistol going off was much louder than Seth had expected. Devynn cried out, hands going to cover the splotch of blood on her midsection, a stain that spread even as he watched with horrified eyes.

"You bastard!" he bellowed.

His first instinct was to run to the man and tear the pistol from his grasp, but Charles was much closer. One hand went up and hit Allenby solidly in the jaw, and the man staggered backward. He fired again, but this time, the bullet went wild, ricocheting off the rocky hillside above them rather than finding its target.

And then Charles got hold of the pistol and flung it off the cliff before battering his opponent with more blows, sending him to his knees.

All this happened in what felt like a single flash of a moment, both men moving almost too quickly for Seth's mind to grasp, and at the same time, feeling like a still frame rather than real life.

But he realized Devynn had sunk to the ground, her breath coming in shallow pants, and he hurried over to her so he could pull her into his arms.

"It's all right," he said. "We'll get you to Helen."

Could Helen cure a gunshot wound to the stomach? She was very talented, but the men of the McAllister clan did their best to avoid confrontations such as this, and that meant Seth didn't know for sure whether their healer ever been called upon to perform that kind of advanced care.

Devynn's lashes fluttered. "I'm so sorry," she murmured. "This is all my fault."

He held her tighter, not wanting to notice how her breathing had already grown more labored, how blood now stained most of her skirt as well.

How could she possibly survive the rough ride down the hill, with the truck bouncing and jouncing her the whole way?

Dimly, he realized that Charles had knocked Lionel Allenby out cold, for the older man was now slumped against the rocky soil, eyes shut. Panting a little, Charles came over to them where they rested on the ground, his face now pale.

"Is she…?"

"She's going to make it," Seth said, his voice sharp. Maybe that was a lie, a pretty fiction his mind had invented because he didn't want to face the truth, but he feared if he spoke the other words out loud, the ones that truly described Devynn's situation, then he would make it all a terrible reality, one he couldn't hide from.

Apparently, his brother understood this was not a point to argue over. Instead, he pulled off his jacket and handed it over, saying, "Hold this against her wound. It might help. And I'll get the truck started."

Yes, the important thing was to get Devynn down the hill and to Helen's house. Perhaps in that time, Lionel Allenby would wake up and flee the scene, but they could deal with him later. Just because the McAllister clan preferred not to resort to violence, it didn't mean they couldn't take care of a troublesome situation when it arose…even if it involved a more permanent solution to a problem than they generally cared to utilize.

Charles hurried over to the truck, and Devynn's eyes fluttered open, fixing on Seth's with an intensity he wouldn't have thought possible in her current condition.

"I wanted…." The words trailed off there, and she pulled in a ragged breath. "I wanted…to tell you…."

"It's all right," he said, and even though he knew it wasn't his gift, he willed with every cell in his body all his strength and his health to her, just so she'd be able to hold on for a few minutes more. Ten minutes, and they would be at Helen's house, and then Devynn would be safe.

A gasp, and this time, there was a terrible rattle to the sound. He'd never heard it before, but he knew what it meant.

Death was coming for the woman he loved, implacable and unmoving as the lengthening shadows that loomed over them as they sat there on the stony ground.

"Kiss me, Seth," she whispered. "Kiss me before I go."

This couldn't be happening. Dimly, as if from another world, he heard the sound of the truck's engine starting, a rumble that might have reassured him if he hadn't known it was already too late.

What could he do except as she asked?

He bent and pressed his lips against hers, lips that still were warm and soft.

The world spun around him, whirling faster and faster into a terrible darkness deeper and blacker than anything he'd ever known. He clung to Devynn, wondering if this was death approaching, not knowing what he could possibly do to hold back the embrace of the Grim Reaper... except, perhaps, to continue to cling to her as tightly as he could and never let go.

A bump, and the darkness receded, leaving them in a place Seth knew he had never seen before. Gone were the rocky hillsides and the dry yellow grass and the indistinct, oddly shaped shadows of nearby agave plants. Instead, he stood on a neat little flagstone path in front of an imposing Victorian house, bigger than even Mabel's near-mansion on Paradise Lane, painted a pale sage color with blood-red and darker green accents on its shutters and cornices. The wind that blew past his cheek was chilly, a far cry from the warm, summery air that had surrounded them on Mingus Mountain.

What was this place?

He staggered a step forward, noting as he did so that this appeared to be a street of similarly handsome houses, although the one in front of him was definitely the biggest of the lot, with substantial columns and stained-glass windows flanking the front door and accenting the third story of the house, right under its peaked gable. The trees planted here were young, not much taller than he, and already blazing in shades of orange and yellow and red.

Autumn, then…wherever he was.

In his arms, Devynn shifted, although her eyes were shut, and her breathing had become even more labored. Her blood had drenched his shirt front, horribly warm, and he knew he didn't have much time now.

But how could he get her help when he had no idea where they even were?

An odd clopping sound came to his ears, and he looked over his shoulder to see a horse-drawn carriage moving slowly down the street past them. The driver didn't seem to have noticed Seth or the woman he carried, because he didn't pause to ask them if they needed any help.

A carriage? Sure, they still used teams of horses or mules at the mine for situations when it made more sense to have them draw a wagon than load up multiple trucks with ore and tailings or such, but Seth couldn't remember the last time he'd ever seen someone using one as a regular daily conveyance.

Not that it mattered right now. What mattered was going up to the door of the house in front of him and knocking and begging for help. Maybe there wasn't anyone at home who could offer assistance, but he had to at least try. Surely whoever lived there would take pity on the dying woman in his arms and send for a doctor.

Possibly too little, too late, but in the absence of his clan's healer, Seth couldn't think of any other options. He still had no idea precisely where he was, but he knew it had to be far, far away from Jerome. His mind didn't quite want to grasp the significance of the autumn color on the trees and the chill in the air, not when it was so obviously summer where they'd come from, so he put that foreboding little detail aside to worry about later.

A staggering step down the neat flagstone path, and then another. The grass on either side of the walkway was neatly trimmed but yellow with frost, another sign that they'd traveled farther than he wanted to admit.

Don't think about that. Just think about knocking on that door.

How could such a slender young woman feel so heavy in his arms?

Devynn's head lolled against his shoulder, and he stared down at her in fright, wondering what he would do if he leaned in and realized she'd stopped breathing. But no, her breath was still there, fast and shallow, which meant she was still with him.

For now.

Just as his foot touched the bottom porch step, the front door of the house opened. Standing there was an imposing man, possibly in his middle thirties, with coal-black hair and eyes, and even, aquiline features. He wore oddly old-fashioned clothing—a black frock coat and crisp white shirt, a vest of dark green brocade—but his appearance wasn't what made Seth freeze in place.

No, it was the wild tingle at the back of his neck that told him the stranger was a warlock. That, and the overwhelming sense of power flowing outward from the man, stronger than anything Seth had ever encountered before, not even from his clan's *prima*.

"Hello," said the stranger, his dark eyes narrowing as he took in the sight of the limp woman in Seth's arms, the blood that stained her dress and his shirt. "It seems you are in need of some assistance."

A pause, and then the man added, the faintest

hint of a smile touching his thin lips, as though he knew the words he was about to say next wouldn't be particularly welcome.

"I am Jeremiah Wilcox."

～

The Witches of Mingus Mountain series continues in Borrowed Time, *releasing on January 15ᵗʰ, 2025.*

ALSO BY CHRISTINE POPE
(SERIES WITH ASTERISKS ARE COMPLETE)

THE WITCHES OF MINGUS MOUNTAIN

(Paranormal Romance)

Stolen Time

Borrowed Time

Killing Time

Wind Called (May 2025)

PROJECT DEMON HUNTERS*

(Paranormal Romance)

Unquiet Souls

Unbound Spirits

Unholy Ground

Unseen Voices

Unmarked Graves

Unbroken Vows

Unholy Night

THE DJINN WARS*

(Paranormal Romance)

Chosen

Taken

Fallen

Broken

Forsaken

Forbidden

Awoken

Illuminated

Stolen

Forgotten

Driven

Unspoken

Hidden

Written

Given

Mistaken

FAMILIAR SPIRITS*

(Cozy Mystery/Paranormal Romance)

Spells and Spaniels

Cauldrons and Cats

Hexes and Hedgehogs

Charms and Chihuahuas

Runes and Ravens

LATTES AND LEVITATION*

(Cozy Mystery/Paranormal Romance)

Caffeine Before Curses

Muffins After Magic

Pastries and Prophecies

Eclairs and Ectoplasm

Sugar Skulls and Specters

Wedding Cakes and Wishes

HEDGEWITCH FOR HIRE*

(Cozy Mystery/Paranormal Romance)

Grave Mistake

Social Medium

Household Demons

Perpetual Potion

Jingle Spells

Wandering Monsters

Uninvited Ghosts

Prophet Motive

Ballroom Bits

Spell Check

Brew Confessions

Charm School (July 2024)

UNEXPECTED MAGIC*

(Urban Fantasy/Paranormal Romance)

Found Objects

Finders, Keepers

Lost and Found

Finding Destiny

THE WITCHES OF WHEELER PARK*

(Paranormal Romance)

Storm Born

Thunder Road

Winds of Change

Mind Games

A Wheeler Park Christmas

Blood Ties

Healing Hands

Wishful Thinking

Smoke and Mirrors

MISS PRIMM'S ACADEMY FOR WAYWARD
WITCHES*

(Fantasy/Academy Romance)

Misspelled

Dispelled

Expelled

The Miss Primm's trilogy is also available in an
omnibus edition at a special boxed set price!

THE DEVIL YOU KNOW*

(Paranormal Romance)

Sympathy for the Devil

Charmed, I'm Sure

A Wing and a Prayer

Wish Upon a Star

THE WITCHES OF CANYON ROAD*

(Paranormal Romance)

Hidden Gifts

Darker Paths

Mysterious Ways

A Canyon Road Christmas

Demon Born

An Ill Wind

Higher Ground

Haunted Hearts

THE WITCHES OF CLEOPATRA HILL*

(Paranormal Romance)

Darkangel

Darknight

Darkmoon

Sympathetic Magic

Protector

Spellbound

A Cleopatra Hill Christmas

Impractical Magic

Strange Magic

The Arrangement

Defender

Bad Blood

Deep Magic

Darktide

THE WATCHERS TRILOGY*

(Paranormal Romance)

Falling Dark

Dead of Night

Rising Dawn

THE SEDONA FILES*

(Paranormal/Science Fiction Romance)

Bad Vibrations

Desert Hearts

Angel Fire

Star Crossed

Falling Angels

Enemy Mine

TALES OF THE LATTER KINGDOMS*

(Fantasy Romance)

All Fall Down

Dragon Rose

Binding Spell

Ashes of Roses

One Thousand Nights

Threads of Gold

The Wolf of Harrow Hall

Moon Dance

The Song of the Thrush

THE GAIAN CONSORTIUM SERIES*

(Science Fiction Romance)

Beast (free prequel novella)

Blood Will Tell

Breath of Life

The Gaia Gambit

The Mandala Maneuver

The Titan Trap

The Zhore Deception

The Refugee Ruse

~

STANDALONE TITLES

Hearts on Fire (Paranormal Romance)

Taking Dictation (Contemporary Romance)

Golden Heart (Gaslamp Fantasy Romance)

Night Music: A Modern Reimagining of The Phantom of the Opera (Contemporary Romance)

Ghost Dance: A Sequel to Gaston Leroux's The Phantom of the Opera (Historical Mystery/Romance)

Flight Before Christmas (Fantasy Romance)

* Indicates a completed series

ABOUT THE AUTHOR

USA Today bestselling author Christine Pope has been writing stories ever since she commandeered her family's Smith-Corona typewriter back in grade school. Her work includes paranormal romance, paranormal cozy mystery, fantasy romance, and science fiction/space opera romance. She makes her home in Arizona.

Don't miss out on any of Christine's new releases —sign up for her newsletter today!

Christine Pope on the Web:
www.christinepope.com

facebook.com/ChristinePopeAuthor
youtube.com/@ChristinePopeAuthor
bsky.app/profile/christinepope.bsky.social